MURDER WITH SPRINKLES ON TOP

Eager to change the subject, Lynette broke out in a wide grin. "Speaking of Salted Caramel . . ."

"Please tell me you brought a carton!" Hayley exclaimed.

"I brought two extra because I would like some of your customers to be able to get some, too!"

Lynette cranked the handle and whipped open the back of the truck, pointing both of her arms with a flourish like a *Price Is Right* model presenting prizes during the Showcase Showdown.

She had been right.

There were two extra-large cartons labeled Salted Caramel in front, as steam from the large freezer swirled out into the early morning air.

Hayley gasped, her eyes popping out, her mouth dropping open.

Lynette spun around to see what had shocked her so badly. When her eyes fell upon the dead body sprawled out on the floor of her truck, Lynette let out a bloodcurdling scream . . .

Books by Lee Hollis

Hayley Powell Mysteries
DEATH OF A KITCHEN DIVA
DEATH OF A COUNTRY FRIED REDNECK
DEATH OF A COUPON CLIPPER
DEATH OF A CHOCOHOLIC
DEATH OF A CHRISTMAS CATERER
DEATH OF A CUPCAKE QUEEN
DEATH OF A BACON HEIRESS
DEATH OF A PUMPKIN CARVER
DEATH OF A LOBSTER LOVER
DEATH OF A COOKBOOK AUTHOR
DEATH OF A WEDDING CAKE BAKER
DEATH OF A BLUEBERRY TART
DEATH OF A WICKED WITCH
DEATH OF AN ITALIAN CHEF
DEATH OF AN ICE CREAM SCOOPER

Collections
EGGNOG MURDER
(with Leslie Meier and Barbara Ross)
YULE LOG MURDER
(with Leslie Meier and Barbara Ross)
HAUNTED HOUSE MURDER
(with Leslie Meier and Barbara Ross)
CHRISTMAS CARD MURDER
(with Leslie Meier and Peggy Ehrhart)
HALLOWEEN PARTY MURDER
(with Leslie Meier and Barbara Ross)

Poppy Harmon Mysteries
POPPY HARMON INVESTIGATES
POPPY HARMON AND THE HUNG JURY
POPPY HARMON AND THE PILLOW TALK KILLER
POPPY HARMON AND THE BACKSTABBING
BACHELOR

Maya & Sandra Mysteries
MURDER AT THE PTA
MURDER AT THE BAKE SALE

Published by Kensington Publishing Corp.

DEATH of an ICE CREAM SCOOPER

LEE HOLLIS

Kensington Publishing Corp.
www.kensingtonbooks.com

KENSINGTON BOOKS are published by

Kensington Publishing Corp.
119 West 40th Street
New York, NY 10018

All Kensington titles, imprints, and distributed lines are available at special quantity discounts for bulk purchases for sales promotion, premiums, fund-raising, educational, or institutional use.

Special book excerpts or customized printings can also be created to fit specific needs. For details, write or phone the office of the Kensington Sales Manager: Attn.: Sales Department. Kensington Publishing Corp., 119 West 40ʰh Street, New York, NY 10018. Phone: 1-800-221-2647.

The K and Teapot logo is a trademark of Kensington Publishing Corp.

First Printing: August 2022
ISBN: 978-1-4967-3649-9

ISBN: 978-1-4967-3650-5 (ebook)

10 9 8 7 6 5 4 3 2 1

Printed in the United States of America

For Linda Parker and Jamie McKown

Chapter 1

Please have the Sea Salt Caramel, Hayley silently prayed to herself. *Please, please, please have the Sea Salt Caramel.*

Hayley was well aware that she was praying for an ice cream flavor. If she were a more noble person, someone with loftier, more far-reaching goals, she probably would have focused her thoughts on praying for world peace or a solution to the climate change crisis. But alas, in the tiny town of Bar Harbor, Maine, there wasn't much she could do about all that.

However, when Lynette Partridge, the enterprising, whip-smart owner of Bar Harbor Ice Cream, pulled her white delivery truck into the gravel parking lot of Hayley's restaurant, aptly named Hayley's Kitchen, Sea Salt Caramel was without apology in the forefront of her mind.

Lynette, blond and beautiful—a potent combination that led people to constantly underestimate her business acumen and creative spirit—hopped out of the driver's side of her beat-up truck. She wore a bulky royal blue sweatshirt with her company logo on it, which somewhat disguised her curvaceous figure, and a pair of tight jeans, which decidedly did not. As if reading Hayley's mind, Lynette flashed her a beatific grin and chirped, "I brought *two* cartons of Sea Salt Caramel for you today, Hayley."

Her prayers had been answered.

Although Lynette's ice cream business had exploded over the last five years, appearing in international tourist magazines as a must-stop destination when visiting Bar Harbor and Acadia National Park, and mentioned in endless "Best Of" articles and blogs for her delectable, wholly original ice cream flavors such as Lemon Poppy Seed Blackberry Jam, or Blackstrap Molasses Banana, or Bay of Figs, it was her more traditional offerings, like Butter Mint, or Pralines and Cream, or Hayley's personal favorite, the aforementioned Sea Salt Caramel, that sent her taste buds into a state of euphoria.

"You're too good to me, Lynette," Hayley spouted, following Lynette like a loyal beagle as she circled around to the freezer in the back of her truck. Lynette slipped a key in the lock, clicked it to the right, and then whipped open the door, as a torrent of steam billowed out from the cold air. Lynette donned a pair of gray work gloves and began effortlessly unloading a half dozen large containers like a longshoreman working the docks.

Hayley's was one of several local restaurants that had cut a deal with Lynette to feature her award-winning ice cream products on their dessert menus. It was a win-win for Lynette. By offering Bar Harbor Ice Cream, the businesses were basically giving her free publicity; plus, as part of the bartering arrangement, the restaurants in exchange would serve limitless free meals to Lynette and her husband, Jamie McGibbon, a history professor at the College of the Atlantic, during the summer season. They would only have to cough up their own money for alcohol and the server's tip.

Hayley was more than happy to have Lynette and Jamie in her restaurant, because she liked them both immensely. She had known the couple for years, long before they had even met each other, fell in love, and got married. However, they'd never really socialized all that much over the years. But ever since Hayley had opened the doors of her new eatery, she and Lynette had found themselves in the same orbit, and now, Hayley wanted to make it a top priority to get to know this vibrant, fun, successful woman, hoping some of Lynette's moxie and business know-how might somehow rub off on her as she tried to get her own fledgling endeavor up and running.

As Lynette hauled the large cartons out of the truck, Hayley leaned over and read the labels. "Oh, good, you brought some more of the Blueberry Sour Cream Crumble. My customers love that one."

Lynette smiled proudly. "It's a classic."

When she was finished unloading, Lynette slammed the door of the freezer shut, then began lifting and carrying the cartons into the restaurant. Hayley was amazed by Lynette's physical strength and stamina. Hayley was practically out of breath just watching her. Feeling guilty, Hayley bent down and grabbed one of the Sea Salt Caramel cartons, and then, huffing and puffing, lumbered after Lynette, who was already in the back, in Hayley's walk-in freezer, sliding two big cartons onto the shelf.

She used one of her gray-gloved hands to wipe wisps of her blond hair away from her face. "How has your summer been so far, Hayley?"

"I certainly can't complain. I'm a new business, so I know there are going to be a lot of unexpected crises to deal with, like a busted water pipe, a leaky roof during that last rainstorm we had, and a delay in a fresh fish delivery that put the kibosh on my salmon special one night, but overall, things have been pretty good. I'm lucky things have been steady."

"I admire you for making such a big change, leaving the security of your job at the *Island Times* to start a new business. Not many people have the guts, especially when so many ventures fail. But you've done it—this place is already a staple in town; you should be very proud."

"It helps to have a very loyal and experienced staff helping me. I wouldn't have stood a chance without Kelton working in the kitchen, Betty up front handling all the reservations, and my waitstaff, most of whom I've known for years."

Lynette shivered from the chilly air in the walk-in freezer, then marched out and headed back to her truck for another load, Hayley close on her heels.

"You're smart to have mostly locals working for you," Lynette remarked, with more than a hint of envy. "I have to rely on a bunch of party-animal college kids from all over the country on my payroll. I swear, I thought I was bad at that age, but kids these days have just gotten so much worse with their TikTok videos, showing up late nursing hangovers, or calling in sick after all night binge drinking, not to mention their endless relationship dramas that they feel the burning need to discuss, dissect, and analyze instead of scooping ice cream, which is the only reason I hired them."

Hayley chuckled. "Is it that bad?"

Lynette stopped at her truck, turned to Hayley, and folded her arms. "Yes, actually it is. Last week, one of my girls had to leave her shift because some tourist ordered a double scoop of the Thai Chili Coconut. Apparently, that's what her ex-boyfriend always ordered, and she said it was a triggering event, and she broke down in a puddle of tears, right there behind the counter. I had to serve ice cream on the house to everyone in the shop, because they were so disturbed by her wailing and sobbing. Have you ever heard of anything so ridiculous? What's wrong with this generation? No one's got any grit or backbone anymore!"

"I do have a couple of college kids busing tables for me, but the older waiters tend to keep them in line," Hayley said, laughing.

"Yeah, unfortunately for me, not a lot of, shall we say, seasoned people, want to scoop ice cream. Too many sore arm muscles at the end of the day, I guess. I suppose it's more of a young people's game," Lynette said.

After hauling the last two cartons inside, Lynette jumped back behind the wheel of her truck. "Don't forget to shoot me a text when you start to run low on supply."

"Of course. Thank you so much, Lynette."

"And we still need to get together for a drink, maybe even allow the husbands to tag along?"

"Sounds like fun!"

Lynette hit the gas and roared away, waving her arm out the window, on the way to her next delivery.

Hayley watched her zip down the street, peel around the corner, and disappear down Cottage Street. She hoped they could make that date happen sooner rather than later. As she wandered back into the empty restaurant, still hours away from opening for dinner, Hayley heard a ringing sound. It wasn't her phone. It was coming from her little office off the kitchen.

Hayley suddenly gasped.

Gemma.

She had made plans with her daughter to FaceTime on the computer at noon. It was already five minutes past twelve. Hayley dashed across the dining room into the kitchen and to her office, where she plopped down in her swivel chair, in front of her laptop, and answered the call.

Her daughter's gorgeous face appeared on the screen.

"Hi, Mom!"

"Hey there; sorry, Lynette Partridge was here, and I lost track of time . . ."

"Did she bring Sea Salt Caramel?"

"Two cartons."

Gemma sighed heavily. "It's excruciating to not be able to come home this summer. New York is so gross and smelly this time of year, everyone flees the city, all the rich people have decamped to the Hamptons, but Conner and I are going to be stuck in our fourth-floor walk-up with a very spotty air-conditioner unit."

Gemma's fiancé Conner had been appearing in a Broadway play, a revival of *A Few Good Men,* for six months now, and Gemma was working hard as a producer for the Food Network. There was a lot of talk, however—given her pretty face, sharp sense of humor, and culinary talent—of transitioning her to a position as an on-air personality, with her own show, which Hayley thought was a no-brainer. But of course, Hayley would also readily admit to having a supremely biased opinion.

Hayley hesitated, then asked, "How are the wedding plans coming?"

Gemma shrugged. "Fine. We're still going back and forth. Maine or Long Island. His parents have launched a pressure campaign to have the whole thing in New York, and you know how Conner is with his parents; he won't stand up for himself, even though he really wants to get married in Bar Harbor, but we're still negotiating, so stay tuned."

Hayley had decided not to insert herself in the middle of all the planning for once, much to the shock of her BFFs Liddy and Mona, as well as her husband Bruce.

No, this was Gemma's day, not hers.

And although she had her own strong opinions, preferring the magnificent views of Frenchman Bay from the majestic lawn of the Bar Harbor Motor Inn, a fantasy wedding she had always dreamed about for her daughter, she was keeping her mouth firmly shut.

Stay out of it, she had told herself countless times.

"I am so bummed I'm not going to get to see Dustin," Gemma whined.

Gemma's younger brother Dustin was flying in from California this week with his girlfriend, whom Hayley had never even met. Her son had moved to Los Angeles to work as an animator after art school, and was currently working on a show airing on the Cartoon Network. Hayley had tried to watch it, but it was loud and frenetic, having something to do with talking food; a very jokey eggplant was in the mix, and lots of constant toilet humor.

Definitely *not* her cup of tea. But she dutifully watched episodes occasionally, so she could talk to him about his work, and was nevertheless extremely proud of him.

"Has he told you yet?"

Hayley suddenly snapped to attention. "Told me what?"

Gemma registered a look of surprise, which she quickly covered. "Oh . . . nothing."

"Gemma, you obviously know something. What is it?"

"I promised not to tell you."

"Well, you brought it up, so now you *have* to tell me."

"I can't."

She normally had no trouble getting Gemma to talk.

Her daughter was a chatterbox who loved to gossip.

An easy mark.

But as she had gotten older and had matured, she was now irritatingly intractable when it came to spilling a juicy secret, if she had made a commitment not to share it.

It was both admirable and frustrating at the same time.

"Gemma, you can't just leave me hanging like this," Hayley pressed.

"I'm sorry, he wants to tell you himself, so I have to respect that."

"Can you at least give me a hint?"

Gemma sighed again. "No, Mom. He's going to be there in like two days."

"Just tell me, is it something big?"

Gemma paused, weighing her response, not wanting to inadvertently share any detail too revealing, before her eyes widened and she leaned in closer until her face filled up the entire computer screen. "Is it *ever*!"

"Gemma, please . . ."

"Gotta go, Mom. Conner's home!"

Her face suddenly froze and then disappeared.

The call was over.

Hayley strongly suspected that Conner had not suddenly arrived home.

That it was just an excuse to cut short the call.

And now, Hayley was left stewing and wondering.

What was Dustin going to drop on her this time?

Chapter 2

Liddy Crawford could barely contain herself as she ran the numbers through her head. "Let's say I get my asking price of just under three million. At a six-percent commission, that's roughly a hundred and eighty grand. Assuming I split that fee with the buyer's agent, I'm still walking away with almost ninety-thousand dollars. Do you know what I can do with that kind of money?"

Hayley waited for Liddy to continue before realizing her question wasn't rhetorical. "Oh. What?"

"A *lot*!"

They were standing on the upper deck of the Seagull House, a sprawling seven-bedroom, five-bathroom, six-thousand-square-foot estate with magnificent, breath-taking ocean views from nearly every room in the house. Liddy had recently been hired as the sales agent for the owners, who were very eager to sell.

Hayley had been on the grounds before—recently, in fact—when they had installed a swimming pool in the expansive backyard the previous summer. She had stopped by to see the contractor working on the project, but had never stepped inside the house, and so she gladly accepted Liddy's offer to give her the grand tour. Liddy was the closest thing Bar Harbor had to a real estate mogul, and so no one was surprised that she had been the one chosen to represent the owners, Jim and Rachel Nash, despite some furious competition.

The Nashes were nationally famous as the married hosts of a cable TV news program, *Morning Politics*, he representing the conservative point of view and she leaning more liberal. Both were blessed with telegenic good looks and had created a party-type atmosphere over cups of coffee every morning from seven to nine, which had resulted in impressive ratings. Rachel's family had roots on the island, having summered in Northeast Harbor for decades, and so when she married Jim, she wanted a connection to the summer home she had lived in since she was a little girl, running around the rocky beaches collecting seashells. They had purchased the Seagull House in 2015, trying to recreate that same idyllic lifestyle for their own two teenaged daughters.

Hayley glanced down at the massive swimming pool that at the moment was covered by a big blue tarp. It was an odd addition to the property, in Hayley's opinion, given the limited amount of weeks one could make use of a pool. This was Maine, after all, not California. "Why are they selling now? They just put that pool in last summer."

"Well, they just bought a new mansion in the Hamptons, twice the size of this one, with their own private beach. Apparently, they just signed a huge multi-year eight-figure contract with the network, so they can afford to splurge. So much for staying connected to the island! But who cares? All that really matters is these people are primed to sell. And I'm the lucky one who gets to unload this place. Do you realize that even if I only get half the asking price, that's still something like forty-five grand in my pocket?"

"Yes, Liddy, I know I was a screwup in school, but I can still do the math."

"Come on, let me show you the library. It's bigger than the public one we have on Mount Desert Street!"

Hayley followed Liddy back inside the main bedroom suite, from the deck and out to the second-floor hallway, where they walked past a few more bedrooms and down the staircase to the library, with its tall ceiling, and along the back wall, row after row of dusty old books, most from a bygone era. Hayley, an avid reader, lit up. "I could curl up with a good book in that old velvet armchair over there and just while away the hours."

"Oh, that's good," Liddy piped in. "I have to remember to say something like that when I'm showing the house." She cleared her throat and waved her arm with a flourish. "And here, you can curl up in that antique chair and crack open a Dickens or Austen or Dostoevsky, and escape into another world, leaving all your day-to-day worries far behind." She excitedly turned to Hayley. "How does that sound?"

"I'm ready to make an offer," Hayley joked.

"You know, this place has such a long history, there could be a lot of super-rich people interested in buying it. I could conceivably have a bidding war on my hands. Can you imagine? If I could play potential buyers off one another, you know, entertain multiple offers, I could jack up the price closer to four million, and half of six percent . . ."

"Which is three percent, just so you know," Hayley said.

"Right, that's a hundred and twenty thousand!"

Hayley could almost see dollar signs in Liddy's eyes. "I'm so happy for you, Liddy; it's a great listing, and I know you will sell it in no time. You're the best of the best."

"Thank you, Hayley; your support has meant so much to me these past few years, especially after that whole nightmare with Sonny."

Sonny Lipton was Liddy's former fiancé, who had left her at the altar, which as it turned out was the best thing he could have done for her, given the multitude of secrets he was hiding about himself.

"But now, *finally*, things are on a total upswing," Liddy said, leading them out the front door and locking it before walking across the front lawn to adjust the FOR SALE sign that included her name and contact information. "Business is booming, I've never been busier, I'm dating someone, there's just a lot of positive things happening in my life right now . . ."

"Wait, back up. You're *dating* someone?"

Liddy smiled coquettishly. "Yes, Hayley, I must have told you!"

"Um, no, you didn't. I would have remembered something like that. Who is he? How long have you been seeing him?"

"You know I don't like to go on and on about my romantic relationships . . ."

"Since when?" Hayley scoffed.

Liddy flashed her a little side-eye before continuing. "Okay, I know I didn't say anything before, but I didn't want to make a big deal about it, or divulge too many details before I was absolutely certain this was something that might last beyond a couple of dates, but it's been almost a month now . . ."

"Who? Who?"

"Hayley, please, it sounds like you're doing an owl impression. His name is George."

Hayley's eyes widened in surprise. "George Emory?"

Liddy scrunched her face. "George Emory! No, of course not! He's ninety-three years old!"

"But he's worth about twenty million!"

"Hayley Powell, are you saying, as my best friend, I would only date a man for his money? What kind of person do you think I am?"

"The kind of person who has spent the last half hour constantly recalculating the amount of your commission based on various sale prices," Hayley responded dryly.

"Well, that's business; this is love!"

"*Love*? You love him?"

"I meant, this is my love life, I didn't say I love him, yet! Don't put words in my mouth," Liddy scolded before softening. "But he really is a sweet guy. His name is George Kittridge. *Doctor* George Kittridge!"

"A doctor! What kind of doctor?"

"He's a doctor of immunological sciences at the Jackson Lab. He just moved here in April."

The Jackson Laboratory was a biomedical research institution that employed over two thousand locals.

"He sounds very impressive! How did the two of you meet?"

"At my Morning Flow Yoga class, can you believe it? He was the only man there, so you can imagine the attention he got, but lo and behold, he rolled out his mat right next to mine, and the rest is history!"

"When can I meet him?"

"He's extremely busy at the lab, but I will talk to him, and we'll set something up soon. But honestly, Hayley, I'm taking this very slow, it's not like I'm thinking about the honeymoon already." As Liddy and Hayley walked to their respective cars, parked alongside the gravel road that led from the main road down to the Seagull House, Liddy turned to take one more look at her newly listed massive property. "Although with a hundred-and-twenty-thousand-dollar commission check, just think of all the places we could go, and fly first class, to boot!"

Hayley had to suppress a chuckle.

Despite her protestations, Liddy Crawford was the most materialistic person Hayley knew, and yet, somehow, it was oddly endearing.

Chapter 3

A Firenze red Range Rover Sport suddenly turned off the main road and barreled down the gravel road toward the estate. Hayley could make out the instantly recognizable face of celebrity newscaster Jim Nash behind the wheel, his pretty, angular-featured blond wife and co-host Rachel in the passenger's seat next to him. Jim rolled down the side window and stuck his arm out, waving at them.

"They're early!" Liddy gasped. "They weren't supposed to arrive until tomorrow!"

Hayley had to admit she was excited to meet the couple, given the fact they were on the TV in her kitchen every weekday morning when she put the coffeepot on, just after seven a.m.

Liddy spun around, her mind obviously racing. "Okay, I want them to think I'm already hard at work trying to sell the place, so I'm going to introduce you as a prospective buyer!"

"What? Liddy, no! Please don't do that. You know how nervous I get when I'm forced to lie. I'm sure they don't expect to have an offer this soon, so promise me you'll just tell them the truth, that I'm your poor friend who could never afford this place in a million years, and you were just showing me around."

Liddy sighed, but didn't commit to anything.

The SUV rolled to a stop, and Jim hopped out. He seemed much taller on television, but his face was even more handsome in person. Rachel remained in the car, her head cranked around as she appeared to be talking to some passengers in the back seat.

"Welcome home, Jim!" Liddy blurted out.

"Hiya, Liddy!" Jim drawled with more than a hint of a Southern accent. Hayley had read somewhere he was originally from Alabama, working years at a local TV station on the Gulf Coast of Florida before moving up to New York for his fame and fortune.

Jim wrapped his arms around Liddy in a bear hug.

Liddy patted him on the back, but Hayley could see her mind racing, debating on how she was going to handle this.

Please, don't, Liddy, please don't, Hayley prayed silently.

When Jim released Liddy and took a step back, his kind eyes flicked in Hayley's direction expectantly. Hayley just stood there with what she knew was a big, dumb, goofy grin on her face.

"Jim, this is my best friend in the whole world, Hayley Powell," Liddy said.

Hayley sighed with relief.

Liddy was not going to lie and make things uncomfortable.

Jim stuck out his hand. "Pleased to meet you, Hayley."

"She's my first showing! She loves the place and is seriously considering making an offer, isn't that right, Hayley?"

Hayley deflated.

Liddy just simply could not resist embellishing the truth of the situation. She wasn't even embellishing; she was flat-out lying. As frustrating as she could be, there was no denying that she was an indefatigable saleswoman.

By this point, Rachel had exited the passenger's side of the vehicle and was walking over to join them, her eyes fixed on Hayley. "I know you; you write the 'Island Food & Spirits' column for the *Times*."

"Yes, that's right," Hayley choked out, agog that someone of Rachel's stature had heard about her column.

"I read you religiously whenever we're in Maine," Rachel added. "I even served your crab-stuffed mushroom recipe at one of our cocktail parties. They were a big hit!"

"Thank you, I'm so happy to hear that," Hayley mumbled, still reeling.

"Hayley's considering making an offer on the Seagull House," Jim said excitedly.

Rachel arched an eyebrow. "Oh?"

There was so much subtext in that one word.

Rachel Nash was clearly confused as to how a local food and cocktails columnist could afford to buy a sprawling three-million-dollar home. There was an awkward pause before Hayley heard herself saying, "I also own a restaurant in town, Hayley's Kitchen."

But even that did little to alleviate the obvious skepticism on Rachel's face. So Liddy, never shy about piling yet another lie on top of a lie, piped in. "Her husband Bruce is a best-selling true-crime writer! He's the one with the money!"

"How nice," Rachel said with a tight smile, still not entirely convinced.

Mercifully, Jim didn't seem as concerned about the veracity of Liddy's claim that Hayley was capable of dropping a few million down, even though she was dressed in jeans that she had bought at Walmart. He glanced back at the Range Rover. "Hey, girls, are you going to stay in there all day?"

Both back doors suddenly flew open, and two young women finally emerged, their faces buried in their phones, one furiously typing, the other casually scrolling.

"Liddy, you know our daughters, Kimmy and Zoe," Rachel said.

"Of course! Hi, girls, nice to see you again!" Liddy cooed.

Both girls were brunette, unlike their blond mother, and appeared to take after their dark-haired father. Even their angular features seemed to resemble his more closely. What was undeniable, however, was their natural beauty, both striking and yet, at the same time, approachable. Kimmy, the older, taller one, who was probably nineteen, maybe twenty, raised her head for a brief moment and flashed Liddy a wan smile. "Hi."

Then her eyes fell back down to her phone.

Zoe, a couple of years younger, closer to seventeen or eighteen, never bothered looking up, even momentarily, to acknowledge any of them, which seemed to annoy Rachel.

"Don't be rude, Zoe, you can at least say hello."

Zoe mimicked the exact same annoyed sigh as her mother. "Mom, I'm working." Then she held out her phone at arm's length, widened her eyes, broke out into a dazzling smile, and took a selfie. Satisfied, she lowered her phone, the smile evaporating and replaced with a dour frown as she typed. "My sponsor is paying me a ton of money to promote this halter top on Instagram."

Kimmy glowered at her younger sister. "Is that a Trina Turk? *I* was talking to them about an endorsement deal before Zoe stole it out from under me!"

"I didn't steal anything," Zoe said, eyes still glued to her phone. "Can I help it if they wanted to go with someone with five million followers as opposed to your pitiful one-point-three million?"

Hayley had read online that Jim and Rachel Nash's two daughters, with their model looks and enviable fashion sense, had both skyrocketed in the ranks of social media influencers of their generation, scoring a number of lucrative brand deals. It was a business Hayley hardly understood but at least could admire from afar.

"Hayley, would you like to come in for a drink?" Jim asked, turning to his wife. "I can unload the luggage later."

"No, thank you, I need to get home and start dinner," Hayley said.

"Well, we will have to have you and your husband over soon; I'd love to hear all about his writing. I keep wanting to write a book of my own about politics in the news business."

"That sounds wonderful," Hayley said, her stomach flip-flopping.

Of course, Bruce did write a true-crime column for the

Island Times, and yes, he had aspirations to write a full-length true-crime book one day, but he had yet to find the time to sit down and actually do it. But now, thanks to Liddy, Hayley feared Jim might ask Bruce's name so he could look it up on Amazon to read about all his mythical best sellers.

A beat-up Volvo suddenly turned off the main road and careened down the driveway.

Hayley noticed both Kimmy and Zoe light up.

Jim, however, grimaced. "Didn't take long for him to show up. We haven't even made it through the front door yet."

The Volvo pulled up behind the Range Rover, and a young man in his early twenties bounded out and ran straight for Zoe, who at the moment was staring daggers at her dad. "I texted him when we got into town. *Be nice!*"

"Hey, baby," he said, eyes twinkling, as he slid his arms around Zoe's waist and drew her closer to him, but still mindful of her parents' presence.

"I could really use a drink right about now," Jim spit out, doing an about-face and stalking off toward the house.

"This is my boyfriend, Chasen," Zoe purred.

Kimmy visibly bristled.

They all nodded as Chasen flashed them a winning smile. Hayley couldn't help but notice that he had the most perfect white teeth. "Ladies."

Rachel seemed a little more impressed with Chasen than her husband, at least enough not to be rude. "Are you staying for dinner, Chasen?"

"Of course he is," Zoe sighed. "We haven't seen each other in weeks." Then she grabbed Chasen's hand and dragged him off toward the house. "We'll be in my room."

"Leave the door open," Rachel warned.

"I'm eighteen!" Zoe called back.

"He's very handsome," Liddy remarked.

"Yes," Rachel agreed. "And he seems to have a good head on his shoulders. At least he has drive and ambition, which is a lot more than I can say about her last boyfriend. I think the only reason Jim doesn't like him is because he doesn't think *anybody* is good enough for Zoe."

Kimmy folded her arms, frustrated. "I just don't know what he sees in her. She's so flighty and shallow. I would think he would go for someone with a little more substance. It's just so disappointing!" She realized she'd just said all of that out loud, and her face reddened with embarrassment. "Excuse me."

She scurried off toward the house.

"She obviously has a secret crush on her sister's boyfriend," Rachel said, sighing. "That's just what we need to kick off our last summer in Maine."

Hayley smiled, sympathetic to how difficult it could be raising teenagers given her own experiences, but she had no clue in that moment just how challenging things were about to get.

Chapter 4

Hayley sensed straightaway from Bruce's ashen face, as he banged into the house through the front door, struggling with two large suitcases, that something was definitely amiss. Making eye contact with Hayley, his stern look of warning sent a clear message that she should prepare herself.

But for what?

When Bruce had called Hayley from the Bangor Airport to let her know that Dustin and his girlfriend MacKenzie's connecting flight in Washington, DC, after arriving from Los Angeles had been delayed, he sounded perfectly fine. But she had noticed a clearly perceptible strain in his voice, an underlying tension, when he called her again to inform her that they had arrived safely in Bangor and were now at baggage claim, waiting for their luggage.

"Is everything all right? You sound weird," Hayley had said into the phone.

There was a long pause before Bruce whispered, "I can't talk now, they're right here, I'll just see you when we get home."

"Bruce, what is it? You can't leave me hanging like this!"

But he had been too distracted by Dustin talking in the background to give her any kind of hint as to what was up. "I gotta go."

And then he had hung up.

Hayley couldn't imagine what could be wrong.

She had spoken to Dustin on the phone just a few days prior, and he had given no indication of any crisis that was brewing. He had simply told his mother that he was looking forward to seeing her, and that he was anxious for her to meet MacKenzie.

Was he hiding some disturbing fact about this new girlfriend?

Was she on the FBI's Ten Most Wanted list or something?

Hayley just could not imagine what the big secret could be. But she didn't have to wonder for long, because after what seemed like two days but had only really been about an hour and fifteen minutes, they had finally arrived home.

Bruce deposited the two suitcases on the floor in the living room, stepping aside so Hayley could see Dustin trundling in behind him with a knapsack. He looked healthy enough, no broken bones or bruised face. He smiled when he saw his mother, which was another good sign. Hayley sprang forward and hugged her son. It had been so long, over a year since he had been home last.

She closed her eyes, squeezing him tight, so happy to see him. When she opened her eyes again, her arms still around him, she got her first glimpse of MacKenzie, and it was instantly clear what the issue was.

MacKenzie was very pretty, maybe wearing a bit too much lipstick and eye shadow, and the red rouge on her cheeks could have been rubbed in a little more so it wasn't so pronounced. She was much shorter than Dustin, the top of her head barely above his biceps, but what really stood out was her big, round, beach ball belly.

MacKenzie was pregnant.

Seriously pregnant.

Like eight or nine months pregnant.

This was the huge news Gemma had already known about.

That Bruce had been so flustered by when he had called her from the airport.

Hayley's baby boy was going to be a father.

At least she hoped he was the father.

At this point, she was not prepared to assume anything.

Dustin finally wriggled free from her grasp. She had been so shocked by the sight of MacKenzie, she hadn't even realized she was still holding onto him.

"Mom, this is MacKenzie," Dustin said laconically, as if there wasn't a giant elephant, or expectant mother, in the room.

"H-hello, M-MacKenzie," Hayley stammered, eyes glued to her protruding belly.

"It's nice to finally meet you, Mrs. Linney, or Mrs. Powell, I'm not sure what name you go by now."

"Hayley's just fine, MacKenzie," Hayley said, still staring.

"I've heard so much about you," MacKenzie whispered shyly with a demure smile.

"I wish I could say the same," Hayley said, instantly regretting it the moment it tumbled out of her mouth.

MacKenzie studied Hayley's stunned face and then turned her attention toward Dustin. "Did you not tell your mother that I was pregnant?"

Dustin shrugged. "I don't know . . . I thought I did."

"No, you did *not*," Hayley said evenly. "I think it's fairly safe to say I would have remembered if you told me you were expecting a baby."

MacKenzie sighed, annoyed. "*Dustin* . . ."

Dustin stared at the floor, a typical reaction from when he was a little boy and got caught doing something he shouldn't. "Um, maybe I forgot . . ."

Dustin had never been the type of kid to share what was going on with him. He kept things to himself a lot, but this, this was beyond the pale.

"I've been asking for weeks if he told you yet, and he kept promising to do it. I just thought by the time we were packing to come visit, he would have done it already," MacKenzie said apologetically.

"I've been really busy at work," Dustin mumbled defensively.

"He's been doing really well," Bruce said, trying to bring down the temperature on this red-hot situation. "I heard all about it on the car ride home. The company has him working as a storyboard artist on three different shows now. Isn't that great?"

"Yes, I'm very proud of him," Hayley said robotically.

But Dustin already knew how proud his mother was of him.

That was not the most pressing issue at the moment.

"How far along are you, MacKenzie?" Hayley asked.

"Almost eight months. I'm not due for another five weeks, so my doctor said it was okay for me to fly."

"Eight months? I can't even count the number of phone conversations I've had with Dustin over the past eight months, so many chances for him to say, 'By the way, Mom, guess what?'"

There was an awkward moment of silence.

Making her own attempt to defuse the tension, MacKenzie interjected, "I'm sorry, may I use your bathroom? I feel like I have to go every ten minutes in my condition."

"Top of the stairs to the right," Hayley said, still glaring at her son, who refused to make eye contact with her.

Seizing the opportunity to escape, Dustin grabbed MacKenzie by the hand. "Come on, I'll show you."

He carefully led her up the stairs, making sure not to go too fast, keeping a protective hand on her waist so she wouldn't trip and lose her balance and fall backward.

Once they had reached the top to the second floor and disappeared around the corner, Hayley grabbed Bruce by the arm and pulled him away from the staircase into the living room. "I don't know what to say; I'm speechless . . ."

"Since when? You haven't stopped talking since they walked through the door," Bruce said.

Hayley threw him a peeved look, then continued on in an urgent low voice, "I know why he hid this from me."

"I do, too. He was afraid you were going to react exactly the way you are reacting now, making him feel as if he's done something wrong."

"He *has* done something wrong! He's been hiding the fact that he impregnated his girlfriend for months now! How could he not tell me something so important?"

"So you're upset he didn't tell you, but you're okay with the fact that he's going to be a father?"

Hayley thought about this, then shook her head. "Of course I'm not okay with it. Dustin's hardly ready to be a father, he's barely twenty-two years old! He's just not mature enough for such a huge responsibility as parenthood. I did everything for him—laundry, cooking, driving him to school. Gemma was much more self-sufficient."

Bruce, suddenly distracted, cleared his throat.

"What?" Hayley asked, following his gaze to the foot of the staircase where Dustin stood, having overheard everything. He had obviously come back down to get their suitcases.

He lifted them up, one in each hand, stared coolly at his mother, and said in a testy tone, "No matter what you say, I *am* ready." Then, obviously hurt, he pounded up the stairs, carrying the suitcases.

Hayley dropped her head, feeling awful.

Chapter 5

"They had this insanely strict policy forbidding any employees dating, so we had to get creative," MacKenzie said with a laugh, as she twirled the last bits of her linguini in clam sauce onto her fork while resting her free hand on her massive, pregnant belly.

Dustin chuckled. "I had to keep my phone hidden underneath my desk so nobody would see us texting back and forth."

"And we would coordinate leaving the office at the end of the day so we wouldn't be seen together," MacKenzie explained. "I was the assistant to Dustin's boss, so the whole thing was dicey, and we lived in constant fear of getting caught."

"But happily, you pulled it off," Bruce noted.

Dustin and MacKenzie exchanged knowing smiles.

"For a while anyway, until I began to show, and then

everybody wanted to know who the father was, the pressure to reveal my baby daddy got so intense!"

"We had let the secret go on for so long, neither of us could ever get any work done; I fell behind schedule with my animatics, I thought I was going to get fired!" Dustin said, shaking his head at the memory.

"It all came to a head last month when the company hosted their annual summer kickoff barbecue in Zuma Beach. The boss's wife Carole caught us kissing in the parking lot when we thought everyone else had already headed down to the beach. We braced for the worst, but it turned out Carole was thrilled for us and threw me a baby shower the following weekend at their gorgeous house in Pacific Palisades. Apparently, Carole found the whole story incredibly romantic, so the rule about no dating kind of evaporated, or was ignored at that point. I guess our boss didn't want to end up sleeping on the couch."

They all snickered as their waitress, Christy, arrived to clear away their plates and offer them dessert—on the house, of course, since the restaurant's owner was at their table. Christy dropped off a few laminated dessert menus for them to peruse and promised to check back in a few minutes before quickly moving on to another table.

Hayley was relieved that her efforts to smooth things over with her son appeared to be working. After Dustin had overheard her remarks about how she thought he was ill-equipped to be a father, there had been an indisputable underlying tension between them. Hayley had suggested she and Bruce take the young couple out for dinner at her restaurant, and although Dustin at first declined, because he could be as stubborn as his mother, MacKenzie finally managed to change his mind, and Dustin begrudgingly agreed to tag along. Now, after an hour and a half of hearing about how they met, the complications of their relationship, and seeing firsthand how deeply they both cared for one another, Hayley sensed that Dustin was loosening up, acting less guarded about the whole situation.

For Hayley's part, she had found her son's girlfriend a bit shy and distant at first, but over the course of dinner, the bright young woman had made a sincere effort to open up and put herself out there, and Hayley was rapidly warming up to her.

When Christy returned, Bruce, Dustin, and MacKenzie all ordered some Bar Harbor Ice Cream. When it was Hayley's turn, she raised a hand in surrender. "Nothing for me, Christy, I'm way too stuffed."

"Oh, come on, babe," Bruce said, cackling. "We know that you're going to regret not ordering anything when Christy brings us all bowls of ice cream, and then you'll ask for an extra spoon so you can sample all of ours, and then after we leave here, you're going to complain all the way home about not getting dessert."

"Bruce, that is a bald-faced lie!" Hayley cried indignantly.

Dustin turned to MacKenzie. "No, it's not. It's exactly what is going to happen."

Christy returned a few minutes later with three heaping bowls of ice cream: Fresh Mint for Bruce, Blueberry Basil Sorbet for Dustin, and Chocolate Pretzel Toffee for the mother-to-be. Hayley sat back in her chair and watched them all start devouring their desserts, instantly regretting not ordering one for herself. She lasted barely two minutes, fearing she might miss out on trying any of the creative flavors at the rapid rate the others were eating them, before she decided to flag down Christy and whisper in her ear.

"One extra spoon coming up!" Christy announced before scurrying to an unoccupied set table nearby, grabbing a spoon, and delivering it to Hayley.

"Thank you, Christy," Hayley said with a thin smile before reaching toward Bruce's bowl. He instantly yanked it out of her reach. "No way, you said you were too full."

"Just a tiny taste!"

"No!" Bruce barked, then turning to Dustin and MacKenzie. "Be careful, she's coming for yours next."

Hayley slammed her spoon down on the white tablecloth and huffed, "Fine, my waistline doesn't need it anyway."

MacKenzie pushed her bowl toward Hayley. "You're welcome to have some of mine, Hayley."

Though tempted, Hayley was not about to give Bruce the satisfaction. "Thank you, MacKenzie, but no. You're eating for two . . . and apparently, so is my husband."

After they were done, Hayley wrote a personal check to Christy for her tip, and then the four of them left the restaurant and strolled through town to work off some of their dinner. Hayley had an enormous craving for something sweet, although she was painfully aware that she was not the pregnant one in the group. She spotted the Bar Harbor Ice Cream signage ahead, and tried to resist the urge to stop in so she could buy a cone, but the closer they got to the shop, the more her willpower seemed to fade away. When they reached the door, Hayley made a grab for the handle. "I just want to pop in and say hello to Lynette."

Bruce turned to Dustin and MacKenzie. "No, she doesn't. She wants the ice cream she didn't order at dinner."

Hayley ignored him.

They all entered the shop.

Oddly, there was no one behind the counter.

They waited for someone to come out from the back, but after a minute or two, no one did. Dustin and MacKenzie stepped forward and began perusing all the tubs of specialty ice creams behind the glass counter, pointing at a few that looked especially delicious.

Bruce turned to Hayley. "Are they open?"

"Yes, it's only seven-thirty; they usually stay open until ten during the summer," Hayley said.

They lingered a few more minutes, and then Hayley heard faint voices coming from above them. "They must all be upstairs. There's a second-floor apartment. Stay here, I'll be right back."

Hayley headed back outside and up the wooden steps leading to the upper level of the building. The door was open, and she could see Lynette and her staff, four college students, gathered in a circle, sitting in metal folding chairs. The room was a fully functioning studio apartment, with a bed in the corner with a small nightstand, a tiny kitchenette, a flat-screen TV on the wall, and a desk and chair instead of a couch and coffee table. Lynette noticed all the eyes of her employees moving toward the door and swiveled around to see Hayley standing in the doorway.

"I'm so sorry to interrupt . . ." Hayley said.

"No, we're just having a flavor development meeting," Lynette said, popping up from her chair. "We meet once a week to brainstorm and come up with interesting ice cream flavors to try." She then turned to the four employees. "Have you met my staff? This is Tim, that's Eric, Bethany, and Miranda."

"Nice to meet you all," Hayley said, smiling. "I'm Hayley."

The kids already knew her from her restaurant, Hayley's Kitchen. It was a small town, after all, even with a million tourists pouring in every summer. Tim and Eric were almost indistinguishable, both lanky with longish hair, eyes at half mast, visibly bored and going through the motions until they could clock out for the evening and go home and smoke a joint. Bethany was short and slight, thick glasses, studious-looking, while Miranda was the opposite, voluptuous and stylish, more Daphne to Bethany's Velma, for any *Scooby-Doo* fans.

"How can I help you, Hayley?" Lynette asked, not the least bit annoyed that Hayley had suddenly crashed their meeting.

"Well, we just stopped in for a cone, and no one was downstairs, so when I heard people talking up here—"

Lynette shot a stern look toward Eric. "I told you to lock the door and put the sign up that said 'Open again at eight.'"

Eric's glassy eyes widened in despair. "I thought I did; I guess I forgot."

"Maybe if you smoked less pot, your memory skills might improve," Lynette said sharply. "Okay. We're adjourned. Go on, everyone get back to work."

Eric didn't move at first.

"What, Eric?" Lynette sighed.

"I'm not sure what you want me to do, lock the door or serve the customers?"

"Serve the customers! That's how you get paid! *Adjourned* means we're through with the meeting! Go!"

Eric finally lifted himself up and slowly ambled out, past Hayley and down the stairs.

Lynette rolled her eyes. "How on earth did that boy ever get into college?"

The other three quietly stood up to leave.

The taller girl, Miranda, turned to Lynette. "Are you going to be making a new batch of Indian Pudding soon?"

Tim and Bethany cracked up laughing.

"Why bother? You're the only one who eats that awful stuff," Tim remarked.

Miranda puffed up, insulted. "I can't help what I like. It's an ancestry thing. For your information, I'm one quarter Native American . . ."

"From the Passamaquoddy tribe, we know, that's why you love Indian Pudding, you've told us a hundred times," Bethany said and playfully sighed.

Lynette noticed Miranda's cheeks reddening. "I think it's wonderful that you're so proud of your heritage, Miranda."

"She's not, really," Bethany said disdainfully. "She just likes scarfing down that weird-flavored ice cream."

Lynette put a protective arm around Miranda's shoulders. "Either way, I'm going to make a big batch just for you."

Dustin suddenly appeared in the doorway. "Uh, excuse me, who's Miranda?"

Miranda looked at him quizzically. "I am, why?"

"You've got a visitor," Dustin explained.

Miranda groaned. "Oh no, I bet it's *him* again."

"Why don't you just tell him to leave you alone?" Bethany suggested, shaking her head.

"I've tried, but he just doesn't seem to take no for an answer."

"Come on, there's safety in numbers," Lynette said, leading them all out. "Tim, close the door behind you."

Hayley and Dustin marched down the stairs ahead of them all, entering the shop to find Bruce and MacKenzie sitting at a small table, and much to Hayley's surprise, her BFF Mona's eighteen-year-old son, Chet, skulking by the door.

"Hi, Chet," Hayley said with a friendly smile.

Chet had not expected to see Hayley, and mumbled, "Oh, hi."

Lynette marched past them, joining Eric behind the counter and grabbing a scooper. "Are you going to order something, Chet?"

"No, I'm just here to see Miranda," Chet said shyly, shuffling his feet.

"I'm sorry, but this is a place of business; I can't have you loitering around here all the time. If you're not going to order anything, Miranda has work to do, so you need to leave."

Chet glanced furtively at Miranda, who swiftly avoided eye contact.

Miranda hastily grabbed a broom from the corner and began sweeping the floor.

Chet opened his mouth to say something to Miranda, but Lynette cut him off. "Goodbye, Chet."

Chet finally gave up, and with hunched shoulders, shuffled out the door, dejected and humiliated.

"I swear, if that kid doesn't leave Miranda alone, I'm going to have Chief Sergio arrest him for stalking," Lynette barked, waving her scoop around.

"He's crushing real hard on her," Tim murmured to Hayley.

Hayley nodded, then peered out the window, watching as Chet now tore down the street at a clip, rudely pushing his way through the gaggle of roaming tourists, shaking his head, fists clenched, filled with what appeared to be abject rage.

A worrying sign, in Hayley's mind.

Island Food & Spirits
BY
HAYLEY POWELL

Recently, I was delighted to hear from Rosana Moretti, who called me out of the blue. Rosana, for those of you who don't know, is the charming wife of my former boss at the *Island Times*, Sal Moretti. I suppose he could still be considered my boss, in a sense, since I continue to contribute my daily food and cocktails column. I just don't clock in every day, unlike my husband, Bruce, who is still a full-time employee.

Anyway, Rosana and I grew very close over the years when I worked at the paper, and have remained best buds, even after my departure to open my restaurant, Hayley's Kitchen.

Rosana wanted to be sure Bruce and I were still planning to attend her and Sal's annual Barbecue & Birthday Bash that they hold in July every summer to celebrate both of their birthdays, which are within a week of each other. It is always a guaranteed good time, with upwards of fifty to a hundred hard-partying guests! I look forward to it every year!

Everyone invited is always asked to bring a tasty side dish, like a lobster salad, a pot of steamed mussels and clams, fresh veggies and fruit, a coleslaw or potato salad, even a bag of chips, all of which would be delicious accompaniments to Sal's out-of-this-world juicy Wagyu beef burgers and platters of spicy Italian sausage, fresh off the grill.

I always prefer showing up with a dessert, something sweet and sinful to cleanse the palate after all that meat and seafood. But with business booming at my restaurant this summer and my free time severely limited these days, I decided this year I would simply bring one of the scrumptious desserts I have in stock at Hayley's Kitchen.

This was decidedly not the case last year, when I had more time on my hands and was far more ambitious. Much to my bemusement later on, I had been creatively inspired at the time to whip up something fabulous for the Moretti soiree by one of the items discovered in a box of junk my dear husband dragged home from a neighborhood yard sale.

An old ice cream maker.

Bruce has always been a self-described "collector." He's always scouring for "the great find" or that "hidden treasure." Most of the time, he just comes home with the junk. The problem was, after we got married, we had to combine two households and suffered from a severe lack of storage space, and so our garage was packed. We couldn't even park our cars in there anymore, and had to leave them outside in the driveway. So when Bruce came barreling into the kitchen with a big, goofy grin on his face, I knew he had not heeded my warning to avoid going to any more Saturday yard sales in town. Apparently, the Ameses on Forest Street were moving to Florida, and they were desperately trying to clean out their house for the new owners, and so Bruce was able to fill up a whole big dusty box for just twenty bucks. Unfortunately, when he opened the box to reveal his treasures, I had to bite my tongue not to say, "They should have paid *you* twenty bucks to take this stuff off their hands!"

I hate to be a nag like my mother—and for the record, I do *not* take after my mother—but I couldn't help berating Bruce for hauling more junk home without cleaning out the garage to make more space for his acquisitions, something he had been promising to do for months, but never seemed to get around to it.

Bruce was barely listening to me. He was kneeling down, examining an old compass, speculating on its value. I remarked that maybe the MADE IN CHINA sticker on the back might give him a clue. That's when something in the box suddenly caught my attention. I hurried over and dug it out.

Sure enough, it was an old-fashioned ice cream maker, still in the manufacturer's box, apparently never opened. Now *that's* a find, in my humble opinion!

I banished Bruce from the kitchen, at least until he finally did something about the state of our garage, so I could have some privacy. I tore open the box and began poring over the little booklet of ice cream recipes that were included. The next thing I knew, I was yanking ingredients out of the fridge, also noticing a bowl of blueberries that needed to be used up soon. I grabbed those, too, and within minutes, that old ice cream machine was churning away on the counter. When it was done, I scraped the delicious-looking blueberry ice cream out and into a plastic container, snapped on a lid, and threw it in the freezer overnight.

The next morning, when Bruce peeked into the kitchen to assess my current mood, I offered him a cheery good morning. A wave of relief washed over his face. He figured it was safe to come in, and then he poured himself a cup of coffee, sat down at the kitchen table, and cracked open the Sunday paper, expecting to be served his usual eggs, bacon, and rye toast, which I always prepared for him on Sundays (I'm not really that much of a dutiful wife; he's in charge of his own breakfast the other six days of the week). What he got instead was a big bowl of bright purple ice cream with extra blueberries sprinkled on top!

Poor Bruce. He looked up at me with a frown, and in a meek, sad voice asked, "Am I being punished?"

"No," I laughed. "You'll get your breakfast. But first, I want you to be my guinea pig and taste this homemade ice cream I made with my new ice cream maker." I neglected to mention my new favorite toy had been in the box of junk that I had yelled at him about for bringing home.

Bruce inhaled a hearty spoonful and nodded happily.

He loved it.

And a monster had suddenly been created.

I ran to the Shop 'n Save to load up on more ingredients to make a wide variety of ice cream flavors. Blueberries, strawberries, and blackberries were all in abundance in Maine during the summer. Not to mention bananas, kiwis, lemons, and of course, nuts, chocolate, and peanut butter.

I was totally hooked.

And then I had this eureka moment.

I could make tubs full of homemade ice cream for Sal and Rosana's party.

When I called Rosana, she assured me they had plenty of room to store my party contribution in their own garage freezer, so I eagerly set about making ice cream to feed a hundred people, storing it in our own freezer chest, after weaving through all the junk in the garage, which was like navigating a maze, in order to get to it.

On the day before the party, I stopped by Mona's house. She had kindly offered to loan me some of her Styrofoam shipping boxes and frozen ice packs that she used to mail her live lobsters to customers all over the United States and even abroad.

When I arrived home, I was surprised to find Bruce waiting for me in the driveway. He helped me with the boxes, and we carried them to the garage. Bruce dramatically swung open the doors, and I stopped in my tracks, in a total state of shock. Bruce had finally cleared out the garage, hauling most of the unusable junk to the town dump! It was sparkling clean and all but empty, except for our large freezer chest. After packing all the ice cream up and stacking the boxes in the freezer, we celebrated with fried clams, fries, and coffee milkshakes at Ocean Drive Dairy Bar, a summertime favorite hangout.

The next morning, the day of the party, I headed to the garage and noticed Bruce had moved the freezer from the back of the garage to the front, where it was more easily accessible. My husband was scoring points left and right! Unfortunately, he was about to lose them as fast as he had just accumulated them, because when I opened the lid of the freezer, to my horror, the ice cream was gone. Not literally gone— *melted* gone. I instantly realized that when Bruce had tossed the heavy frozen ice packs in, they had smashed the top containers open, so there was ice cream melted and dripping everywhere.

But why had it all melted?

It didn't take long to solve that mystery.

A quick inspection revealed that when Bruce moved the freezer, he forgot to plug it back in.

I heard myself screaming.

Bruce came running out of the house wearing only his boxers, his face covered in shaving cream and a razor in his hand. Well, Bruce felt terrible about his blunder. I tried not to blame him—it could have happened to anyone—but he was determined to fix it.

Luckily, Bruce called Lynette Partridge at Bar Harbor Ice Cream, who was more than happy to provide three tubs of Salted Caramel ice cream on the house for the party, and she delivered them herself. I have to say, Lynette's ice cream was a much bigger hit with the guests than my own attempt at Blueberry Swirl ever could have been!

And for the record, the freezer debacle did not deter me in the least! I was back to churning out ice cream every weekend for the rest of that summer, my favorite being Hayley's Easy Blueberry Ice Cream, a treat I always enjoy with an accompanying cocktail!

HAYLEY'S BOOZY BLUEBERRY FLOATS
(Makes two adult-size floats for those
warm summer days)

INGREDIENTS:
½ cup blueberries
5 ounces blueberry vodka
1 cup lemon or lime sparkling water
4 scoops vanilla ice cream (I have used 6 scoops
   before for the die-hard ice cream lovers in my
   home).

Add your blueberries, blueberry vodka, and
sparkling water to a blender and mix until
blended.

Scoop two scoops of ice cream each into two
glasses. Divide your blended mixture into both
glasses. Garnish with extra blueberries if you like.

HAYLEY'S EASY BLUEBERRY ICE CREAM

INGREDIENTS:
4 cups fresh blueberries
2 cups sugar
1 tablespoon vanilla
Pinch of salt
1 cup whole milk
1 cup half-and-half or whipping cream
2 cups whipping cream

Puree blueberries in a blender. Add the pureed blueberries and sugar to a saucepan on medium-low heat and stir until the sugar dissolves.

Place the mixture in the refrigerator until nice and cold.

Remove and add the vanilla, salt, milk, and half-and-half or whipping cream, and stir until combined.

Pour into an ice cream maker and churn. (Be sure to follow your ice cream maker's directions.)

Scoop into a clean plastic container with lid and place in the freezer for at least 6 hours—but overnight is best, if you can wait that long!

Chapter 6

Hayley scrunched up her nose after licking her ice cream cone. "Oh, this is not for me."

"Why did you order such a weird flavor?" Bruce asked as they strolled along the sidewalk down Main Street, Dustin and MacKenzie a few steps behind them.

"I wanted to be adventurous, and Lynette thought I might like it. Bakaliowe. It sounded so exotic."

"What is it?"

"She said it's Polish, all dried nuts and fruits. I should have taken my cue from all her employees, who were shaking their heads, trying to warn me off, when Lynette was pushing it on me." Hayley tried one more taste.

"Why do you keep eating it? Are you hoping the taste will grow on you?" Bruce asked.

"I just hate wasting food," Hayley said. She made one last attempt, one more lick, then shivered and tossed the whole cone into a trash bin they were passing by. "No, I'm done. So much for being adventurous."

"Hey, Spanky!" Dustin called out from behind them. Hayley glanced across the street to see a tall, lanky kid, in cargo shorts and a ratty T-shirt, waving at them. He dashed across the street, almost getting run down by a car with Florida plates, the driver angrily blasting the horn. Spanky ignored it and gave Dustin a big bear hug, and then Dustin introduced him to MacKenzie.

Hayley couldn't believe her eyes. This was Spanky McFarland, Dustin's childhood best friend. She had hosted him at her house countless times for sleepovers when he and Dustin were kids. She was shocked at just how tall he was now, at least six feet four inches, his sharp lanky features such a contrast to the cherubic little moppet she remembered from all those years ago.

God, she felt old.

Hayley still saw Spanky's mother, Carla, on occasion, usually just in passing at the grocery store or the post office, but she hadn't laid eyes on Spanky in such a long time. He and Dustin had slowly drifted apart when they entered high school. Hayley remembered at one point asking Dustin about him, but her typically morose, uncommunicative teenage son had just shrugged and mumbled something about them hanging in different circles. After chatting a few minutes with Dustin and MacKenzie, Spanky finally turned to acknowledge Hayley and Bruce.

"Hi, Mrs. Powell," he said with a perfunctory nod.

Bruce put an arm around his wife. "It's Mrs. Linney now. I'm Bruce, the stepfather, but I swear, I'm nothing like the one in those blood-splattered horror movies."

Spanky stared at him blankly.

"You never saw those? The stepfather is a psychotic killer who marries the perfect family, and then when they don't live up to his expectations, he goes crazy and grabs a knife and—"

"Bruce," Hayley said with an admonishing look. "Those movies came out way before they were even born."

"I guess I'm really showing my age right now," Bruce said.

Hayley nodded, then turned back to Spanky, noticing the word MARSHMELLO on his T-shirt. "Did you know *marshmallow* is misspelled on your T-shirt, Spanky?"

Spanky glanced down at his shirt. "No, it's not. Marshmello is a famous DJ; he's kind of my hero."

"I heard you were a DJ now," Dustin said.

"Yeah, I love creating my own remixes, working up a crowd; it's like a passion with me," he said, looking completely engaged for the first time, but then he paused, and the enthusiasm slowly began to drain from his face. "But mostly my gigs have been junior proms and homecoming dances, small-time stuff. I didn't think I'd still be hanging around high-school kids at this point . . ."

"Like Matthew McConaughey in *Dazed and Confused*—that's got to be one of my favorite movies of all time!" Bruce blurted out.

"Again, *not* born yet," Hayley said evenly.

"I saw it on Netflix or something not too long ago," Dustin said, not wanting Bruce to feel bad. "I remember laughing a lot watching it. McConaughey was this guy in his twenties who was still hanging out with all the kids in high school."

"Thanks for humoring me, man," Bruce said, grinning.

"Well, I'm sure Spanky is *nothing* like the character in that movie," Hayley insisted, trying to be mindful of Spanky's feelings.

Bruce realized his faux pas. "No, of course not. I didn't mean to imply . . ."

Spanky raised a hand. "No, it's cool. Maybe I am a little like that. I've been stuck here for so long, but I've been saving my money to get out of Bar Harbor, maybe go to New York or LA, see what I can make happen. I was seeing someone, but we broke up recently, so there's really nothing keeping me here anymore. I could use a fresh start."

"Well, I wish you great success, Spanky, you deserve it," Hayley said. "I remember both you boys were always so creative when you were kids; I love seeing you pursue your passions."

Spanky gave her a genuinely grateful smile. But there was something amiss, a haunted look in his eye, like there was a lot more bubbling beneath the surface.

"I'm sorry," MacKenzie interjected, a hand resting on her belly. "My feet are getting tired. I'd love to find somewhere to sit down for a spell."

Dustin suddenly snapped to attention, gently taking MacKenzie by the hand. "We better go. Spanky, do you still have the same number?"

"I've had the same number since I got my first phone for my twelfth birthday, which is kind of sad," Spanky said with a self-deprecating chuckle.

"I'll text you my new contact info so we can stay in touch. If you make it out to LA, definitely let us know," Dustin said hurriedly as he led MacKenzie toward an unoccupied bench in the Village Green.

"Congrats on the whole dad thing!" Spanky yelled after him, before turning to Hayley and Bruce. "Nice to see you again, Mrs. P—I mean L."

"Bye, Spanky, say hi to your mom," Hayley said, waving as he bounded back across the street, again nearly getting mowed down by a car, this one with New York plates.

"Seems like a nice kid," Bruce remarked.

"Yes, he was always so sweet, but I don't know, he seems a little lost," Hayley noted.

"He's in his twenties. We were all lost in our twenties."

Hayley suspected there might be more to it than that.

After resting for about fifteen minutes while watching summer tourists stroll by in the Village Green, MacKenzie was finally ready to continue the half-mile trek back home to Hayley's house.

When they arrived, Hayley's shih tzu, Leroy, was jumping up and down in the kitchen to greet them. Dustin escorted his girlfriend up the stairs and into his room so she could lie down, and Bruce retreated to the dining room to finish his *Island Times* column that had to be filed by midnight. Hayley poured herself a glass of Chablis and wandered out to the deck to sit down and look up at the clear night sky dotted with stars and constellations. A few minutes later, the screen door swung open, and Dustin joined her, popping open a can of beer. Hayley eyed him warily.

He stopped himself from taking a sip to remark, "I'm over twenty-one, Mom."

"I know, it just takes some getting used to," Hayley said, sighing.

Dustin waited, eyes fixed on Hayley.

She turned to him and smiled. "I'm sorry; go ahead and enjoy your beer. I won't say a word."

He happily took a chug of his beer and then leaned back in the white wooden lounger, his feet outstretched. "It was good to see Spanky. Talk about a blast from the past."

"You've both grown up so much," Hayley said.

There was a long silence as Dustin followed his mother's gaze up to the stars.

Hayley took a small sip of her wine, and then set the glass down on the deck. "I really wish you had told me about MacKenzie."

"I did. I said on the phone about a month ago that I was dating someone," Dustin said defensively.

Hayley gave him a hard look. "I mean about the *pregnancy*."

Dustin had no answer for her. He just squeaked out a barely audible, "Sorry."

"Do you know the baby's sex yet?"

Dustin shook his head. "We want to be surprised."

Hayley hardly agreed with him. She would absolutely prefer knowing ASAP in order to properly plan for the birth, but that was their decision, and so she was not about to share her own personal views on the subject. For now.

Dustin folded his arms, eyes still glued to the stars. "I guess maybe I was a little afraid."

Hayley turned to him. "Afraid of what?"

"How you were going to react."

"About MacKenzie being pregnant?"

"No. More about you being a grandmother who is still in her forties."

Hayley considered this, then burst out laughing.

Her son had a point.

The thought had crossed her mind more than once since their arrival.

In her mind, she was *way* too young to be somebody's grandmother, or Nana, or Grammie. Just the idea of that was very unsettling and almost too painful to think about.

But she was determined to get her mind around it, because like it or not, in a month or two, that was going to be her new reality, her new normal.

"Dustin, I want you to know, I'm happy for you. For both of you. Really, I am," Hayley said.

"Thanks, Mom." He reached out and squeezed his mother's hand. "And don't worry, I am ready for this."

Hayley silently prayed that he was right.

Chapter 7

"I can't believe you're going to be a *grandmother*!" Debbie Pierson shouted to the heavens from behind the counter at The Top Shop, a local boutique specializing in baby clothes.

"Say it a little louder, Debbie; I don't think they heard you all the way up in Bangor!" Hayley moaned as she rifled through the sales rack, checking the price tag on an adorable little jean jumper.

MacKenzie quietly chuckled behind her while sifting through a pile of colorful tiny knitted sweaters.

"I would have thought Gemma would be the first one of your kids to become a parent. I mean, Dustin is *so* young!"

Hayley nodded in agreement. She carried the jumper and set it down on the counter in front of Debbie. "Can you hold this for me while we continue to browse?"

"Of course," Debbie said, setting the piece aside. "Boy or girl?"

"They want to be surprised," Hayley said, frustrated.

"Oh, I could never do that. I'd want to know. I'm an obsessive planner. I have to be totally prepared," Debbie exclaimed.

Hayley turned and said pointedly in MacKenzie's direction, "If we knew the baby's sex, we wouldn't have to go with so many neutral colors."

MacKenzie held up a darling gray baby cardigan. "I love this!"

Hayley snatched it from her. "Great, I'll add it to the pile."

"Wait, we're on a tight budget, so I can't be buying everything I see that I like," MacKenzie said.

"I understand. But I can. Please, I need to start practicing spoiling my grandchild," Hayley said, examining the cardigan. "This would look so cute in pink."

"It's your lucky day! We have it in pink!" Debbie chirped from behind the counter.

"It would be so much easier if we knew the baby's gender," Hayley couldn't resist commenting. She noticed MacKenzie's face tightening, so to avoid coming across as the interfering mother-in-law, she quickly added, "But who cares what color babies wear nowadays—pink, blue, cranberry, whatever, does it really matter? We shouldn't be so hung up on the whole pink-blue tradition, right, Debbie?"

"My four-year-old nephew Carl *loves* wearing pink polka dots!" Debbie gushed, ever the saleswoman.

"I, for one, believe colors should not be exclusive to the gender of the baby," Hayley said emphatically in MacKenzie's direction, before turning back to Debbie and holding up the gray cardigan. "We'll take this, and another one in pink."

Debbie plucked the sweater out of Hayley's hand and laid it on top of the jumper.

Hayley wandered back over to MacKenzie, who had just moved on to a rack of rompers, carefully inspecting each one. She stood on the opposite side of the rack, pretending to peruse the selections, but she was more interested in peppering her future daughter-in-law with a few more nosy questions. "How long will you be taking off for maternity leave?"

"At least five months. Dustin wants me to take more. I said we can't afford it—my mother lives in Van Nuys, so she can babysit when I go back to work—but Dustin is adamant about me being a stay-at-home mom, for at least the first year. He said he could pick up a few extra freelance assignments in addition to working on staff, so we have more money coming in."

Hayley nodded, poker-faced, trying not to drop her jaw open in surprise. This did not sound like the same Dustin who lasted forty-five minutes on his first day bagging groceries at the Shop 'n Save because the cheap polyester jacket they forced him to wear itched too much.

"I can't imagine doing this with anyone else. Dustin is so steady and calm and, what's the word, inflatable?"

"Unflappable, I think you mean," Hayley said, smiling.

"Oh, right, yeah, unflappable." MacKenzie chortled.

Hayley struggled to comport this version of Dustin that his girlfriend was describing to the spoiled, often lazy boy she had raised, who she feared might have trouble adjusting out in the real world. But perhaps leaving the nest was just what he needed to finally grow up.

MacKenzie picked up a romper hanging on the rack. "Look at this one with all the little snowmen. It'll remind Dustin of growing up in Maine during the cold winters." MacKenzie searched the openings for a price tag. "I can't find how much it costs."

Hayley grabbed the romper from her before MacKenzie changed her mind and put it back on the rack. "He'll love it. Let's get it."

After adding four more tops, some pants and leggings, a few more one-pieces, and a precious khaki bomber jacket, Hayley and MacKenzie were finally ready for Debbie to ring up the final total. Hayley charged the amount to her credit card, thankful that business at Hayley's Kitchen was currently booming. After Debbie had filled two large white paper bags with handles and the store's logo on the side, they left the shop and were out onto Main Street, where Hayley could see the town clock.

"It's almost eleven. My brother Randy is about to open for lunch. He serves the best fried clams in town," Hayley said.

"Good, I'm starving, and I've been craving fried clams. And shrimp. And scallops. Actually, anything fried."

"Perfect. He makes the best onion rings, too, the thin kind, not too thick. We can always order a side salad, so we don't feel *too* guilty afterward."

MacKenzie laughed as Hayley made a grab for the bag of baby clothes she was holding.

"Here, let me take that. You should take full advantage of your condition and let other people pamper you."

"I'm fine, Hayley," MacKenzie said, her eyes flicking to something across the street. "Hey, isn't that the boy from the ice cream shop? What's he doing?"

Hayley followed MacKenzie's gaze over to an alleyway, where Mona's son Chet was poking his head out continuously in an odd manner, as if he were spying on someone.

Hayley knew instantly what he was up to, because just across the street was the Bar Harbor Ice Cream Shop, and Hayley would bet anything that Miranda, Chet's current object of affection, was at this moment working her shift.

"Come on," Hayley said, leading MacKenzie through the crosswalk to the opposite side of the street and over to the alley, where she waited for Chet to poke his head out again. When he did, she was ready for him.

"What are you doing, Chet?"

Chet jumped back, startled, his eyes nearly popping out of his head. "Hayley, I didn't see you there . . ."

"What's so interesting at the Bar Harbor Ice Cream shop?" Hayley casually asked.

"Nothing. I wasn't looking at that. I thought I saw somebody I knew going into The Hemporium next door . . ."

"Oh, really, who?"

"Just a friend! I gotta go, Hayley," Chet said, pushing past them and dashing away.

There was no mystery to solve here.

Hayley knew exactly what he was doing.

And she feared it might be developing into a real problem.

Perhaps it was time to talk to his mother Mona.

Chapter 8

"She seemed sweet. I liked her immediately," Randy said while wiping the counter of his bar at Drinks Like A Fish.

"That's because she was so complimentary of your fried clams. You're such a sucker for flattery," Hayley said, sipping her sparkling water.

After bringing MacKenzie into Randy's bar for lunch earlier, she had dropped her son's girlfriend off at the house, because she was feeling tired and wanted a rest. Then Hayley had run some errands for her restaurant, and doubled back to Drinks Like A Fish to meet with Liddy, so they could plan a small cocktail party in order for her and Bruce to finally be able to meet Liddy's new beau.

Liddy, on the stool next to her, was enjoying a more potent Manhattan. "I can't believe our little Dustin is going to be a father. It just doesn't seem real."

"Believe me, I'm still trying to get my mind around it, but in the end, it's his life, and my job is to just be his loving and supportive mother. Truth be told, I did have fun today shopping for baby clothes with MacKenzie."

"I can see it now, you're going to spoil that kid rotten," Randy concluded, refilling Hayley's water from the fountain.

Hayley shrugged.

He wasn't wrong.

She swiveled back around toward Liddy. "Is Friday good for you?"

Liddy nodded, knocking back the rest of her drink, then setting the glass down and sliding it toward Randy so he could make her another. "Yes, I spoke with George, and he was a little resistant at first. He's very shy and introverted and doesn't really socialize all that much . . ."

"Boy, it's true what they say, opposites really do attract," Randy said, chuckling, as he picked up the glass and began making Liddy another Manhattan, first pouring the whiskey, then some sweet vermouth.

"*Anyway,*" Liddy hissed, eyes narrowing. "When I explained to him how important you are in my life, how you're my best friend in the whole world, well, he couldn't say no, so I'm happy to confirm we are definitely on for Friday."

"Excellent, I'll let Bruce know," Hayley said before glancing at Randy, who had come back with a fresh Manhattan for Liddy. "What about you and Sergio? Do you guys want to meet Liddy's new fella?"

"As much as I would love to, I can't," Randy said, genuinely disappointed. "Michelle's driving down to Hartford to visit a sick aunt, so I'm covering her shifts all weekend, and Sergio's got a town hall meeting to discuss policy, training, use of force, and community programs, stuff like that, so you'll just have to report back to us what he's like."

"I can assure you he's lovely," Liddy said, a bit defensive. "Seriously, I know I have dated a lot of men . . ."

"A *lot*," Randy agreed too quickly.

Another slow burn look from Liddy. Then she continued, focusing more on Hayley. "I know I haven't had much luck in the relationship department. I've obviously made a few mistakes . . ."

"I'll say. I mean, let's face it, you've made a *huge* number of bad decisions in your life, Liddy, but choosing Sonny as a husband might just top the whole list!"

Liddy whipped back around to Randy. "I'm sure you have other customers to tend to; don't feel you have to hover around us all night."

Randy got the message and gave her a playful wink, heading back down to the other end of the bar.

"I don't know, George feels different. I hate to say it, because I'm afraid to jinx it, but . . ."

Hayley leaned forward expectantly. "But what?"

"I . . . I think he may be *the one*."

"Oh, Liddy, I'm so happy for you."

Suddenly, the door to the bar flew open, and Mona hustled in.

Liddy grabbed Hayley's shirtsleeve and whispered urgently, "Hayley, please don't mention the cocktail party to Mona. I love her to death, but you know how she can be, especially when she's had a few beers. I'm worried she might scare George off. I want him to meet her, of course, but I would prefer slowly easing him into it . . ."

"But—"

Liddy squeezed her arm. "*Please!*"

Mona ambled up to the bar and shouted, "Bud Light, Randy. I got two minutes, so make it snappy!"

"Evening, Mona," Liddy drawled, trying to act natural.

Mona grunted a reply.

Randy popped the top off her beer with a bottle opener and handed it to her.

She took a swig. "So, Hayley, what time is your little soiree on Friday?"

Liddy's jaw nearly hit the floor.

Hayley gave Liddy an apologetic smile. "I may have mentioned to Mona earlier to keep Friday open, because I was thinking of hosting a small gathering at my house."

"To meet the poor unsuspecting fish that Liddy finally managed to hook and reel in," Mona roared, guzzling her beer.

"Promise me you will be on your best behavior, Mona!" Liddy pleaded, slamming her hand down on the counter.

"Don't worry, Liddy, I'm always the life of the party!"

"Yes, you are, the kind of parties where the police are called in and arrests are made for disorderly conduct!" Liddy sniffed.

"Relax, I'll try not to embarrass you . . . too much," Mona cackled; then offhandedly, almost inaudibly, she followed with, "Mind if I bring a date?"

It suddenly felt as if the entire bar froze in some kind of sci-fi movie time warp.

But it was only Hayley and Liddy, who were usually the loudest people in the bar.

"*What?*" Hayley gasped.

"A date?" Liddy asked. "You mean a *man?*"

"No, Liddy, I'm coming with Lady Gaga. Of course I mean a man!" Mona snapped.

"Mona, I had no idea you were seeing someone," Hayley said, still in a slight state of shock.

"I'm not, really, it's just a guy I met a few weeks ago while I was walking my dogs along the shore path. I've had him over to dinner a couple of times, and what can I say, he's not horrible."

"High praise indeed," Liddy cracked.

Mona ignored her. "He doesn't make me want to punch him in the face every time he opens his mouth. In other words, he's not Dennis!"

Dennis was Mona's ex-husband.

Hayley had so many questions, she could barely contain herself. "Do we know him? Is he local? What's his name?"

"Chuck," Mona said.

"Chuck, Chuck what? What's his last name?"

"Just Chuck. I didn't ask his last name, because I didn't think it would last past the first date, and now I'm too embarrassed to ask him."

Liddy sighed. "Well, what does he do?"

"He's a janitor."

Liddy seemed to relax, relieved to know that Mona's boyfriend didn't have a better job than her own impressive paramour, the doctor.

"In answer to your question, Mona, yes, you can bring him, I'm sure we'd all love to meet him," Hayley said.

"Good, now I gotta go. I left Chet manning the lobster shop, and you know how bored he gets. I don't want to show up there and find all the lobsters out of the tanks in a drag race across the floor!"

As Mona downed the rest of her beer, slammed the empty bottle on the counter, and bounded for the door, Hayley jumped off her barstool and intercepted her.

"Mona, wait, how is Chet?"

Mona looked at her blankly. "He's fine, why?"

Hayley hesitated, not sure how she should proceed. It was a delicate matter, and she wasn't even sure it was anything to worry about yet, but she felt the urge to say something.

The question was, what?

So Chet was obsessed with a girl.

What teenaged boy wasn't, or girl, for that matter?

"Hayley, can this wait? I'm kind of in a hurry!"

"Yes, go, we can talk later."

Mona then barreled out the door into the night.

When Hayley turned to return to her barstool, her eyes fell upon a young woman at the opposite end of the bar, whom she instantly recognized.

Kimmy Nash, the daughter of Jim and Rachel Nash, the cable TV news stars. She was pleading with Randy, who had his phone out and was trying to make a call. Liddy had struck up a conversation with another woman who had just come into the bar, a loan officer from the First National Bank whom she dealt with all the time in her real estate deals. Hayley wandered down toward Randy and Kimmy to see what the problem was.

"Please, don't call the cops, I promise to leave and not come back!" Kimmy wailed.

"Randy, what's going on?"

Kimmy glanced over at Hayley, trying to place her.

"She ordered a cosmo, I asked for ID, she gave me this," Randy said, holding up a laminated card. "Totally fake, and not even a good fake ID, so I'm calling Sergio."

"No, I'm begging you, please don't," Kimmy cried, her eyes brimming with tears. "I can't go to jail. If I lose my sponsors, I will lose everything!"

Randy gave Kimmy a quizzical look.

"She's a social media influencer," Hayley explained.

Kimmy stared at Hayley, wiping the tears from her eyes, her brain searching for why Hayley looked so familiar.

Suddenly, Liddy, who had finished her conversation, noticed the scene unfolding down at the opposite end of the bar and decided to investigate. She was surprised when she spotted Kimmy.

"Kimmy, what are you doing here?"

"Liddy! Thank God! Please, you have to stop him from calling the police! Please, I'll do anything!"

"She tried passing off a fake ID," Hayley quietly explained.

Liddy hugged a sobbing Kimmy, gently patting her back and whispering to Hayley, "*Do* something!"

Hayley stepped up to the bar and leaned forward, speaking softly to her brother. "She's the daughter of Liddy's clients. She made a bad mistake. Can't you let her off this one time with a stern warning? For Liddy, for me?"

Randy folded his arms, not entirely convinced. "You do know I could lose my liquor license if I ever got caught serving a minor."

There was no debating that.

He was totally right.

But she also knew her brother was a big softie.

And finally, after a few agonizing seconds, he barked at Kimmy, "If I see you in here again before you're twenty-one, I won't be so nice next time!" And then he stalked off to wait on a customer of legal age.

"I just realized who you are—you're Liddy's friend, the one thinking about buying our house," Kimmy said.

Hayley had completely forgotten about Liddy's little white lie that Hayley had a few million bucks to burn, but she did confirm the "friend" part.

Kimmy hurtled forward and threw her arms around Hayley. "Thank you for saving my butt. You have no idea how much that means to me. I owe you big time."

"Just don't try anything like that ever again, okay?"

Kimmy nodded, her head planted on Hayley's shoulder.

Liddy, enormously relieved and grateful that she wasn't going to have to call Jim and Rachel Nash to come and bail their older daughter out of jail, simply mouthed the words to Hayley, *Thank you!*

Chapter 9

Hayley wasn't sure what to expect when she met Dr. George Kittridge, but the short, slight, soft-spoken, bespectacled, birdlike man in front of her was certainly not anything like what she had envisioned. Physically, he was not remotely close to Liddy's usual type. She had always been attracted to men taller than herself, beefier, more manly. Her ex-fiancé Sonny Rivers had a nice build and exuded confidence and strength, as did most of her other former boyfriends. But George, God bless him, probably wouldn't stand a chance against a stiff north-easterly wind. He seemed pleasant enough, smiling politely and nodding a lot, letting Liddy do most of the talking at Hayley's cocktail party, completely oblivious that he was actually the guest of honor, that the whole gathering had been planned so everyone could meet him.

Bruce tried his best to engage with George, peppering

him with questions about his job at the Jackson Lab, as they stood in the living room among the other guests.

"Liddy tells me your specialty is immunological sciences," Bruce said, handing George a bourbon and water.

"Yes," George muttered.

Long pause.

"That must be interesting work," Bruce commented.

"Yes."

Liddy, sensing Bruce's frustration in carrying on a conversation with her new man, jumped in. "George is going to deliver a very important speech at some big medical conference in Barcelona this fall, can you believe it? Fingers crossed he can bring a plus one!"

"Oh, what is your speech about?" Bruce asked, curious.

"Normal microbiota as a microbiological barrier and stimulator of the immune system," George said softly.

"Sounds riveting," Bruce cracked.

But he was happy he at least got George to say more than a one-word response.

George took a small sip of his bourbon, then had a coughing fit, hacking and choking. His eyes were watering, and his face was red, but when Bruce stepped toward him to see if he was okay, George held up a hand to keep him at bay.

"George doesn't often drink alcohol," Liddy noted. "It's one of the many things I respect about him."

Bruce raised an eyebrow. This coming from the woman who spent an hour of her day, almost every day, nursing a cosmo at Drinks Like A Fish.

Hayley, who had been eavesdropping on the conversation, was also making sure her other guests were having a good time. She made an effort to keep the list small. She didn't want a huge crowd that would stay late into the night, especially since she still wanted to swing by her restaurant to check in on her staff before closing.

Besides Liddy and George, she had invited Lynette and her husband Jamie, and Dustin and MacKenzie, of course, as well as Mona and her new boyfriend Chuck, although the latter couple had yet to show up.

Liddy was now clapping George on the back with the palm of her hand as he continued hacking and choking.

Hayley stared at the poor wheezing man. "What's wrong with him?"

"Nothing," Liddy said calmly. "This happens all the time. He sometimes swallows the wrong way when he's eating or drinking."

Hayley offered a plate of her canapés to Lynette and Jamie, who were chatting with Dustin and MacKenzie. They all took one, and then Hayley made a beeline back toward Bruce, Liddy, and George, who was now bent over, hands on his knees, breathing heavily in and out; but mercifully, he seemed to have finally stopped choking.

"You okay, buddy?" Bruce asked George, placing a comforting hand on his back.

George suddenly stood erect, but the top of his head was barely above Liddy's right shoulder. He nodded, forcing a smile. "Yes."

"Can I get you a glass of water?" Hayley asked.

"No."

Dr. George was definitely a man of very few words.

Luckily, he was accompanied by a renowned chatterbox, who was more than happy to do all the talking for him.

"George is super impressive. He studied at Imperial

College in London, got his PhD at MIT, did his residency at Mass General . . ." Liddy gushed.

"Wow, you must have had your pick of places to work; what brought you to the Jackson Lab?" Bruce asked.

"He grew up in New England; this is home to him. He was born in Worcester, but they don't have a major-league research facility like we do, so of course, Bar Harbor was the perfect fit," Liddy explained. "Isn't that right, honey?"

"Yes," George said with a curt nod.

Dustin appeared at Hayley's side. "Mom, do you have any more of those bacon-scallop bites? Mac can't get enough of them. She devoured the whole plate."

"Yes, give me a minute, they're in the kitchen," Hayley said, starting off just as Liddy grabbed her by the sleeve of her sweater and stopped her.

"So, what do you think of George?"

"I like him."

"I feel there's a *but* coming."

"No buts. He's just very shy."

"Yes, I know. That's what I love most about him. It's so darn cute," Liddy said, smiling. "It is cute, isn't it?" Liddy paused, then redirected her loving gaze in Hayley's direction. "Don't you think it's cute, Hayley?"

"Oh, yes! Sorry, I didn't think you were waiting for me to actually answer. Yes, Liddy, it's cute. Very, very cute."

"I will tell you, it is so refreshing not to be with a man who constantly loves to hear himself talk."

Especially when the woman he's with actually loves to hear herself talk. But that wasn't a thought Hayley had any intention of sharing with her BFF. "Excuse me, Liddy, I need to put more food out."

Hayley had a tray of mushroom-onion tartlets cooking

that still needed to be served. She glided into the kitchen, grabbed some mitts, and pulled the tray out of the oven, setting it down on top of the stove for the tartlets to cool.

Hayley's phone buzzed in her back pocket. She pulled it out and saw a new text. "Oh, no . . ."

"Something wrong?"

Hayley swiveled around to find Lynette hovering in the kitchen doorway. "Mona just texted. She's not coming."

"That's a shame. Did she say why?"

"Apparently she just had a fight with her new boyfriend."

"I didn't know she was seeing someone new," Bruce said, surprised, suddenly appearing in the kitchen and grabbing another beer from the fridge.

"His name is Chuck. He's a janitor. That's all we really know about him so far. But unfortunately, it looks like that's all we ever will know, because she just broke it off with him," Hayley said, disappointed.

"You know what a hothead Mona can be. I'm sure once she lets off some steam, she'll calm down and come around, and they'll somehow work it out," Bruce remarked, before popping the cap off his beer with a bottle opener and heading back down the hall to the living room.

Hayley turned to Lynette. "I hope he's right. Mona's kids are growing up and leaving home; it would be nice if she found a companion that makes her happy."

Lynette walked up next to Hayley. "Can I help you serve those delicious-looking hors d'oeuvres?"

"No thanks, Lynette, I got it," Hayley said, noticing Lynette lingering near the kitchen counter. There was something clearly on her mind.

"Is there anything you wanted to talk to me about, Lynette?"

Lynette glanced over her shoulder to make sure everyone at the party was still socializing in the living room, and then scooted over close to Hayley, whispering intently, "Yes, Hayley, I have been hoping to get you alone so we could have a private chat."

"Okay," Hayley said tentatively.

Dustin wandered down the hall to the kitchen. "Mom?"

"Bacon scallops, yes, on the counter!"

Dustin smiled with approval as he spotted the plate.

"Do me a favor, take those and offer a few to the guests before you and MacKenzie scarf the rest down."

Dustin grabbed the plate and headed out, Hayley knowing full well he wasn't about to share them with anybody else but his baby mama.

Hayley turned back to Lynette with a concerned look on her face. "What is it, Lynette—what's wrong?"

Lynette gathered her courage, took a deep breath, and then just spat it out. "I think Jamie is having an affair."

Hayley reeled back. "What? I don't believe it. With who?"

"One of his students."

"No! Jamie would never . . ."

"A customer came into the shop the other day, and casually mentioned that she had seen Jamie with a young woman, who looked like she could be one of his students at the college. I didn't think much of it at first; I mean, Jamie is always meeting with students to mentor and advise them, there is nothing unusual about that. But this customer—and I trust her, because she would have no reason to make this up—she said she was jogging around Eagle Lake on a carriage trail, miles from town, and she spotted the two of them sitting together on a rock at the edge of the lake, immersed in what looked like a very deep and personal conversation. If she was a student who just wanted to discuss a grade or a paper, why not just meet in his office? Why did they have to go all the way out there, like they didn't want to be seen together?"

"There could be a whole host of reasons. It doesn't necessarily mean something untoward is happening between them," Hayley insisted.

"I have been extra busy running the shop this summer, and I haven't exactly been present in our marriage. I've noticed that Jamie's been bored lately. He's been filling his time teaching a few summer classes and doing work around the house, but he has a lot of free time on his hands. But the last thing I ever expected was that he would cheat on me!"

"Lynette, listen to me, you can't speculate on what you know nothing about. Just talk to Jamie, give him a chance to clear the air. I'm sure you'll discover it's something completely innocent."

"But Hayley, what if I discover it's *not*," Lynette said, worry lines forming on her brow.

Chapter 10

"That can't be right," Hayley said out loud to herself as she gaped at the princely sum on her digital calculator. She scooped up the stack of receipts from the previous evening at Hayley's Kitchen and began adding them up again.

Sure enough, she got the exact same total.

The verdict was officially in.

Her restaurant was a bona fide hit.

Hayley wished someone were around to share in this victorious moment, but alas, she was alone in her cramped office, just off the kitchen of her restaurant. She had come in early to catch up on some paperwork, having decided after the last of her guests had left her cocktail party the previous night not to swing by and check up on her staff. Her manager and cooks and waitstaff were all highly capable and hardworking and could probably use one night where the boss wasn't obsessively hovering over them, inspecting their work.

But she was bursting to tell someone that her restaurant had just broken a record for the most business in one night.

She debated who to call first.

Unfortunately, it wasn't even seven a.m. yet.

Who could she call who would already be up and out of bed?

Not her husband Bruce; that was for certain. She had just left him at home, snoring loudly, dead to the world.

Mona would certainly be up this early.

Mona.

She really needed to talk to Mona.

After the party last night, it had been way too late to reach out to her and find out exactly what happened with her new man Chuck, so now was as good a time as any.

Hayley grabbed her phone off the desk and called Mona's number but got her voice mail. She decided to try her house phone, and after a few rings, someone picked up and mumbled in a groggy voice, "Hello?"

"Hi, it's Hayley, who's this?"

"Chet."

"Good morning, Chet, is your mother home?"

"No, she left a couple hours ago to haul traps with my brothers," Chet said. "I'll tell her you called."

"Chet, wait!"

Hayley paused but heard nothing.

"Chet, are you still there?"

"Yeah, I'm here," he sighed, annoyed.

Obviously wishing he wasn't.

"How are you? Are you enjoying summer vacation?"

"I guess so."

"I hear Mona's got you working in the lobster shop."

Chet grunted something unintelligible.

This kid was even less chatty than Liddy's new beau George.

Truth be told, she was very worried about Mona's son, especially after catching him loitering outside the Bar Harbor Ice Cream Shop. She didn't want to tattle to Mona that her youngest boy may have an unhealthy obsession with a college-age girl, but she also didn't want to ignore it, either.

Especially if it was developing into a real problem.

"Well, I hope she's not being a taskmaster, and you're allowed to have a little fun this summer . . ."

"She gives me Wednesdays and Fridays off . . ."

"That's right, I saw you last Wednesday, outside the Bar Harbor Ice Cream Shop."

There was a long silence, and she could picture him tensing up on the other end of the call.

Finally, he growled in a low voice, "I wasn't outside the ice cream shop, I was all the way down the street."

"I know there are a few pretty girls who work there, one in particular I think you may have your eye on—"

Click.

"Chet?"

Hayley paused.

"Chet, hello?"

He had hung up on her.

Hayley set her phone back down on her desk and pondered her next move. She hadn't had the chance to discuss any of this with Mona, and perhaps she should refrain from butting in and just mind her own business, but a big part of her believed that Mona would really want to know.

Still, except for Miranda complaining about Chet hanging around all the time, he had done nothing yet to raise any serious alarm bells.

Her thoughts were interrupted by a loud honking noise outside.

Hayley shot up from the desk and walked out the back door of the restaurant to the gravel parking lot, where she saw Lynette in the driver's seat of her white ice cream truck, pulling up out front.

Lynette jumped out of the truck and ambled over to greet Hayley. "I really want to replace that obnoxious horn with one that plays 'Turkey in the Straw' and draws all the kids in the neighborhood out like a real honest-to-goodness ice cream truck!"

"Kids? I'd probably knock them out of the way to be first in line for a Salted Caramel cone!"

Lynette chortled, then strolled to the back of the truck. "Hey, thanks for the party last night. Jamie and I had a wonderful time."

"We loved having you," Hayley said. "By the way, did you have a chance to bring up what we discussed with Jamie?"

"Uh, no," Lynette said, her hand resting on the handle of the truck's back door. "It was late when we got home, and he was tired, and so he went straight to bed. He had an early faculty meeting to prepare for the fall semester, and he was up and gone before I was even awake. I promise, I will talk to him."

Hayley offered her a thin smile, not entirely convinced she would.

Eager to change the subject, Lynette broke out in a wide grin. "Speaking of Salted Caramel . . ."

"Please tell me you brought a carton!"

"I brought two extra, because I would like some of your customers to be able to get some, too!"

Lynette cranked the handle and whipped open the back of the truck, pointing both of her arms with a flourish like a *Price Is Right* model presenting prizes during the Showcase Showdown.

She had been right.

There were two extra-large cartons labeled Salted Caramel in front, as mist from the large freezer swirled out into the early morning air.

Hayley gasped, her eyes popping out, her mouth dropping open.

Lynette spun around to see what had shocked her so badly. When her eyes fell upon the dead body sprawled out on the floor of her truck, Lynette let out a blood-curdling scream.

There was no mystery as to who it was.

It was one of her young employees.

And the object of Chet Barnes's affections.

Miranda Fox.

Island Food & Spirits
BY
HAYLEY POWELL

Anyone who has known my brother Randy for a long time knows that before becoming a bar owner, he desperately wanted to be an actor. He even moved to New York City to study at the American Academy of Dramatic Arts before realizing just what kind of a commitment and dedication it was going to take to make it, and that the odds were overwhelmingly stacked against him accepting an Academy Award before his twenty-first birthday, which was why he moved back to Bar Harbor and opened the doors to our favorite local watering hole, Drinks Like A Fish.

But what most people don't know about my brother is his uncanny talent with numbers. Yes, he's always been brilliant when it comes to math problems. Back in the day, Randy was a math genius! And still is, which is why his business ledgers are always balanced right down to the penny. He rarely talks about this God-given talent, because it just isn't as glamorous or exciting as being an actor in his mind. It was just a passing phase.

But boy, was he good at it.

Case in point.

Pi Day, which every year comes on March 14th, was Randy's favorite holiday as a kid. I am no math whiz by any stretch of the imagination, so all I can gather from Randy's many, many attempts to enlighten me is that Pi Day is March 14th—March is the 3rd month, and the date is 14, so the digits 3-1-4 represent the first three digits of pi, and that also happens to be Albert Einstein's birthday. But all of this is way above my pay grade, and I get a headache just thinking about it.

Okay, so Pi Day is not technically a holiday. But you know how the Super Bowl isn't really a holiday, but people still go nuts during the buildup to the big day? Cheering on their favorite teams; screaming over every touchdown; agonizing over every fumble; chowing down on endless hamburgers and hot dogs and chicken wings and pizzas; storming off to bed after every loss; staying up late celebrating by pounding down beers after every victory; exhausting themselves until only two teams are left to battle it out for the much-coveted trophy, which takes place on one glorious Sunday every year, like it's an actual holiday? That's what Randy went through on Pi Day.

I'll wait for you to stop laughing at the absurdity of this, but Randy took Pi Day very, very seriously. He would even insist our mother make homemade pies to mark the occasion. Not just dessert pies like apple and coconut cream, but shepherd's pies, pizza pies, any pie her creative brain could come up with.

Because I know this is one part of his past that Randy would now like to forget, I always show up every March 14th on Randy's doorstep with one of my own tasty pies (this year was peanut butter cup ice cream pie, but more on that later) to remind him of his hilarious childhood obsession with math.

And if he tries to deny it, I am always there to remind him of an embarrassing story from his math glory days, which I did again this year as Randy and I, along with Randy's husband Sergio, sat down to dig into my delectable peanut butter cup ice cream pie.

Since the third grade, Randy had impressively won every math competition he entered. Every inch of his bedroom walls were covered in blue ribbons. He never lost. Not once. Until his freshman year in high school. Our math team had already won the state competition and was preparing to go on a trip to Washington, DC for the nationals. Mostly only the juniors and seniors were allowed to go, but this year, the principal had decided to include one freshman in the mix, and they would decide who that lucky person would be with a difficult exam using the hardest math problems imaginable. Randy desperately wanted to go; he had never been farther than Bangor, so DC to him was like Mecca. Although if it had been up to him, Hollywood, California, with the Walk of Fame, would have ultimately won out.

Anyway, Randy was his usual cocky self. He knew he would ace the test and be on his way to our nation's capital in no time. But then the unthinkable happened. He came in second!

When Mr. Richards, the math teacher, announced that a new student, Sharon Alley, had gotten the highest score, a jaw-dropping one hundred percent, everyone was stunned, especially Randy. As an excited and screaming Sharon mowed past him (he had already stood up, assuming his name would be called, when they were about to announce the winner), to collect the golden ticket to DC, well, to say Randy was inconsolable would be a gross understatement.

But soon after, that crushing sadness gave way to seething anger, and Randy began asking himself who this new student Sharon Alley was, and how dare she take away his dream of seeing the theater where Lincoln was shot!

After asking around, Randy discovered Sharon had moved to the island a few months ago with her family when her father was stationed at the Coast Guard base in Southwest Harbor. Kids described her as friendly, but a bit of a braggart about all of the places in the world she had lived. She made no secret of the fact that she was unhappy about moving to a small town on an island in the middle of nowhere and tended to whine on and on about how much more sophisticated her friends were in the big city of

Virginia Beach, where her father had last been stationed. However, the big revelation Randy had been looking for quickly came to light. According to three different girls who were in Sharon's Algebra I class, she was an average student. One girl caught a glimpse of her last quarterly report card and swore on her life she saw a C minus!

Randy smelled a rat. And he began formulating a plan to get back what in his mind should have been his rightful first-place win. He would befriend Sharon, play upon her vanity and cluelessness until he got her to openly confess that she had cheated while secretly recording her, and then he would very dramatically play the evidence over the school's loudspeaker right after the national anthem before first period.

He slyly complimented her blouse in study hall, insisted that a boy she had her eye on had been staring at her all through English class, and by lunch, they were sharing his bag of Lay's potato chips and had cute nicknames for each other.

Still, Randy only had three weeks to expose her before the mathletes left for DC, and so the clock was ticking. No matter how much time they spent together, gabbing and laughing and opening up to each other, Sharon remained frustratingly tight-lipped when it came to the controversial math test.

With only four days left to go, Randy was about to give up his mission. They were sitting in the cafeteria doing homework together, and

Sharon slapped her pen down and declared, "I just don't get this!"

"What don't you get?" Randy asked tentatively.

Sharon tapped her paper with her index finger and whispered, "This." Then she made her fatal mistake—trusting Randy. She leaned over, eyes darting around to make sure no one was eavesdropping, and whispered in her new best friend's ear, "Math. I have never been any good at it. I cheated on that test."

Randy was kicking himself that he had forgotten to turn on his tiny voice recorder, but he couldn't very well ask her to go back and repeat what she had just said. Sharon continued blabbing on, explaining why she had done it. She hated moving to the island and leaving her friends in Virginia, and her parents wouldn't let her go back to see them until Christmas, so she thought that if she could get to Washington, DC, then she could use her stipend money to hop a bus to Virginia Beach. Her parents would never even know! But now that she had met Randy, and had made a close friend here in Bar Harbor, it didn't seem so important anymore. Sharon was happy here, but now she had made a big mess of things and didn't know how to get out of it. She jumped up and ran crying out of the cafeteria.

Well, this changed everything. Now Randy felt bad for her and decided not to tattle on her and reclaim his first-place position. He would keep mum and let her go on the trip and see her friends. But things worked out differently.

The next morning, Randy heard his name called out over the loudspeaker and was told to report directly to the principal's office. There he found Principal Good and the Mathlete Coach Mr. Richards, and Sharon dabbing her eyes with a Kleenex from Mr. Good's desk. She had come clean and confessed everything. She had been disqualified, and Randy would now be taking her place.

In the end, Randy got what he wanted, and Sharon said she got what she wanted—a new best friend. In fact, Randy and Sharon remained close all through high school, and Randy still hears from Sharon when she drops him post-cards from all kinds of exotic locations, since she became a renowned photographer who works for a travel magazine. And most importantly, I got what I wanted, which is to have any excuse to eat pie, and I have Pi Day to thank for that.

What better way to start celebrating Pi Day than a pie-inspired cocktail? This is one of Randy's absolute favorites!

RANDY'S APPLE PIE MARTINI

INGREDIENTS:
Ice and a shaker

1½ ounces Baileys Apple Pie liqueur
1 ounce Crown Royal Apple Whisky
¼ ounce Torani caramel syrup
Cinnamon stick for garnish

Add all of the above ingredients except cinnamon
stick to the shaker and shake until chilled. Pour
into a martini glass, garnish with a cinnamon
stick, and enjoy!

HAYLEY'S PEANUT BUTTER CUP ICE CREAM PIE

INGREDIENTS:
½ tub of Cool Whip
¼ cup peanut butter ice cream
1 pre-made Oreo cookie crust
4 or 5 peanut butter cups, roughly chopped (6 if
   you're like me)
½ cup hot fudge ice cream topping

Microwave your hot fudge topping according to
the directions and allow to cool while still
stirrable.

In a large bowl, mix the ice cream and Cool Whip
using an electric mixer until smooth.

Pour the mixture into the Oreo pie crust, and
then pour on the chocolate topping and swirl,
using a butter knife.

Top with your peanut butter cup pieces. Place
into the freezer and freeze at least 6 hours.

When good and frozen, remove from freezer,
slice, and dig in! You will thank me!

Chapter 11

Lynette Partridge's adorable spotted dachshund, Sprinkles—the irony of the name was not lost on anyone—raced along the rocky beach of Frenchman Bay with Hayley's aging shih tzu, Leroy, who was desperately trying to keep up but nevertheless struggling. The tide was coming in, and so both dogs had to scamper sharply to the right every minute or so to avoid getting swept up by the waves rolling in. Hayley and Lynette walked side by side along the shore, in bulky wool sweaters and jeans, since the temperature had dropped considerably and a heavy mist was in the air.

They had spent a good part of the day at the police station, answering questions, after finding Miranda Fox's dead body in the back of Lynette's ice cream truck. Chief Sergio and Lieutenant Donnie, along with Officers Earl and Tina, a recent new recruit, had arrived on the scene within minutes of Hayley calling 911, doing an initial sweep of the scene before the county crime scene investigators arrived. Hayley and Lynette were briefly interviewed by the chief in the parking lot, and then he requested that they come down to the station for further questioning. The two women were taken in separately, presumably to make sure there was no opportunity for them to "get their stories straight." However, Hayley figured it was just routine, since she could not fathom her own brother-in-law, the chief, suspecting her of anything nefarious.

When they were finally told they were free to go, Lynette raced back to her shop to alert her other employees to the devastating news about Miranda, and Hayley, exhausted, drove to her house to feed Leroy and call Bruce with an update. She had been home maybe an hour when Lynette called and asked if she would accompany her while she took Sprinkles on a walk along the beach so they could discuss the day's events. Hayley readily agreed. She was going stir crazy waiting for Bruce to come home, and Leroy needed to get out, anyway.

"How did your staff take the news?" Hayley asked, hugging herself to keep warm from the numbing chill in the air.

"They're in shock, just like me," Lynette said breathlessly. "Nobody can believe it. They're also very worried about being considered suspects, since Bethany, Tim, and Eric were the ones who loaded up the truck last night."

"Where was Miranda?"

"She was right there with them, helping. Then when they were finished, they all left, Miranda included. I just don't understand how she could have wound up stuck in there. You can't lock the door from the inside, it has to be done from the outside, which means someone else had to have been there. It couldn't have been an accident. I can't stop thinking, what if she was still alive? I'm haunted by the image of her trapped in there, banging on the door for help, nobody around to hear her, and then slowly freezing to death. How awful that must have been!"

"You can't let your mind go there, Lynette. We don't know what exactly happened yet. We'll find out after the autopsy. Has her family been contacted?"

"Her parents died in a plane crash when she was a little girl; she was an only child, and was raised by an elderly aunt, who passed away a few years ago. She was working her tail off to put herself through college so she could get a good job, make a happy life for herself. Oh, Hayley, I'm just heartbroken over this."

"Where did the employees say they went after finishing up their shift last night?"

Lynette shrugged. "The boys say they went to Drinks Like A Fish for a beer. Bethany and Miranda walked home. They're all renting a house together for the summer on School Street. Bethany told me Miranda went upstairs to bed, and that's the last time she saw her. How on earth did she wind up in my truck's freezer this morning? It doesn't make any sense!"

Lynette, shaken, stared into space, lost in thought.

Hayley noticed Leroy and Sprinkles were far down the beach and called out to them. Both dogs stopped, ears perked up, alert, then began sprinting back towards them, Leroy once again bringing up the rear, tongue panting, doing his best, poor thing. He was ten years old, whereas Sprinkles was a spry and energetic three and a half.

"There's something else," Lynette mumbled, so low Hayley almost missed it.

"What?"

"When I got back to the shop from the police station this afternoon, I found a sealed manila envelope addressed to me on the counter. There was no postage or return address on it. Someone just left it there anonymously. Inside were some printed-out digital photos."

Hayley could feel her stomach tightening. "Of what?"

"Jamie," Lynette said solemnly, her voice hoarse. "He was on a hiking trail in the park . . . with a young woman . . . her face was clearly visible . . ."

"Who?" Hayley asked, although she already had a strong suspicion at this point.

"Miranda," Lynette choked out.

"Oh, dear . . ." Hayley whispered.

"I know," Lynette wailed. "What if it turns out Jamie has been unfaithful with a student, with one of my own *employees* . . ." She stopped, her mind racing. "And what if . . . what if Miranda threatened to tell me about the affair, and Jamie suddenly felt cornered and got desperate . . . Oh god, I'm too scared to even think about it!"

"Lynette, don't get ahead of yourself. The first thing you need to do is talk to Jamie."

Sprinkles arrived, tail wagging, a big, doggie grin plastered on his face. Lynette bent over and petted him on the head, her hand trembling. "Good boy."

"Like I said before, there could be a simple, reasonable explanation for those pictures," Hayley said, barely convincing herself. She had always tried to give everyone the benefit of the doubt, but for those photos to turn up on the same day Miranda's dead body was found in the back of his wife's ice cream truck—well, it was a troubling sign, to say the least.

"We've been happily married for seven years now, but I know I've been immersed in my business, and there have been times when perhaps I haven't been as present and attentive as I could have been, but he's always been so understanding, because I was working so hard for us, for our future . . . What if he really wasn't as understanding as I believed? What if I don't know my own husband at all? What if I've been completely blind, and I'm married to a cold-blooded kill—"

"Lynette, stop! This is ridiculous! There is no way Jamie is guilty of something so awful! We just need to wait until we learn the cause of death! In the meantime, talk to him!" she begged Lynette.

"If I bring this up, and I'm wrong, it will destroy him. Maybe you could . . ."

"Oh no, no way."

"Please, Hayley, you're so good at this sort of thing. Just find out if they were romantically involved, for my own peace of mind. And if there was nothing inappropriate going on, and it was just a platonic teacher-student relationship, then Jamie will never have to know I ever suspected him."

"I am not a private investigator."

"You may not have a license, but everybody in town knows you kind of are. I'm begging you, Hayley. If I come out and ask him, Jamie might never forgive me for thinking the worst of him, for even entertaining the thought that he was capable of such a vile, despicable act. That he might be a *murderer*."

"He's *not*, Lynette," Hayley said.

This seemed to calm her down.

But then again, Hayley thought to herself, *his own wife is suspicious of him.*

So how could Hayley, who only knew Professor Jamie McGibbon socially on rare occasions, defend him with such confidence?

She really couldn't.

And that disturbed her.

Chapter 12

Hayley could hear the raucous partying from two blocks away. There was no mystery where it was coming from. Lynette had already told her that most of her college-age employees were renting a house together on School Street. Even though it was a Thursday night, just after the ice cream shop closed, they were still smack-dab in the middle of the freewheeling summer season. There were no early morning classes to worry about, so why not host a nonstop festival of late-night beers and bongs every night of the week until it was time to travel back to their various campuses in different parts of Maine and beyond?

Hayley was certainly not one to judge.

She had indulged her wild side plenty when she was that age, especially during the summer months after high school, when she, too, scooped ice cream during the day and waited tables in the evening for a couple of years. She fondly recalled her heated romances with young, granola-eating, laid-back hikers from abroad eager to hit the hard, intense mountain trails before dawn and cuddle up with a nice local girl after dark, or the experienced, wealthy city boys on break from the Ivy League schools, begrudgingly tagging along with their parents on a family vacation, who were in search of a diversion, something more interesting than blueberry picking.

Nothing had really changed in Bar Harbor since those days.

Same crowd of kids, except now, they all had smart-phones.

As Hayley rounded the corner onto School Street, she spotted a gaggle of young men and women hanging around on the front lawn of a stick-style house typical of the late nineteenth century architecture in New England, and named for its linear stickwork on the outside walls. The house overall was in dire need of a home makeover, but Hayley figured the owners were not about to cough up much for improvements until their hard-partying tenants vacated after the summer season. Music blasted from inside the house, some hip-hop confection; perhaps Drake, Hayley couldn't be sure.

She felt funny passing by the tight-knit group of kids on the lawn and walking up the rickety steps and into the house, because she was so much older than everybody else. Decades older, in fact. But she was a woman on a mission. She had made a promise to Lynette. So like it or not, she was going to crash this party.

Inside the house, Hayley crinkled her nose, taking in a distinct odor, and then instantly began choking on smoke—pot, to be more specific. In the living room were about six kids in their late teens, early twenties, sharing a blue bong. A couple looked up at her with friendly, albeit glassy, eyes, and she acknowledged them with a wave and continued on to the kitchen, where two kegs were set up, a crowd of boys lined up to refill their cheap plastic cups.

Hayley recognized two of them, Tim and Eric, from Lynette's ice cream shop. Both were stumbling and laughing and acting silly with each other, no doubt from too much alcohol.

Tim glanced over at Hayley and lit up. "Hey, sexy, wanna beer?"

Hayley stiffened.

Sexy?

Just how drunk was this kid?

"No, thanks."

"Oh, come on," Tim insisted. "It's a party!"

He went to grab a cup from the stack on the counter and knocked the whole thing over onto the floor. He bent over, nearly losing his balance, as he scooped one up in his hand. "One-second rule! You should be fine!" He handed it to Eric, who was closer to the keg. "Fill 'er up!"

Eric giggled as he flipped the lever and white foamy beer from the keg's nozzle began pouring into the cup.

Neither of them seemed to recognize Hayley in the slightest, even though they had previously met.

Eric handed Tim the cup of beer, and Tim shuffled over to Hayley and gave it to her with a big, goofy grin. "You're beautiful; wanna dance?"

Oh, lord.

"I can't. I have to go home to my *husband* soon."

He stared at her curiously, swaying back and forth. "You're married? Okay. We can still dance, can't we?"

He started showing off his embarrassingly drunken dance moves, and Hayley knew at that moment she had seen quite enough. She took one sip of the warm, rancid beer and dumped the rest of it in the sink, then scooted out of the kitchen, eyes searching for someone who might be able to fill in a few of the blanks about the mysterious Miranda Fox.

"Hey, I know you," a voice said off to her left.

Hayley turned to find Zoe Nash, the daughter of Jim and Rachel Nash. She was hanging off the arm of her boyfriend, the handsome young Chasen, whom Hayley had also met at the Seagull House.

"I heard you did my sister a solid. That was very cool of you," Zoe commented.

"She told you about that?"

"No, she wouldn't dare. She's too afraid I'd post about it on Instagram. But I have eyes and ears all over this town," Zoe said, chuckling. "You could have tattled on her to my parents, and you didn't, so you get major points in my book."

"What did Kimmy do?" Chasen asked, curious.

Zoe gave him a sly smile. "I'll tell you later."

He then redirected his attention to Hayley. "It's nice to see you—what's your name again?"

"Hayley."

"Hayley, right, you're friends with Jim and Rachel's real estate agent. I'm surprised to see you here. This doesn't strike me as your kind of scene."

"You're right, it's not," Hayley explained. "I'm here to try and find someone . . ."

A blindingly drunk, bleary-eyed, hefty kid barreled through them, nearly knocking Hayley to the ground. She quickly recovered. "I'm trying to find someone lucid and sober enough to string a few sentences together and tell me about Miranda Fox."

The name gave both of them pause, but neither missed a beat. Zoe jumped in first. "I didn't know her well at all. I mean, of course I met her—Chasen lives here, so I've met all of his roommates—but I didn't even know her name until after, you know, after she died," she said. Then she felt the urge to add, "It's so sad what happened."

"Yes, it is," Hayley agreed.

She turned to Chasen, waiting for him to speak.

But he didn't.

He just kept his eyes fixed on his girlfriend, with whom he clearly was head over heels.

"What about you, Chasen?"

He finally snapped out of his reverie. "Me? She seemed nice enough, kept to herself mostly. I rent a room down the hall from her, but we barely spoke. I mean, she was closer to the girls in the house . . ."

"Chasen's hardly around here, anyway; he spends most of his free time with me," Zoe said with a playful, coquettish smile.

Chasen leaned in and kissed her longingly on the lips.

Hayley was starting to feel nauseated.

And not from the one sip of beer.

"Is there a particular girl in the house she was closest to?" Hayley asked.

Chasen shrugged. "I don't know. Talk to Bethany. She's kind of like the den mother around here."

"Thanks," Hayley said, moving on through the sea of loud, sweaty, obnoxious kids, her eyes scanning for Bethany.

She found her by the staircase, chatting intensely with

another girl Hayley didn't recognize. As Hayley approached, Bethany noticed her and instantly stopped talking.

"Bethany, hi, I'm not sure if you remember me . . ."

Bethany nodded. "I remember you. What are you doing here?"

The girl preferred getting right to the point.

"I'm sorry to crash your party, but I was hoping you might help shed a little light on Miranda . . ."

Bethany squeezed her friend's hand. "I'll catch up with you later."

The young woman was curious and wanted to stay, but reluctantly moved on outside to join the kids on the lawn.

"What do you want to know? I already told the police that she went straight to her room after we got home from work that night, and that's the last time I saw her."

"Do you remember anyone coming to the house that night to see her?"

"Maybe. I mean, it's possible. But I never heard a thing. I went straight to bed, and I'm a pretty heavy sleeper. I take Ambien, and it usually knocks me right out."

"Did she ever talk about seeing anyone—a boyfriend, perhaps?"

Bethany hesitated, then nodded. "We were hanging out in the living room once, about a month ago, watching TV, and she got a call. You could just tell from the look on her face that she was excited over a guy. She went upstairs to take it so I couldn't overhear. When she came back down, I pressed her to spill the details, but she refused, she wouldn't divulge anything about him. Which was odd, because normally, if one of the girls in the house met a guy, it's all they would talk about."

"Why do you suppose she was so secretive about this mystery man?"

"Who knows? I thought maybe he was married, a local in the community, so they had to keep their affair under wraps, but I was just guessing. I didn't know for sure."

A married man.

Like Professor Jamie McGibbon?

Hayley's mind did not want to go there.

Just yet.

"Bethany, do you think it would be all right if I took a look around her room?"

Bethany bristled. "Why?"

"I promise I'm not trying to stir up any trouble, I just want to piece together what happened to her. She has no family around to ask questions, and the circumstances of her death are so unusual, I just feel like she deserves some kind of inquiry, so we can get some answers."

Bethany was still not sold, but finally, she relented with a frown. "Upstairs, third door down on the left. Don't be in there too long."

"Thank you," Hayley said, bounding up the steps.

Miranda's room was pretty bare. Just a bed, a chair with ripped upholstery, a small nightstand, and a tiny desk pushed up against the window, with a fan on the sill. It didn't take long for Hayley to case the place, because there was nothing much to case. Some clothes hanging in the closet. Toiletries in a bag under the bed. An aging laptop on the desk. A robe hanging on a hook behind the door.

Definitely a minimalist, with very few possessions.

Underneath the desk was a small metal trash can.

It was the only thing left to check.

Hayley bent down, pulled the can out, and began rummaging through a pile of crumpled-up papers and discarded fashion magazines. At the bottom, she found an empty aspirin bottle and some packaging for one of those rapid pregnancy tests. Hayley's eyes widened in surprise. She frantically hunted around for the white stick to no avail. She popped back up to her feet and hurried down the hall to the bathroom, where she began searching the trash can in there.

Eureka!

At the bottom was a white test stick, and on the digital display was the word YES with a plus sign.

Hayley stumbled back, in a state of shock.

Miranda Fox had been pregnant.

Chapter 13

Hayley plowed down the stairs, her mind racing. Miranda's pregnancy opened up a whole new set of questions. Could this revelation have had anything to do with what happened to her? It was a chilling, disturbing thought, but one that needed further investigating. Navigating her way through the crowd of partiers toward the front door, Hayley was just about home free when someone grabbed her by the wrist and dragged her onto the makeshift dance floor in the middle of the living room. It was Tim, one of the drunken housemates, and the copious amounts of alcohol he had been consuming all night had only strengthened his resolve to trip the light fantastic with Hayley.

Tim, following the lead of the surrounding couples, all of whom were bumping and grinding up against each other to some throbbing dance beat Hayley was too old to recognize, slapped his hands on her hips, drawing her closer to him. He closed his eyes and pursed his lips. Horrified, Hayley instantly planted a hand on his chest and gave him a quick, forceful shove back. He stumbled a bit but didn't fall.

"Not happening, sorry," Hayley said sternly.

He pouted, a hurt look in his eyes. "I'm just really into older women—so much life experience, you know what I'm saying?"

"Well, I'm not into boys young enough to be my son, so keep your body parts to yourself," Hayley warned.

A big football-player type suddenly appeared at Hayley's side. "Is he bothering you?" He turned to Tim, whose eyes were at half-mast, unaware his whole body was swaying listlessly back and forth. "Dude, you need to back off. She's not interested."

"You make a great bouncer," Hayley said, sizing up the giant kid, who grabbed Tim by the arm to hustle him away. "It's okay, I was on my way out."

"Please don't call the cops, they've already given us one warning," the big kid said. "We had a party here a few weeks ago that got pretty rowdy. Some windows got broken; the lady across the street caught someone taking a leak in her flower bed; we had to drag out that stupid drunk guy bothering Miranda . . ."

This stopped Hayley cold. "What guy?"

The big kid shrugged. "I don't know his name, but he was always showing up here, hanging around outside, watching the house. I remember that night he worked up the courage to crash the party and started harassing Miranda, which really freaked her out. Miranda lives here . . . or lived here . . . She . . ."

"Yes, I know all about what happened to Miranda," Hayley said, fishing for her phone. She found a photo of Mona and her entire brood in front of a Christmas tree, one that Hayley had taken last December, and zoomed in on Chet's face.

She held up the photo for the big kid to see. He blinked a couple of times, trying to focus. "To be honest, ma'am, I can't see very well without my glasses."

Hayley suspected his blurry vision had less to do with corrective lenses and more to do with the amount of beer he had been downing all night, like everybody else.

"Come on, Tim," the big kid said as he threw a massive arm around Tim and escorted him away.

Hayley was about to put her phone away when someone said from directly behind her, "That's him."

Hayley spun around to find Bethany hovering over her shoulder, staring at the photo on Hayley's phone.

"He was here that night. It was one thing him showing up at the ice cream shop or hanging around outside the bar when we'd go out for a drink, but when Miranda saw him here in the house, she just lost it. She ran upstairs and locked herself in her room until he left. Clint—that was the guy you were just talking to—and a couple of others had to physically escort him out."

"Are you sure it was him?"

"I don't drink. I'm stone-cold sober tonight, and I was that night, too. So yeah, it was definitely him."

Hayley nodded appreciatively. "Thank you, Bethany."

She knew where she was going next.

Despite Chet's stubborn resistance, it was time he admitted to his infatuation with Miranda Fox, because there was now overwhelming evidence that Mona's youngest son was stalking this young woman, both at work and at home.

And Hayley had to know if that's as far as it went.

Or did he take his obsession to another level that may have cost Miranda her life?

Chapter 14

There was a playful twinkle in Mona's eye that Hayley had never seen before.

"You're back together?" Hayley asked, slack-jawed.

"Yup," Mona answered as she stirred some marinara sauce in a big pot on the stove with a wooden spoon. "He showed up at my front door, got down on his knees, and begged me to take him back. He has such a sweet puppy-dog face, I couldn't stay mad at him, so I said I'd give him one last chance, but I warned him not to screw it up again!"

Sweet puppy-dog face?

Those words coming out of the mouth of Mona Barnes were, to say the least, distinctly out of character.

They were in Mona's kitchen, trying to talk over the ruckus in the living room. Mona had managed to corral most of her kids, the ones still residing in town, over for a family dinner. Her three oldest boys, now grown men who were helping run their mother's lobster business, were shouting and whooping at a baseball game that was playing on the seventy-five-inch flat-screen TV hanging above the fireplace, Jodie, the baby of the family, was upstairs in her room, and Chet, her youngest boy, had been recruited to set the table. He was scowling as he sullenly counted out forks and spoons from the silverware drawer. As for the rest of her brood, Hayley could barely keep track of the number of kids Mona had popped out over the years. Two were away at college, one was in Boston trying to be a musician, and another was working a desk job at Bangor Hydro, last she checked.

"Mona, I've never seen you be so . . ."

"Forgiving?"

"I was going to say *smitten*."

"No, I hate that word. Smitten. Who says smitten? What is this, *Bridgerton*? I may be many things, but smitten will *never* be one of them!"

"I think you're smitten."

"Keep it up, and you won't get any spaghetti."

"I can't stay for dinner; I just dropped by to say hello."

Okay, half of that statement was true.

She definitely could not stay. Bruce, Dustin, and MacKenzie were all at home, waiting for her to cook dinner for them. But she didn't just drop by to say hello. She had her eye on Chet. She was waiting for the right opportunity to get him alone, so she could talk to him.

"If you must know," Mona said with a sigh, "the more I thought about it, the more I thought I *may* have over-reacted when Chuck said he couldn't come to your cocktail party the other night. I don't know what got into me. I rarely get worked up; I usually just go with the flow."

Hayley impulsively burst out laughing.

Mona menacingly waved the wooden spoon at Hayley. "This can be used as a weapon, FYI!"

"Okay, Mona, I won't argue; you're the poster child of calm and clear-headedness. Did Chuck say why he couldn't come to the party?"

"The official story was he had a headache, but I suspect he was nervous about meeting you all. He knows how much you guys mean to me—you and Bruce especially, Liddy not so much. Anyway, I think he got cold feet at the last minute and left me high and dry, and that's what set me off."

"Well, I'm glad you talked it out and got things back on track," Hayley said, eyeing Chet, who had wandered out to the dining room to arrange the place settings on the long oak table, which seated twelve people.

"I got my hands full, Hayley," Mona said, stirring the sauce while opening the oven door to check on her two large loaves of garlic bread. "There's a colander in the sink; could you drain the spaghetti for me?"

"Sure, happy to help."

Hayley did as instructed; then, without prompting, began tossing the salad on the kitchen counter. "So when are we finally going to meet him?"

"I'm working on that. He's usually done with work every day at five. Janitors never have to work late, I guess, so he's free to come over here to hang out, or we cook dinner at his place, whatever we feel like that day. I'll talk to him—maybe we can plan a lobster feast here this weekend, keep it simple, just the four of us."

"Bruce and I would love that. Dustin wants to introduce MacKenzie to some of his high school friends this weekend, so that would be perfect."

Mona grunted some kind of reply as she slurped some marinara sauce off her wooden spoon, which Hayley translated as Mona-speak for "Sounds good."

"If you don't need me for anything else, I'm going to go help Chet set the table."

Before Mona could insist that the boy needed to do it himself in order to cure his inherent laziness or something like that, Hayley scooted out of the kitchen to the dining room, where she found Chet lining up the large soup spoons to the left of the turquoise Fiestaware plates and next to the forks, one at a time.

"What can I do to help?" Hayley said with smile.

Chet glanced up at her and frowned. "You can leave me alone."

"I remember the days when you actually liked having your Aunt Hayley around."

"And I remember the days when you didn't butt into my personal business."

"Fair enough."

"And you're not really my aunt."

"That's true."

She paused, watching him grumpily move down the side of the dining table to the next place setting, slamming the spoon down hard to make his point that he was definitely not happy with Hayley being here.

Hayley took a breath, flicked her eyes toward the kitchen to make sure Mona wasn't within earshot, and then fixed them back on Chet. "We've danced around this long enough, Chet, you need to come clean and tell me what's going on."

"I told you, *nothing's* going on, I don't know why you keep harassing me!"

"Apparently you were the one doing the harassing, according to a number of Miranda Fox's friends. They say you followed her home, crashed a party you weren't invited to, and I personally saw you loitering outside her workplace. This is serious, Chet. Now you can talk to me, or I can call Chief Sergio."

"Go ahead, call him, I dare you."

He wasn't intimidated.

So Hayley had no choice but to go for the nuclear option.

"I can also bring your mother into this conversation at any time."

That did it.

If there was anyone Chet feared more than the police, it was his short-fused mother, whose legendary temper struck fear in the hearts of her children, and most residents of Bar Harbor, for that matter.

Chet swallowed hard and whispered frantically, "I didn't do anything, I swear! I could never hurt Miranda! She was . . ."

"She was what?"

"Perfect," he said, eyes downcast, fingering the spoon he had just set down at the head of the table.

"You loved her, didn't you?"

He shrugged, still staring at the spoon, pressing his finger on it, making it go up and down like a seesaw. "I guess."

"Did you ever tell her how you felt?"

He looked up at Hayley, incredulous. "What? No. I was afraid if I said anything, she'd just laugh at me. I didn't want to like her, I hated the way it made me feel inside, but I couldn't help myself. I couldn't stop thinking about her, I wanted to see her, so I'd just show up where I thought I might run into her. There was no real plan. I was too much of a wimp to talk to her, but I can see how that came off as, I don't know, a little . . ."

"Stalker-y?"

Chet shrugged again, embarrassed. "That night, when I crashed the party at her house, I didn't think anyone would notice me. I mean, they had parties practically every night, and it was so crowded, but the moment Miranda saw me, she got so upset and ran away, and the next thing I knew, these big guys were grabbing me and throwing me out the door and yelling that if I ever showed my face again, they'd bust me up real bad. It was so humiliating."

"Then why did you keep showing up, like at the ice cream shop, the night I was there with Bruce and Dustin and MacKenzie?"

"I was hoping to talk to her, explain that I wasn't this crazy, weird guy that she thought I was. I didn't want her to be scared of me . . . Her friends, Tim and Eric, they finally told me to forget it, she'd never give me the time of day, that she only had eyes for some other guy."

"Who?"

"They didn't know."

"She never told them?"

Chet shook his head. "No. One of them—Eric, I think—he said nobody knew who it was, because Miranda went out of her way to keep his identity a secret. Sometimes they'd get drunk at the house and try to get her to slip up, but she never did. She was determined not to give up the guy's name."

"And no one in her circle knew why?"

"Nope. All I know is, this mystery boyfriend, he was a lucky guy. I would've given *anything* to be him."

Miranda's secret boyfriend was hardly a new piece of

information. Everyone she lived with talked freely about him.

But why the big secret?

What was it about him that had to be kept under wraps, even from her closest friends, like Bethany?

Hayley was convinced this secret, whatever it could be, was the key to why Miranda wound up dead in the back of Lynette Partridge's ice cream truck.

Chapter 15

Professor Jamie McGibbon stared at Hayley, dumb-struck, his mind obviously reeling. "Am I what?" Jamie asked, as if he had misheard the question that she had just asked him in his small office crammed with text-books and research folders and a now-cold big mug of coffee on his battered wooden desk.

Hayley repeated her question. "Are you, or were you at any time, having an affair with one of your students?"

Jamie leaned back in his creaky metal chair, eyes still fixed on Hayley, mouth agape, and then, after a long dra-matic pause, let out a burst of uncontrolled laughter. Such loud, hearty, gut-busting guffawing that tears began stream-ing down his cheeks, and he had to reach for a box of tissues to wipe them off his face. "That's a good one, Hayley."

Once his cheeks were dry again, he balled up the tissue

and launched it toward the trash can across the room like
LeBron James taking a three-point shot in the last two
seconds of a game. Except Jamie missed. It bounced off
the edge of the can and landed on the floor next to it. He
turned back to Hayley, who was stone-faced, and his
mood suddenly darkened. "You're serious."

Hayley nodded.

"I knew you didn't just drop by my office at the college because you wanted to get my grandmother's South
Carolina peach cobbler recipe."

"I do want that, but you're right, that's not why I
came."

"Who told you I was having an affair?"

"No one actually told me anything, but . . ." Hayley
reached into her bag and pulled out the photo of Jamie
and Miranda taken in the park and set it down on the desk
in front of him. "What's that old saying, a picture is worth
a thousand words?"

With his index finger, Jamie dragged the picture closer
until it was right in front of him. He studied it intently and
then shook his head, defiant. "This doesn't prove a thing.
And for the record, I am *not* cheating on my wife now,
nor have I ever, not in a million years! I love Lynette with
all my heart and would never do anything to hurt her!"

He certainly sounded convincing.

Jamie never struck her as the philandering type.

In fact, whenever she saw him and Lynette together, he
followed her around like a devoted puppy dog, always
eager to please.

Jamie tapped his finger on the photo. "Where did you
get this, Hayley?"

"Someone left it anonymously in the apartment above
the Bar Harbor Ice Cream Shop."

Jamie bolted upright, grabbing the photo and waving it in front of her. "The ice cream shop? So Lynette saw this? Was *she* the one who sent you here to grill me? Was she too afraid to ask me herself?"

He reached for his phone, but Hayley shot out a hand to stop him. "Wait, don't call her yet. Just explain to me why you met up with Miranda multiple times . . ."

"*Two* times. I met with her only two times. She was applying for a scholarship. She has no family, very little money, she's always begging Lynette to give her more shifts at the shop, because there is a strong possibility she may have to drop out of the college because she can't afford the tuition this fall. We offer a full-year academic grant to worthy students, and I was counseling Miranda on her application essay. She's one of my top students, I believe in her, and I wanted her to be able to put her best foot forward when the committee reviews her application next month. That's all. I had no interest in sleeping with her!"

"Then why not just meet her here in your office? Why sneak around and rendezvous in such a remote location in the park?"

Jamie sighed. "Because Miranda insisted we meet off campus. She said she had a friend, another one of my students, who was also applying for the same scholarship. This girl was real competitive about it, I mean viciously competitive, with no qualms about sabotaging Miranda's chances, and Miranda didn't want her finding out that I was helping her on the side. I assured her I would happily assist *any* of my students who asked for my help, including this friend, so we didn't have to be so secretive about it. That's when Miranda admitted that there was another reason, which she didn't want to divulge at first, but after some prodding, I forced it out of her."

Hayley leaned forward, dying of curiosity. "Which was?"

"Apparently this roommate has a 'huge crush' on me; those were Miranda's words, not mine. Anyway, this girl could get very jealous, obsessively so, enough for Miranda to be scared about how this girl might react if she saw us meeting together, and so she didn't want to have to deal with that headache on top of competing with her for the scholarship money. Either way, it was a lose-lose situation for Miranda, so I ultimately agreed to meet her on the down-low."

Hayley glanced down at the photo. "It looks like all of your clandestine efforts were for naught."

"Yeah, she found us anyway. She must have already been suspicious and was following Miranda around, which probably wasn't hard; they were roommates." Jamie sighed.

"*Roommates*?" Hayley gasped.

Jamie nodded. "Damn, I knew in my bones it was a dumb move to meet in the park, but I wanted Miranda to get that scholarship so bad, she was so smart and had so much potential, and she honestly deserved it . . ." He stared at the photo wistfully. "She was planning on going for her master's in human ecology. She eventually wanted to get her PhD, maybe become a food scientist or nutritionist. Such a waste . . ."

There was a long, sad silence.

Hayley didn't have to do much deducing to come up with the name of this mystery roommate. There were only two girls who lived in that house on School Street. Miranda and . . .

"Bethany?"

Jamie, still lost in thought, finally looked up. "Hm?"

"The friend, Miranda's roommate, was it Bethany?"

"Yes. They also work together at the ice cream shop."

Which would explain how those photos ended up in the second-floor apartment above the shop.

As an employee, Bethany would probably have had access to a key.

A ruthless competitive streak.

Obsessively jealous.

What else was this girl hiding?

Chapter 16

"**P**lease, please, don't tell Lynette! If she finds out it was me who left those photos, she'll probably fire me, and I desperately need this job! I'm barely making ends meet as it is, and I still only have about a third of my tuition saved up for this fall!" Bethany begged as she stood behind the counter at the ice cream shop. She was the only employee on duty at the moment, and there were no other customers in the shop besides Hayley.

Hayley felt sorry for Bethany.

When she had shown up at Bar Harbor Ice Cream to find Bethany working alone after leaving Jamie's office at the college, she knew it might be her only opportunity to confront her about the fraught relationship she had with her late roommate Miranda. Bethany had at first adamantly denied leaving those photos for Lynette to find. She gave an admirable performance, acting indignant and insulted that anyone would suggest that she would ever do something so hurtful and underhanded, but when Hayley calmly mentioned that she had just spoken to Professor McGibbon, Bethany's tough facade quickly began to crumble.

"What? You *talked* to him? About *me*? What did he say?" She gasped, her cheeks blushing, a brief girlish giggle escaping her lips.

"He said Miranda told him about your . . . how did he put it? Your 'huge crush' on him."

"Oh god, no! She didn't! He *knows*? I'm so embarrassed! How will I ever be able face him again?"

Hayley was thrown for a total loop.

She had just accused Bethany of attempting to sabotage her boss's marriage in order to bring down her coworker, but Bethany's primary concern at the moment was how Professor McGibbon had reacted to the news that she harbored a secret longing for him.

"So, when he told you, was he smiling, or did he look upset? I would just die if he was really bothered by it," Bethany opined.

"Bethany, my advice to you is, stop worrying about Professor McGibbon and start thinking about what Lynette will do when she finds out it was you who left those photos on the desk upstairs."

And that's when the severity of her situation finally began to sink in, and Bethany began pleading with Hayley not to tattle on her so she could stay gainfully employed.

"Why did you do it?" Hayley pressed.

Bethany shrugged. "I don't know, I wasn't thinking, I

guess. I was jealous. I confided to Miranda one night about how I had spent my whole sophomore year of college pining over Professor McGibbon . . . Jamie . . . and then I find out Miranda was sneaking around behind my back seeing him, it was like a gut punch, a massive betrayal of our friendship! So I followed her and took those photos and left them where I knew Lynette would see them."

"For what purpose?"

"I was hoping Lynette would fire Miranda, and then she'd be out of the way, and maybe Jamie would pay more attention to me."

"But there was nothing going on between them. Miranda was just meeting with Professor McGibbon because he was helping her apply for a scholarship . . ."

"I know. She left her essay with Jamie's notes on it in her room, and I happened to see it. It was like a double whammy. First, she's horning in on my relationship with Jamie, and now she was out to steal that scholarship, the one I wanted so badly, my one shot at being able to pay for school before I had to drop out."

"But Bethany, there was no relationship with you or with Miranda. Professor McGibbon is a happily married man, and, not to point out the obvious, he's married to your boss here at the ice cream shop!"

"I know, it's complicated, my life has always been so messy, I just can't help it."

"Well, it's about to get a whole lot messier if it turns out that Miranda's death was a homicide."

"What do you mean?"

Hayley sighed. This girl did not strike her as all that bright for a college student. No wonder Miranda was the frontrunner for that scholarship.

"Bethany, if we're talking about murder, you will automatically shoot to the top of the suspect list. You didn't just have one motive, you had two! You believed Miranda was having a clandestine affair with the man you were secretly in love with, you were admittedly consumed with jealousy, and you were competing with her for a scholarship, which your entire future depended on you getting for yourself. That's more than enough for the police to haul you in for questioning!"

"But I'm innocent! I never did anything to Miranda! I just left those photos I took for Lynette! That's it! I don't have a clue how Miranda ended up in the truck's freezer! I could never, I would never—!"

Suddenly, Bethany's mouth dropped open as she glanced out the store window. Lynette was pulling up out front in her ice cream truck.

She locked eyes with Hayley. "Please, I'm begging you, don't say anything yet! I will explain everything to Lynette and apologize; I just need a little time to figure out what I'm going to say!"

"Don't wait too long," Hayley sighed.

"I won't! Thank you, thank you," Bethany said breathlessly.

Lynette barged through the door to the shop, happy to see Hayley. "Looking for a late-afternoon sugar high?"

"Yes, I was debating between my usual favorite Sea Salt Caramel, or maybe something a little more adventurous, like the Spicy Chai," Hayley said.

"I vote for the Butter Mint!" Bethany cheerfully offered, covering up her meltdown moments earlier.

"Sold!" Hayley said, pointing at her.

"I'm going to go upstairs and get through some paperwork," Lynette said. "Hayley, once you get your cone, why don't you come up so we can chat for a minute?"

"Sure," Hayley said, keeping eye contact with Bethany, who was now panic-stricken.

Lynette thankfully didn't notice and bounded out and up the stairs to the second-floor apartment.

Hayley gave Bethany a reassuring smile.

She wasn't going to finger her just yet about the photos.

Lynette was undoubtedly more interested in what Hayley had found out about her husband, and Hayley was more than happy to report that in her unvarnished opinion, Jamie McGibbon was a loving and faithful husband, always has been and always will be. The identity of the person who ignited all of Lynette's concerns was less important at this time.

But that did not necessarily mean that Bethany was in the clear. Not by a long shot. Hayley firmly believed in the notion of innocent before proven guilty. However, given Bethany's frantic state of mind, obvious motives, and multiple opportunities, she was, at the moment, the number one suspect, if indeed they were dealing with foul play.

And that was now the burning question in the forefront of Hayley's mind that needed to be answered.

Was Miranda Fox murdered?

And if so, how?

Island Food & Spirits
BY
HAYLEY POWELL

There are three solid subjects that are of the utmost importance to any teenage girl on her sixteenth birthday—a party, boys, and a car. Unfortunately for my daughter Gemma on that momentous day in her young life, she only got two out of the three, which I did not think was so bad, since I only got one when I turned sixteen, and it was definitely not a boy or a new car! I got a lame party with a few girls from school, some warm Kool-Aid, and a sickeningly sweet carrot cake. I don't even like carrot cake, but my mother confused my taste in birthday cakes with my brother Randy's.

Gemma fared slightly better. Her party was packed with friends, she was dating a nice handsome fella named Tad, but the car was definitely a no-show, much to her chagrin and disappointment. I explained to Gemma that her father and I had talked (okay, to be fair, *I* talked, and he just had to agree), and we felt strongly that she needed more time to practice behind the wheel of a car. But we told her that if she kept her grades up, and proved that she was responsible enough, then when summer came, she could get a job and save her money. When she earned the agreed-upon amount, then her father and I would chip in the rest and help her purchase a reliable first car. That seemed to make up for the rather boring JCPenney gift certificate she had found in her birthday card from me.

As summer approached that following year, Gemma and her boyfriend Tad were totally inseparable. It would not be a Friday or Saturday night if I didn't see the two of them at our dinner table, holding hands and mooning over each other as her younger brother Dustin made gagging and choking noises in their direction while rolling his eyes in disgust. The lovebirds excitedly made all sorts of fun plans to do on their days off from their summer jobs—romantic bike rides, intimate dinners, barbecues with friends.

Gemma landed a job scooping ice cream at the town's most popular ice cream joint, a hole in the wall—and I mean literally, it was a hole in the wall that was quite popular with locals and tourists, because all you had to do was line up right outside on the sidewalk, order through the open windows on either side, and simply grab your cone and go. This was long before the wildly popular Bar Harbor Ice Cream opened for business.

Tad worked only a few doors down on an

open lot with a garage, where they rented mo-
peds to tourists who enjoyed zipping around the
town and all through Acadia National Park, out
in the open air, instead of being stuck driving in
a car.

The first two weeks went smoothly for the
happy couple, but not so good with me, since I
had already packed on five pounds from buying
too many double-scoop ice cream cones for me
and Dustin every night, which made a huge
dent in my weekly miscellaneous expenses budget.

One day, my BFF Mona showed up with a
basket of lemons one of her customers had
gifted to her from the array of lemon trees on
his property. Mona was far too busy to know
what to do with them, and she was always hearing about my experimenting with recipes, so
she dropped them off and told me to use them
up before they spoiled. I had the perfect idea. I
borrowed the ice cream maker that her kids
had given her for Christmas last year with the
expectation she would make them tons of ice
cream all year long, but she wasn't falling for
that sugar-rush trick again. I, on the other hand,
was all in on making delicious, tart lemony
cocktails and decadent bowls of lemon ice
cream! I was already five pounds fatter since
May; what's another five to ten pounds? Plus, it
would be a lot cheaper than buying ice cream at
Gemma's shop every night of the week.

Meanwhile, Gemma was laser-focused on
raising money for her new car. She picked up

double shifts, scrimped and saved all of her pay-
checks and tips, and was well on her way to hit-
ting the magic number she needed to buy her
first car. At first, Tad was understanding about
all the time Gemma was spending working at
the ice cream shop, but as the weeks dragged
on, his visits became shorter and fewer in between. And Gemma was so dead tired after her
long shifts, she didn't notice at first that Tad
was less available to take her calls. Finally, she
decided to take a day off and focus on her relationship. Unfortunately, Tad told her he had to
work. Well, when she walked by the moped
rental shop, he was nowhere to be seen. That
triggered a little suspicion, but at the time, she
decided to let it go.

But then the next day, all hell broke loose.
Gemma and her coworker were out straight
scooping ice cream into cones for ravenous
tourists stopping by the windows that over-
looked Main Street. Gemma was just handing
out two double-scoop chocolate fudge ripple
cones to a woman and her five-year-old daughter
when she heard a familiar voice. She glanced out
into the street and saw Tad driving by on a
moped, carefree and chatting with a bombshell
of a girl around the same age, who was sitting
on the back with her arms wrapped tightly
around his waist, her luxurious long blond hair
whipping in the breeze, as she laughed uproari-
ously as if he had just said the funniest thing in
the world.

Gemma gasped and let go of the ice cream

cones. One hit the sidewalk with a splat, while the other landed right on top of the little moppet's head. The girl burst into tears as the chocolate fudge ice cream dripped down the side of her face. Gemma, unable to control herself, joined in with her own tears and wails. That poor mother had no idea what to do.

Later, when Gemma arrived home, still sobbing and inconsolable, I tried cheering her up with frosted lemonades that I had been trying to perfect all day as well as a few bowls of my homemade lemon ice cream. It was starting to work, until Tad called and told Gemma he was busy and couldn't see her at all next week. When Gemma confronted him about this new mystery girl, Tad immediately got defensive, claiming he never would have started anything with her if Gemma wasn't working all the time and paid a little more attention to him.

Well, as they say, that was the final nail in the coffin as far as Gemma was concerned, especially since Tad didn't have the decency to at least break up with her before he started his new summer fling. She told him in no uncertain terms that they were kaput, and he was never to call her again. Then she slammed down the phone, turned to me, and said, "I think it's time for me to get that car!"

And she did. With a little help from me and her dad in Iowa, and her Uncle Randy, who accompanied us to the used car dealership because he was, in his own words, "a masterful negotiator," Gemma drove off the lot in a reliable Honda Civic right before Labor Day, and truth be told, it was richly deserved. She had worked very hard for it.

Tad had already started calling, trying to apologize, begging Gemma to take him back, especially now that his summer fling had gone back to school in Boston. But Gemma was having none of it. She didn't budge and refused to talk to him.

About two weeks after Gemma got her car, we had a horrible rainstorm all night, but luckily, it had finally subsided by morning. I warned Gemma to drive with extreme caution to school, because the roads could be flooded after such a strong storm.

Just as I settled down at my desk at the *Island Times*, Mona called, cackling on the other end of the phone, barely able to recount what she had just witnessed, because she was laughing so hard. Apparently, Mona's oldest son had missed the bus that morning, so Mona had to drive him out to the high school, since she had taken away his driving privileges for too many "senior skip days." They were about two miles out of town when they spotted a boy standing on the side of the road next to a moped, trying to flag cars down. Mona figured his moped must have flooded out in one of the giant puddles that were all over the road.

She recognized the boy as Tad, Gemma's ex-boyfriend, and just in front of her was a Honda Civic, which Mona realized must be Gemma coming to his rescue.

"Boy, was I wrong!" Mona howled.

"Why? What happened?" I asked.

"Your daughter can certainly hold a grudge. Instead of stopping to help him, she just waved an arm out the window, and then swerved into the biggest puddle I have ever seen on Eagle Lake Road! This giant wave of water just went straight up into the air and came right back down, completely dousing that poor boy as he just stood there helplessly, not knowing what to do. And then she beeped the horn a few times and kept going!" Luckily, after Mona whizzed past him, she saw in her rearview mirror that the truck behind her pulled over to assist the soaked boy in distress.

I didn't know whether to be upset with Gemma or proud of her. In the end, I just chalked it up to a woman scorned, and called it a day.

Now, I'd like to share with you two of my very favorite lemon treats, and believe me, this pair of recipes have become a beloved staple in the Powell household, having been sucked down and devoured over many heartbreaks, celebrations, and just plain fun times during our summer season.

FROSTED LEMONADE

INGREDIENTS:
½ cup fresh-squeezed lemon juice
¼ cup granulated sugar
½ cup cold water
3 cups vanilla ice cream

Pour your lemon juice, sugar, and water into a pitcher. Mix until all of the sugar dissolves. Place in your refrigerator for an hour to chill.

Remove the chilled mixture from refrigerator, add to a blender, and add your ice cream. Blend until smooth and creamy.

Pour into two glasses and share with a loved one.

LEMON ICE CREAM

INGREDIENTS:
1½ tablespoons lemon zest
½ cup fresh-squeezed lemon juice
1 cup sugar
3 eggs
1½ cup whipping cream
1 cup whole milk
1 tsp vanilla
Pinch of salt

In a saucepan, add your lemon zest, lemon juice, sugar, and egg and whisk together.

Add your whole milk and vanilla and whisk.

Cook your mixture over medium heat, stirring constantly, until it comes to a simmer.

Strain the mixture through a sieve into a bowl and then cover with plastic wrap and place in the refrigerator at least an hour or until cold.

Remove mixture from refrigerator and pour mixture and whipping cream into an ice cream maker and mix according to the manufacturer's directions.

When done, scoop out into a clean container and freeze for a couple of hours or until you are ready to serve.

Chapter 17

Hayley had always gotten along with everyone in her high school class. One notable exception had been Sabrina Merryweather, best described by Liddy years later as "the meanest of the mean girls." Sabrina had seemed to revel in tormenting Hayley, gossiping about her behind her back, leaving her off the guest lists for her blowout parties that she would host when her parents were out of town, intentionally snubbing her in the hallway before classes. Hayley had never really figured out why Sabrina disliked her so much, especially since they had been quite good friends in middle school, before Sabrina began running around in more rarefied circles their freshman year in high school. But she knew there was nothing much she could do about it, so she just carried on with a stiff upper lip and tried to ignore Sabrina's intentionally malicious behavior.

Only later, years after their high school graduation, did they reconnect as adult women with a lot of life experience under their belts. Suddenly, their past feud seemed so petty and unimportant. Sabrina had become Hancock County's medical examiner, which was right about the time Hayley had discovered her predilection for investigating local crimes—murders, to be more specific—and so she made a concerted effort to patch up their differences. After all, having a friend in the county coroner's office would be an invaluable asset, especially when Hayley's brother-in-law Sergio, the police chief, would put his foot down on sharing key information on a particular case. Hayley could just call up her "good buddy" Sabrina to chat and perhaps sprinkle a few pertinent questions that she needed answers to when Sergio was stonewalling. Sabrina, for her part, had somehow developed amnesia when it came to their highly fraught teen years. According to Sabrina's own memory, she and Hayley were "the best of friends," and there was nary a cross word ever spoken between them. She had an uncanny ability to rewrite history, recalling those same recollections that Hayley had found so painful as "happy times."

Instead of confronting her and forcing her to come to terms with her spiteful, nasty side, Hayley allowed Sabrina to leave it all in the past, especially since in the present, she was getting so much out of it. Besides, although Sabrina was still very flighty and controlling and manipulative, she had noticeably mellowed, and actually seemed to like Hayley calling her and asking for her help. Perhaps deep down, she was working hard to make up for her past sins.

So Hayley was understandably distressed when Sabrina up and quit her job eight years ago and left town. Her key contact in the coroner's office was gone, and her replacement was hardly as accommodating as Sabrina had been. Solving local murders was suddenly far more challenging without easy access to the exact cause of death.

Sabrina had blown back into town on several occasions over the past few years, most notably as a bridesmaid at Liddy's ill-fated wedding, but the last Hayley had heard was that Sabrina had met a man, fourteen years her junior, at an all-inclusive resort in Cancun, and impulsively married him. They moved to Phoenix to live happily ever after while Sabrina worked to realize her new dream, using her medical expertise to write crime novels, determined to become the next Patricia Cornwell or Tess Gerritsen. After sixteen months working diligently on her first manuscript, her effort failed to get published. Her marriage lasted even less time, crashing and burning in less than a year when she discovered that her young husband was having an illicit affair with the comely, blue-eyed, typist/copyeditor Sabrina had hired to help make her work publishable.

There were rumors floating around town that Sabrina was looking to move back to Bar Harbor, and when the current county medical examiner tendered his resignation to take a higher-paying position in Worcester, Sabrina swooped in and was welcomed back with open arms.

She had only been back in town for a few weeks, and had just started up again at the coroner's office, so the Miranda Fox case was her first autopsy back on the job. Hayley had also heard from Liddy that Sabrina had recently purchased a hilltop house on the outskirts of Acadia National Park with sweeping views of Frenchman Bay.

Hayley showed up at the sprawling house and rang the

bell. There was a Tesla in the driveway, so Hayley assumed Sabrina was home.

Of course Sabrina was driving a Tesla.

Only the best for her.

The front door swung open, and Sabrina's face lit up at the sight of Hayley. "I was wondering when you would finally get in touch with me!" Her hair was pulled back in a ponytail, and she was in jeans and an oversize flannel shirt as she hugged Hayley and dragged her inside her giant new house.

There were sealed boxes everywhere, and the large furniture pieces had yet to be arranged. "I'm still getting my bearings; there's so much to do, I haven't had a moment to unpack, and they've already got me working twelve-hour days, can you believe it?"

Hayley could tell Sabrina was overjoyed to be back in Bar Harbor and to have reclaimed her position as county coroner.

And to be honest, so was Hayley.

"Can I get you some coffee?" She didn't wait for an answer before heading to the kitchen as she blathered on. "I'm so busy, but we must plan a girls' night, you, me, Liddy, and Mona, to catch up. I need my posse to help get me back into the social scene around here."

Okay, Hayley, Liddy, and Mona had *never* had a girls' night with Sabrina.

Ever.

And they had never *ever* been her posse at any point in their shared history.

But why quibble when she was here for a reason?

"I suppose you heard about my disastrous eleven-month marriage to that Nick Jonas wannabe I met in Mexico! God, Hayley, sometimes I make the *worst* decisions when I've had one too many Manhattans, and unfortunately, that resort in Cancun was all-inclusive, alcohol included! I was too buzzed to read all the warning signs! He said he was a physical therapist; well, it turned out when I took him home to Arizona that he was an unlicensed massage therapist, who only worked on women under thirty! Hello? I didn't need Angela Lansbury to solve that mystery!"

"I'm so sorry it didn't work out," Hayley said.

"Don't be! That little vixen I hired turned out to be a godsend! If she hadn't batted her eyelashes and unbuttoned her blouse every time he walked in the room, I might still be in the total dark while he bled me dry! Catching them in the laundry room was the best thing that ever happened to me! I hope you and Bruce keep separate checking accounts! That's my word of advice to you! Do not, repeat, do not open a joint account! You will live to regret it! You're running a successful restaurant now, Hayley, you need to keep track of what you're hauling in, just in case things go south with Bruce, do you hear me?"

"Loud and clear," Hayley said, nodding amiably.

Sabrina finished pouring grounds in the top of her coffee maker and pressed the ON switch. "Anyway, enough about my train wreck out west. I'm just so tickled pink to be back in Maine. Single and ready to mingle!" She grabbed two coffee mugs out of an open box filled with kitchenware on the counter. "I'm sorry I don't have any muffins or croissants to offer you, I've basically been subsisting on caffeine, frozen dinners, and protein bars these last two weeks."

"I'm fine, thank you, I really just stopped by to—"

"Find out my conclusions in the Miranda Fox autopsy?"

Hayley reared back, stunned.

Was she *that* transparent?

"Well, I also wanted to welcome you home . . ."

Sabrina smiled knowingly. "How sweet."

She was way too smart to buy that.

"I just filed my report with the police. It was definitely a homicide," Sabrina said casually as she watched the coffee percolate and begin filling the pot.

Hayley's mind raced. "Was it hypothermia? She must have been locked in that freezer all night."

"She was, according to my timeline, but she died from poisoning," Sabrina remarked matter-of-factly.

Hayley gasped. "*Poison?*"

Sabrina nodded, yanking the pot from the coffee maker too soon as coffee continued dripping onto the base. She poured some into the mugs. "Cream or sugar?"

"No, black."

"Me too. Strong. Dark. Nothing fancy. Gets the job done. That's how I want the next man in my life to be, too, just like my morning coffee."

Hayley was mystified as to how to respond to that, but luckily, she didn't have to, because Sabrina just continued talking.

"Tetrodotoxin, the kind of poison found in the puffer fish, kills about fifty Japanese people a year. It's not easy to get it here in the States, but it's possible."

"How on earth did Miranda ingest a substance as rare as that?"

"Through something she ate. I found traces of an ice cream cone in her system—Indian Pudding flavor—yuck, who eats that? Anyway, she licked it right in, and she died shortly thereafter. Whoever laced the ice cream with the toxin must have dragged her body to the delivery truck's freezer and locked her inside, where you and Lynette Partridge found her the next day," Sabrina said while nonchalantly slurping her coffee.

"That's so cruel and heartless; who would do such a thing?" Hayley pondered, shaken.

"A cold-blooded killer, that's who, but it's not my job to find him or her, it's Sergio's, and yours, I suppose."

"It's just such a tragedy, especially considering she was pregnant, too," Hayley said sadly.

"*Pregnant*? What makes you think she was pregnant?"

"I found a positive pregnancy test that I assumed belonged to her in a trash can where she lives."

"It has to belong to someone else, Hayley, because I conducted a thorough autopsy, and trust me, Miranda Fox was definitely *not* pregnant at the time she was murdered."

Chapter 18

"Ew, who eats Indian Pudding ice cream?" Dustin asked, his face scrunched up as he twirled spaghetti onto his fork at the dining room table.

"That's what Sabrina said. What does everybody have against Indian Pudding ice cream?" Hayley asked, tearing off a piece of garlic bread.

Bruce shrugged. "What's wrong with good old-fashioned chocolate? Why do there have to be so many fancy flavors? When I was a kid, there were basically three at the drug store around the block where I lived: chocolate, vanilla, and strawberry."

After leaving Sabrina's new house, Hayley had dashed home to put a pot of water on the stove to boil some pasta and thaw some frozen marinara sauce in the microwave for dinner. She had been craving Italian ever since she had turned it down at Mona's the other night.

She didn't have time to swing by the restaurant and check on her staff before coming home, but while she was driving, her manager Betty had texted her that business at Hayley's Kitchen was steady but not overwhelming, and she should just go home and have dinner with her family.

MacKenzie had helped set the table, and Hayley had to admit to herself that it was a nice breather to just enjoy some pasta and wine in the company of her husband, son, and his girlfriend instead of running around town trying to dig up answers about Miranda Fox, or sweating in the kitchen of her restaurant, trying to get orders out to her customers' tables in a timely manner.

"Well, the point is, Sabrina's autopsy report concluded that the most likely scenario was that the poison that killed Miranda had been put it in the ice cream she ate shortly before she died. The day Dustin and MacKenzie arrived in town, and we all went to dinner and stopped by Lynette's shop for dessert, I overheard Lynette's employees teasing Miranda about the fact that she was the only one who ate the Indian Pudding flavor. Which means, now that Sabrina has ruled the cause of death as a homicide, it makes perfect sense that the killer injected the poison into the carton of Indian Pudding, knowing that Miranda would be the *only* one who touched it!" Hayley exclaimed.

Bruce, Dustin, and MacKenzie all stopped eating to ruminate on that plausible theory.

"Yeah, that does make a lot of sense," Bruce agreed.

"Of course it does!" Hayley said emphatically.

"So the killer has to be one of the kids who works in the ice cream shop!" MacKenzie concluded.

Hayley shook her head. "Not necessarily. One of the employees could have inadvertently shared that information with the killer, or maybe the killer was around when they were joking about it and found out that way. It might be a coworker, or housemate, or just a friend. Someone who knew her habits. There were dozens of people at that party, going in and out of the house where she lived. It could have been any one of them."

"I rang Sergio at the police department right before you got home, hoping to get a statement for my column tomorrow, but he's obviously dodging my calls," Bruce said. "He hasn't even made the news public that this is now a murder investigation."

Dustin turned to MacKenzie with a grin. "That's my mother. Always one step ahead of the police."

"Your Uncle Sergio is a terrific police chief, very capable. I just have a long history in this town; I was born and raised here, and so I know everybody, everybody knows me, and some people just feel comfortable talking to me more, that's all," Hayley said.

"That's your mom, humble-bragging about what a good amateur detective she is," Bruce cracked.

Hayley shot him an annoyed look.

Dustin and MacKenzie chuckled.

"So you've done this before, Mrs. Linney? Investigate murders?" MacKenzie asked, wide-eyed and curious.

Hayley took a bite of garlic bread. "There have been one or two times I may have insinuated myself into a specific case . . ."

Bruce spit out some wine, then grabbed for his napkin to wipe it off his face. "Excuse me?"

Dustin put a hand on MacKenzie's arm. "It's a lot more than one or two times, but she'll never admit it."

Now it was Dustin's turn to face the wrath of a sore look from his mother.

"Well, I think it's awesome that your mom's such an intrepid crime fighter," MacKenzie said, before sitting up straight and placing a hand on her belly. "Oh, the baby just kicked."

"Won't be long now," Bruce said.

Hayley zeroed in on MacKenzie, reminded of something.

Bruce picked up the bottle of Chianti and held it over Hayley's glass. "More wine, babe?"

Hayley just kept staring at MacKenzie's stomach.

"Babe?"

She suddenly snapped out of her thoughts. "What? No, thank you."

"No? Now I'm really starting to worry," Bruce joked.

Bruce set the wine bottle back down on the table, and then Hayley absentmindedly picked it up and poured some more in her glass, totally distracted.

Bruce, Dustin, and MacKenzie all exchanged knowing smirks.

"Something's been nagging at me. I found a pregnancy test kit in Miranda's room. The stick was in a trash can in the bathroom down the hall. It was positive," Hayley said.

This was fresh news for everyone at the table.

All of their ears perked up.

"Miranda was pregnant?" Bruce asked, eyebrow arched.

"Not according to Sabrina. She swears Miranda was definitely not pregnant at the time of her death, which begs the question, if Miranda wasn't pregnant, what was she doing with a positive test?"

"Maybe it was a false positive," MacKenzie said.

"Or maybe it belongs to one of her housemates," Dustin guessed.

"Maybe . . . but then how did the packaging find its way into Miranda's trash can?" Hayley pondered. "I suppose someone else could have tossed it in there. Maybe Miranda was simply offering moral support to a friend who was there in her room while she took the test . . ."

"Bethany?" Bruce offered. "She is the only other woman living in that house besides Miranda. The rest are guys, right?"

"Yes. I just have a strong instinct that the murder has something to do with this mysterious secret boyfriend Miranda had, and that positive pregnancy test."

MacKenzie leaned forward, setting her fork down. "I know this sounds crazy, but when Dustin and I first started dating, there was this assistant who worked in the cubicle next to me at the animation company. I confided to her that I was falling hard for Dustin and wanted to marry him and spend the rest of our lives together, but I wasn't sure where his head was at, and I was scared I might lose him. Well, this girl—I'll never forget it—she suggested I fake a pregnancy in order to force his hand! Can you believe that?"

"Who was that?" Dustin gasped, stunned.

"Becky Wilcox, in accounting."

"Oh, her. That's not a big surprise," Dustin said.

"I was so appalled she would even say something like that. I asked her if she was joking, and she gave me this weird look and said with a completely straight face, 'No, of course not.' I basically stopped talking to her after that; I just found the whole idea so vile and deceptive. What kind of person would ever do such a thing?"

"Well, the irony is, just a few months later, MacKenzie

actually *did* get pregnant, but there was no reason to trap me, because I'm elated I'm going to be a father!" Dustin crowed as he leaned over and bussed MacKenzie on her cheek.

"The reason I'm even telling you this story is because there is the possibility that Miranda got her hands on a positive pregnancy test in order to falsely claim she was expecting."

A deception.

Hayley had never considered that.

It was absolutely plausible.

Was this kind of a shotgun wedding–type scenario?

If so, then that would bring the secret boyfriend to the forefront of this investigation.

And it was becoming vitally important that Hayley unmask this elusive man of mystery, who, she was now convinced, held the missing piece to this entire puzzle.

Chapter 19

"Oh, man, yummy, these are delicious," Lieutenant Donnie said, his feet up on his desk, bits of cookie tumbling out of his mouth as he spoke. "My girlfriend Sally's oatmeal-raisin cookies taste like chalk. She's a lousy baker—but don't tell her, she wouldn't appreciate me talking smack about her baking skills!"

"I'm also sure she wouldn't appreciate you talking with your mouth full," Hayley scolded.

Donnie swallowed what was left in his mouth and offered a meek "Sorry."

She held out the Tupperware container toward Donnie. "Would you like another before I drop the rest off in the chief's office?"

"Yes, ma'am," Donnie said, lighting up. He grabbed one, then two, then a third, banking on the fact that Hayley would not object.

And he was right.

She was not going to say a word about Donnie leaving his boss only three cookies.

Because Donnie knew that she had not dropped by the Bar Harbor Police Department out of the goodness of her heart, to make sure all the officers got a tasty little treat in the middle of the afternoon. No, Lieutenant Donnie and Officer Earl, who was working the reception desk and also helped himself to three of the oatmeal-raisin cookies, were well aware that Hayley was here to get information about a case.

This was Hayley's typical modus operandi.

And they had been around long enough to expect it and not forcefully object, especially when Hayley always arrived bearing a sweet, mouthwatering bribe. Several months ago, it had been a cardamom cream-filled Bundt cake; before that, a gluten-free apple rose tart. The boys at the station figured if the head honcho Chief Alvares didn't have a problem with it, why should they?

"Give my best to Sally, will you, Donnie? I'm just going to go drop this off in the chief's office."

"He's not there. He's busy in the interrogation room."

"Oh?"

Donnie hesitated, not sure if he should divulge any more.

Hayley picked up one of the three remaining cookies and handed it to Donnie. "Here, I know Sergio's been trying to cut back on sweets. He thinks he's been getting a little too thick around the middle lately, so why don't you take this one home to Sally?"

"Gosh, that's awfully kind of you, Hayley; maybe it will inspire Sally to work harder on improving her own baking skills," Donnie said, chuckling. He set the cookie down on top of the others he had hoarded before continuing. "He's been questioning Lynette Partridge's employees at the ice cream shop again all morning. Right now, he's with one of the girls."

Bethany.

He had to be referring to Bethany.

She had been the only other female worker besides Miranda.

"Thanks, Donnie!"

Hayley made a big show of walking down the hall to Sergio's office and placing the Tupperware container on his desk, where he would see it when he returned, but instead of heading for the exit, she made a quick beeline down the opposite hall and to the large two-way mirror that looked into the interrogation room. She knew every inch of this precinct, having infiltrated the building many times before.

She knew Sergio and Bethany could not see her, so she wasn't worried about standing there and watching. There was an intercom to the right of the mirror, which she clicked on so she could hear what they were talking about inside the room.

"I've already spoken to Tim and Eric, and their stories match up," Sergio said, leaning back in the metal chair across the table from Bethany, his arms folded, stone-faced. "And to be blunt, they both pretty much pointed the finger at you as the most likely suspect."

Bethany, agitated, her face colorless, spit out, "They don't know what they're talking about! They're just scared and panicky, and are looking for someone, anyone but themselves, to blame!"

"Maybe, but neither Tim nor Eric had a clear motive. But you did. You were competing with Miranda for that scholarship. You believed she was having an affair with Professor McGibbon, who could tip the scales in her favor. And you knew that Indian Pudding was Miranda's favorite ice cream flavor in the shop and that she was always sneaking a scoop. With Miranda out of the way, she would no longer be a threat to your successful future. That's what I would call damning evidence."

"No! I would never do something like that! I couldn't! I'm not that kind of person!" Bethany wailed.

"You had no problem leaving those suggestive photos on your boss Lynette's desk when you thought her husband and Miranda were having an affair. Is it fair to say you're at least that kind of person?"

Bethany's eyes pooled with tears.

She sniffled.

"I knew that was wrong. But I was jealous. I didn't know at the time they were not actually . . . I regret that. If I could take that back, I would. But I can't. It happened. And there's no way for me to change it. I know when Lynette finds out it was me, she'll probably fire me. But sabotaging Miranda and killing her are two totally different transgressions! Yes, I was willing to do awful things to get that scholarship, but I am not—repeat, *not*—guilty of murder!"

The waterworks started.

Bethany covered her face with her hands and sobbed uncontrollably.

Sergio sat quietly for a moment, then gently asked, "I have some tissues in my office. Would you like me to go get them?"

She nodded behind her hands.

Sergio stood up and walked out of the room.

His back was to Hayley as he headed down the hall.

When he rounded the corner and was out of sight, Hayley seized the opportunity to slip into the interrogation room. She knew she only had a minute or two, tops, before Sergio returned.

"Bethany?"

Bethany lowered her hands, surprised to see Hayley standing in the doorway. "What are you doing here?"

"Are you pregnant?"

The question blindsided her. "*What*?"

"There was a positive pregnancy test in Miranda's trash can in her room, and I found the stick in the bathroom you two shared. Did it belong to you?"

"No, of course not. I'm not pregnant. I'm not even dating anyone."

"So it had to have belonged to Miranda," Hayley murmured, confused as to why Sabrina's autopsy would conclude otherwise. She peeked out the door. She could hear Sergio talking to someone in his office. He must have taken a phone call. She spun back around to face Bethany. "If you didn't do it, and I believe you didn't, then who? What about this secret boyfriend? Do you have any idea who he might be?"

Bethany slowly shook her head. "Miranda liked a lot of boys. I mean, we lived with three good-looking guys. She was always flirting with Tim and Eric, but that's pretty much all it was, teasing and joking around. As for Chasen, she did seem to think he was cute, but he already had a girlfriend. He was all over Zoe and didn't really give Miranda a second look. I can't think why any of them would have a reason to kill her."

"What about someone outside of the house?"

Bethany sat up in her chair. "You mean like the stalker, that weirdo who was always hanging around the ice cream shop, trying to talk to her? If anyone fits the profile of a demented killer, it would be that guy, yeah."

Mona's son, Chet.

It was hard for Hayley to comprehend the possibility.

She had known the kid since he was born.

But she also was not privy to what was going on in his head.

What thoughts or impulses might be driving him?

Did Mona know?

She loved her son to death, but there were a lot of clue-less mothers out there who wound up shocked when their child committed some kind of irrational, unfathomable act. She had seen them interviewed on TV, in a state of cloudy confusion, swearing they never saw it coming.

Had Mona just missed the signs?

"Cookie?"

Hayley whipped around to see Sergio towering behind her outside the interrogation room, a box of tissues in one hand and Hayley's Tupperware container in the other.

"Oh, I see you got them. Good. I was just heading out when I passed by Bethany here and stopped in to say hello."

Sergio glanced down the hallway. "The exit is *that* way."

"You know how turned around I always get in here."

Sergio eyed her suspiciously. "Yes, our two hallways can be quite a maze."

He knew exactly what she was doing.

Hayley gave Bethany a little wave. "'Bye."

And then she squeezed past Sergio, who was half-blocking her path. "I know how much you love cinnamon, so I put a little extra in that batch. Enjoy!"

And then she made her escape.

Hayley knew whom she had to talk to next, as much as she was dreading it.

But luckily, they already had plans to get together this evening.

Chapter 20

Hayley had never seen Mona Barnes looking so elegant.

Yes, elegant.

That was the first word that came to mind when Mona had opened the door of her house to greet Hayley and Bruce. She had discarded her usual wardrobe of choice, a frumpy sweatshirt and mom jeans, for a flattering green plaid flutter-sleeve top that could have come right out of an Ann Taylor catalog. And although she still wore her signature jeans, they were more fitted than baggy, with not a grease stain in sight. Mona, who normally eschewed makeup of any kind, had a hint of lipstick and a tiny amount of blush on her cheeks, although Hayley suspected she would vehemently deny it if called on it. As for Mona's pageboy haircut, there wasn't much to be done about that on such short notice, but Mona had gone to the trouble of pulling her bangs out of her eyes with a matching green barrette.

Even Bruce was momentarily taken aback. "Mona, you look so . . . so . . ."

"What, Bruce? Spit it out, we haven't got all night!" Mona barked.

"Nice."

That was the best the professional writer could come up with, but you could hardly blame him for his down-right lack of articulation.

"All right, that's enough. Get in here, I gotta get the lobsters in the pot, and we still have to go over some ground rules!" Mona announced, ushering them inside.

Hayley and Bruce froze in the foyer as they looked around the normally chaotic mess of a house. First of all, there were no screaming kids running around. Second, the house looked, well, tidy, for lack of a better word. Mona's mother Jane had always said her house typically resembled one of those hurricane-ravaged homes in Florida whenever she stopped by for a coffee and a chat with her daughter. Mona's excuse was that she was a busy working woman, who didn't have a lot of free time for monotonous chores like housework. She had a family to feed. But somebody had gone to the trouble of dusting and vacuuming for tonight.

"Who cleaned?" Hayley asked.

"I paid Chet and Jodie fifty bucks each to make the place look presentable. I know, I shouldn't have to pay my kids to do simple chores, but I was in a tight time crunch," Mona explained, bounding toward the kitchen.

Bruce and Hayley dutifully followed.

"Where are Chet and Jodie?" Hayley asked.

"Banished to the basement. I ordered them pizza from Napoli and told them to stay down there and watch a movie and don't come up for any reason until I say the coast is clear."

Mona whipped open the refrigerator, grabbed two lobsters—whose claws had been tied shut with rubber bands— and deposited them into a big pot of boiling water. It was admittedly a barbaric ritual, one Mona would never give a second thought to, but Hayley always struggled with it whenever she cooked lobsters. However, she could always manage to work through her angst by picturing herself gorging on all that delicious lobster meat later.

"Can we help, Mona?" Bruce offered.

"Yes, help yourself to something to drink. I still have to melt the butter and make the coleslaw."

"You mentioned something about ground rules?" Hayley asked.

Mona slammed the lid down to cover the pot of boiling lobsters. "Yes. Chuck can be shy, so don't hit him with too many questions. And no silly comments like 'Oh, you two make such an adorable couple' or something like that. I don't want to embarrass him."

"I would never say anything like that," Hayley argued.

"Yes, you would, Hayley! Please, I've known you since kindergarten!" Mona bellowed.

Bruce fetched two beers from the fridge, popped the tops off with a bottle opener, and handed one to Hayley. "What about politics, is that allowed?"

"Oh, for the love of god, no!" Mona snapped.

Bruce took a swig of beer. "Why not?"

"Because I don't know if he's a Republican or Democrat or whatever, and if you two bleeding hearts start spouting off, I don't want to make him uncomfortable if he doesn't automatically agree with you!" Mona barked, giving them a disbelieving look, as if her reasoning were obvious.

"Nothing personal; no politics—what about the weather, is that off limits, too?"

"That's fine, I suppose," Mona huffed.

"Mona, there is no reason for you to be so nervous," Hayley said gently.

"I'm not nervous; who said I was nervous?"

Even Mona didn't believe what she was saying.

She was uncharacteristically jumpy.

Hayley could tell she just wanted the evening to go well.

Mona checked her watch. "He's late. Maybe he's not coming."

Hayley glanced up at the wall clock in the kitchen. "What time did you tell him to be here?"

"Six-thirty."

"It's six-thirty-two. Bruce and I were early. Bruce always wants to show up early when there are lobsters involved. He wants to scout out the biggest one for himself."

"She's right," Bruce admitted. "I'm starving. Is there something I can munch on while we wait for Mr. Right to arrive?"

"Stop saying stuff like that!" Mona warned. "I put out some mixed nuts in the living room; go in there and stop crowding me!"

Bruce chuckled and wandered out.

Hayley lingered, waiting for the opportunity to inquire more about Chet, to see if Mona had any kind of inkling yet that he had been obsessed with Miranda Fox, stalking her, or if she had seen any kind of indicator that might reveal if her son might have had a role in what happened to her. But Hayley also knew that Mona was a mama bear, willing to do just about anything to protect one of her cubs, and would probably kick Hayley out of her house if she thought Hayley was going to somehow get her son into any kind of serious trouble.

"Mona, how has Chet seemed to you lately?"

Mona lifted the lid on her pot to check on the lobsters. "What do you mean?"

"Has he been acting odd or moody?"

"Yes, he has."

Hayley perked up. "He has?"

"Of course he has. He's a seventeen-year-old boy! They all act odd and moody, not to mention stubborn and stupid and lazy! I can keep going, if you want."

This was not going to be easy.

"I know boys can be a handful—I went through all that with Dustin—but I have noticed recently that Chet has been acting rather strange and peculiar, even more so than usual. Have you picked up on that?"

Mona thought about it for a couple of seconds and then shook her head. "No." She then scurried back to the fridge for two sticks of butter, which she dropped into a small pan before firing up the burner. She was far more preoccupied with her dinner than her son's current mental state.

"I don't mean to raise the alarm, or cause any concern,

but I happen to know that he had been heavily fixated on Miranda Fox right before we found her in the back of Lynette Partridge's ice cream truck."

"Yeah, I know all about that."

"You do? How?"

"He told me."

"Chet told you he had a crush on Miranda?"

"Yeah. Well, not in so many words, but he talked about her enough. A mother knows these things. But you can stop right there, Hayley. If you're trying to tie my Chet into that awful thing that happened to that poor girl, you're dead wrong! Chet had nothing to do with it! And it's going to be a problem between us if you keep pushing that idea, do you hear me?"

"Of course, Mona. I know Chet's a good boy; I'm just trying my best to piece together what happened."

"Be my guest, but leave Chet out of it!"

The doorbell rang.

"He's here," Mona gasped, eyes wide, suddenly ruffled. "One more rule to remember. No accusing my Chet of murder in front of Chuck. Can I count on you at least to follow that one?"

Hayley sighed. "Of course, Mona."

Mona blew past Hayley out of the kitchen. Hayley, curious, slid in behind her, trailing her to the door. Bruce was chewing some nuts and washing them down with his bottle of beer in the living room.

Mona took a deep breath, then opened the door where Chuck stood on her porch, smiling and holding a bottle of wine.

"Sorry I'm late," he said.

"You're late? I hadn't even noticed!" Mona sang.

As Chuck stepped inside and gave Mona a quick peck on the cheek, Hayley stood behind her, slack-jawed and speechless.

Because she had met Chuck before.

But not as Chuck.

She had met him as George Kittridge.

Liddy's new boyfriend.

Chapter 21

As Chuck, or George, or whatever his name was, hugged Mona, his eyes wandered over to Hayley. Upon seeing her, they bugged out, nearly popping right off his face like those of a character in a Looney Tunes cartoon.

Hayley offered him a tight smile as Bruce joined her, his own welcoming smile fading as it slowly registered just who this Chuck actually was.

Mona dragged him inside, her arm around his shoulders. She was much bigger and towered over him. "Sorry I didn't warn you about inviting more people to dinner. I bet you wanted it to be just the two of us so you could get fresh with me." Mona winked at Hayley and Bruce as she pinched her boyfriend's cheek. "He can get very handsy, if you know what I mean." After guffawing and slapping him hard enough on the back that he jolted forward a few inches, Mona returned her gaze to Hayley and Bruce.

"Hayley, Bruce, this is Chuck. Chuck, this is my best friend Hayley, and her husband Bruce, who I tolerate." Mona snorted. "Just joshing. You'll like him when you get to know him. He's just an acquired taste." Mona giggled some more, quite pleased with herself.

There was a painful silence as they all stared at each other, none of them knowing what to say.

"This is the part where someone says, 'Nice to meet you'," Mona gently prodded.

"N-N-Nice to meet you," Chuck stammered, reaching out to shake Bruce's hand. Bruce numbly accepted it and gave him a wary nod.

Hayley remained frozen, having no clue what to do.

"You all get acquainted; I'm going to go check on the lobsters," Mona said, scooting off to the kitchen.

Hayley waited until Mona was out of earshot before whipping her head back around toward Chuck and urgently whispering, "Okay, just who *are* you?"

"George," he explained, wringing his hands and shifting his weight from foot to foot uncomfortably.

"Then why is she calling you Chuck?" Bruce asked.

"Chuck's her nickname for me. She says I remind her of her father's favorite movie actor. Charlton Heston."

"She also said you were a janitor?"

This seemed to surprise George. "She did?"

"Yes. Why did you lie?" Hayley demanded to know.

"I didn't! I told her I worked at the Jackson Lab, and that's the God's honest truth."

Hayley folded her arms. "As a *doctor*?"

"Of course!" But then he thought about it. "I mean, maybe. Come to think of it, she never actually asked me what I did. I assumed she just figured it out on her own."

Bruce pivoted toward Hayley. "Why would she assume he was a janitor instead of a doctor?"

"You know Mona! If she thought a man was interested in her and he said he worked at the lab, she would probably just assume he was a janitor and not a doctor! She's always selling herself short in her own mind!"

"This is terrible; I had no idea you all know each other," George mumbled, more to himself.

"Liddy, Mona, and I have been the best of friends since we were five years old!" Hayley exclaimed.

"Oh, dear . . ." George continued wringing his hands, his whole body spasming, teeth chattering, a bundle of nerves.

"You have to tell Mona the truth; she has to know you're dating both her and Liddy!"

George appeared as if he were about to dissolve into a puddle on the floor. His eyes darted back and forth, hands beet red from all the wringing. He slowly nodded, and it looked as if he were agreeing with her, that it was time to come clean and tell Mona the truth, but then the nodding abruptly stopped, and he started shaking his head, slowly and then vigorously, almost violently. "No, no I can't do this now!"

And then he bolted out the front door.

Bruce walked over to the door and watched him fleeing down the sidewalk until he disappeared around the corner. He turned back to his wife. "What just happened?"

Mona returned from the kitchen, a puzzled look on her face. "Where's Chuck?"

Another painful silence.

"He . . . uh . . . he left," Hayley said.

Mona crinkled her nose, confused. "He left? Where?"

Hayley eyed Bruce, who signaled to her that there was no way he was going to be the one to do it, so it was entirely up to her. Bruce closed the front door and walked back to the living room, where Hayley was standing with Mona.

"Mona, as it turns out, Bruce and I have met Chuck before, but he said his name was George at the time we were first introduced."

"Oh, right, you know, I call him Chuck so much I sometimes forget George is his real name. So you all met before? Well, it's a small town . . ."

"We met him because Liddy introduced us," Hayley said, proceeding with extreme caution.

Mona was slowly starting to sense something was amiss now. "Liddy knows him, too?"

"Yes; quite well, in fact," Hayley said gently. "Mona, why don't you sit down?"

Mona's whole body stiffened. "I don't want to sit down. What are you trying to tell me?"

Hayley took a deep breath. "Liddy is also dating him."

Mona gaped at her. "What?"

"He's two-timing you, Mona," Bruce said, jumping in.

Hayley threw him an admonishing look.

Mona burst out laughing. "That's the craziest thing I have ever heard! There is no way Liddy would ever date a janitor at the lab!"

"You're right," Hayley said. "But the thing is, he's not a janitor, he's a doctor, a very important one."

"No way!" Mona scoffed.

"It's true," Hayley said quietly.

Mona stood in the middle of the room, her mind reeling, letting this bombshell sink in. After what felt like an eternity, she slowly turned to Bruce. "This isn't one of your lame jokes, is it, Bruce?"

"It's no joke, Mona," Bruce said solemnly.

She then flicked her eyes to Hayley, who could see the anguish on her face.

"Mona, I'm so sorry," Hayley muttered.

Mona's eyes started pooling with tears. She despised showing any kind of emotion besides anger, so it was unexpected when she blurted out, "I have a headache, Hayley! I'm going to go lie down. Don't waste the lobsters! Why don't you and Bruce go fetch Chet and Jodie from the basement and enjoy them!"

And then she dashed upstairs to her room, slamming the door shut behind her.

Hayley started after her, but Bruce stopped her by taking hold of her arm. "I really think she wants to be alone right now, babe."

As much as she wanted to dismiss him, Hayley knew Bruce was right, and she had to respect Mona's wishes. So instead, she went to the basement door and called down to Chet and Jodie to come upstairs for some lobster.

Mona's youngest, Jodie, was the first to ask about her mother, and Hayley quietly explained that she wasn't feeling well, but that she wanted them all to feast on the lobsters she had prepared while she rested. Both kids seem to buy the excuse and eagerly sat down at the table. Hayley made sure she was next to Chet, and while Bruce peppered Jodie with questions about her summer vacation and what fun activities she had planned, Hayley was left alone to grill Chet, handing him a gravy boat of melted butter for him to dip his lobster tail in.

"Here, everything tastes better with butter—am I right, Chet?"

He eyed her suspiciously, a smart enough kid to pick up on her true motive. Then he dunked his lobster tail in the butter. "I know you're just being nice so I'll answer more questions about Miranda. Well, I've already told you a hundred times, it wasn't me! Yes, I was, like, really into her, and maybe I crossed a line, hanging out near her all the time, hoping she'd notice me, but she wanted nothing to do with me! I finally got the message, okay? I stopped following her! It wasn't me, Aunt Hayley!"

He was shouting now, which drew the attention of Bruce and Jodie.

Hayley gave him a reassuring smile. "I believe you, Chet. But I was hoping you might know, since you were around her a lot, was there someone else you saw that she might have been secretly dating?"

"No, I was watching her all the time . . ." He noticed Hayley's wary expression. "I know it sounds creepy, but I liked her so, so much . . . But if she was seeing some other guy, I would have known about it. I would have spotted them out together, but outside of the guys in the house, I never saw her with anybody—well, except . . ."

"Except who?"

"Spanky McFarland; he had it bad for her. Even more than me. There may have been something between them before, but it was definitely over, which was why I thought I might have a chance. I'm such an idiot."

"No, you're not, Chet. You're a handsome, charming young man who is going to find the perfect girl someday."

"You have to say that; you're like my aunt." Chet sighed.

Hayley squeezed the back of his neck with her hand. "Trust me, someday you're going to be a real heart-breaker."

She was grateful he had finally opened up to her after all this time, but slightly disturbed that Dustin's child-hood best buddy, Spanky McFarland, might be somehow involved in this whole mess.

Which meant she had to find out more.

Island Food & Spirits
BY
HAYLEY POWELL

Not too long ago, I was cleaning out some of the clutter in my kitchen cupboards, when I came across a half-used jar of instant coffee. Well, I immediately got a huge craving for some of my easy homemade coffee ice cream. Luckily, I already had all the ingredients, because I remembered the last time that craving hit me, I had to run to the store to pick up what I needed for the recipe, and that particular day turned out to be one for the books.

It was back when my son Dustin was still in high school. He and his friend Spanky had walked into town to hang out for the afternoon, and I was going through some old recipes my mother had collected and sent me over the years. That's when I spotted the easy homemade coffee ice cream recipe.

I stared at it longingly.

"Put it back; you don't need those extra calories," I told myself.

I put it back.

Well, five minutes later, I was fishing it out again and searching my kitchen for all the ingredients, which I luckily had, except for one—the instant coffee.

I glanced at my watch. If I hurried, I could drive to the store, grab the coffee, drive home, whip up a batch, and throw it in the freezer, so it would be done in time for that evening, when Mona and Liddy were scheduled to come over to watch the Saturday night Lifetime movie, which we had planned the moment I saw the listing in my channel guide. This week's movie was starring my favorite TV actor obsession—Mark Harmon! Even as a deranged serial killer, he was still heart-stoppingly gorgeous!

Off I went to the Shop 'n Save. I held my breath as I pulled into the lot, because during the summer, at the height of the tourist season, you can never find a parking space. The lot is always jammed with cars. But I got lucky. At that precise moment, a car just happened to be pulling out, and I was able to grab the open spot. I was in and out of the store in less than five minutes, thanks to Lady Luck also providing me with an empty express lane when I was ready to check out with my can of coffee.

That's when all my good luck came to a screeching halt.

When I returned to the spot where I had parked my car, there was a Toyota Prius with a New York license plate parked there instead, and no sign of my Kia Sportage. I thought perhaps I was confused about the exact space where

I had parked my car, and began wandering around the lot, looking for it. I couldn't imagine it had been stolen. Cars never get stolen in Bar Harbor, Maine. It just doesn't happen. And even if one was, it would never make it off the island before it got intercepted by the police at the Trenton Bridge. But after I'd circled the lot three whole times, the reality of the situation finally began to sink in. Someone had stolen my car!

I quickly called the chief of police, who happened to be my brother-in-law. He arrived on the scene within minutes in his squad car, with the flashing blue lights getting all sorts of attention from the wide-eyed tourists and locals passing by. Most stopped to listen as he questioned me, and pretty soon, a large crowd had gathered around, since it wasn't every day a vehicle got stolen from the Shop 'n Save parking lot in broad daylight.

Chief Sergio asked me to start from the beginning, and I recounted everything: how I had stumbled upon my mother's easy homemade coffee ice cream recipe; how I needed a jar of instant coffee; the plans to watch a Lifetime movie with Liddy and Mona; my obsession with Mark Harmon. Sergio calmly asked me to hurry the story along and get to the part where I arrived at the Shop 'n Save, so I skipped ahead to how hard it always is to find a parking space in the summer, which garnered lots of nodding and mumbles of agreement from the crowd of onlookers. How I had jumped out of the car, ran into the store for five minutes at most, and then returned to discover my car missing.

That's when Sergio interrupted and asked if I had left my keys in the car.

"Of course not!" I cried, indignant.

I reached into my purse to grab my keys, felt around, but couldn't find them. I could feel everyone's eyes on me. I started frantically shaking my purse as a sinking feeling started to overwhelm me. Finally, I leaned into Sergio and whispered sheepishly, "I think I may have left the keys in the ignition because I was in such a hurry."

This admission had the crowd gasping out loud. I wanted the parking lot to open up and swallow me whole. How embarrassing! My car had been stolen, and it was all my fault!

Well, Sergio wasted no time putting out an all-points bulletin. He asked for my license plate. I told him it was on the registration, which unfortunately, was in the glove compartment of my stolen car.

That's right about the time my brother Randy squealed into the parking lot, honking his horn and yelling out his window, "Wait!" He stopped in front of us, jumped out of his car, then flung his vehicle's back door open, sternly ordering the occupants in the back seat to get out and explain themselves.

My son Dustin and his friend Spanky slowly crawled out of Randy's car, their faces beet red, as Randy nudged them towards me. Apparently, as the boys explained to the chief, they saw me pull into the parking lot and decided to catch a ride home with me, but when they got in the car, Dustin spotted the keys in the ignition and thought it would be hilarious to move my car and watch my reaction when I came out of the store to find it gone. But when they pulled out of the parking space, they couldn't find another free space, so they had to park it out on the street in front of Jordan's Restaurant. Thinking I'd be in the store longer than five minutes, they went into Jordan's to buy a couple of Cokes to go, and by the time they had come out, the police were already there, surrounded by this huge crowd. The boys panicked and didn't know what to do, so they ran down the street to Randy's bar and nervously explained what had happened. They hoped that if Randy was the one to tell me what they did, I might stay calm and not lose my temper.

Fat chance.

After receiving a stern lecture from Sergio, the chastened boys shuffled off to my car, knowing they would be getting another even sterner lecture from me on the way home.

Thankfully, the crowd of people was already thinning out, with some of them shaking their heads in disbelief, but most of them getting a good chuckle out of the whole drama.

I hugged Sergio and Randy, promising them that I would stop by the next day with some homemade coffee ice cream for both of them to show my gratitude.

And the next day, I made good on that promise, arriving at their house with a huge vat of my easy homemade coffee cream. Randy made his new favorite happy-hour concoction, spiked coffee, and the three of us sat on their front porch, roaring with laughter, recalling the previous day's events and promising we would never tell Dustin just how funny we all thought the prank really was, especially since he was so consumed with guilt, he had actually offered to do some yard work, which he always hated. So in the end, some good did come out of the whole ordeal. Dustin learned his lesson, I got a freshly mowed lawn, and everybody enjoyed some delicious coffee ice cream!

RANDY'S SPECIAL COFFEE

INGREDIENTS:
1 ounce bourbon
½ ounce Kahlúa
Dash of vanilla extract
Sugar to taste
6 ounces hot coffee
Whipped cream (optional)

In a large coffee mug, add the coffee, then add your favorite bourbon, Kahlúa, and a dash of vanilla.

Add sugar to your taste and a splash of cream, if desired.

I love coming home after a busy day of work and making myself this delicious pick-me-up for the long evening ahead.

MOM'S EASY HOMEMADE COFFEE ICE CREAM

INGREDIENTS:
2 cups heavy cream
14 ounces (1 can) condensed milk
1 teaspoon vanilla
3 tablespoons instant coffee

Pour your heavy cream into a stand mixer (or mixing bowl, if using electric beaters) and beat for about 5 minutes until stiff peaks are formed.

Dissolve the instant coffee in a small bowl with one tablespoon water.

Add the condensed milk, vanilla, and coffee, and mix until combined.

Pour your mixture into a bread pan and place into the freezer for at least 6 hours or until frozen.

When frozen, remove, scoop into a bowl, and let it melt in your mouth!

Chapter 22

Carla McFarland was a talker. So much so, in fact, that Hayley had to marvel at just how long she could speak without stopping to take a breath. She must have the sturdy lungs of an Olympic swimmer. During the days when both Hayley and Carla served on the school's PTA board, Hayley had always been mindful to have some extra time on her hands when she called Carla about a bake sale or new soccer uniforms, in order to allow Carla to get whatever crisis she was dealing with in her life off her chest before Hayley could jump in and steer the conversation toward the reason for her call. But since Carla divorced her husband several years ago, she had mellowed somewhat. Her son, Spanky, still lived at home, which was a lifeline for Carla, who was admittedly lonely and feeling unmoored now that she was navigating life as a single woman again. Hayley would hardly call her and Carla close friends, but they always stopped to catch up whenever they ran into each other at the bank, grocery store, or post office. Hayley had detected a lingering sadness in Carla, who had struggled after divorcing Gray, who cruelly told her there was no other woman to blame for the breakup of their marriage, that he just couldn't stand being around her anymore. That had to have hurt deeply.

And so, when Hayley showed up on Carla's front porch and rang the bell, and Carla answered the door looking fabulous in a smart summer ensemble and her hair done up in a stylish bob, her face bright-eyed and cheery, as if she had discovered a whole new lease on life, Hayley could not have been more thrilled for her.

"Hayley! What a lovely surprise!" Carla cooed.

"I'm sorry to drop by unannounced. I usually have much better social skills, but I really needed to talk to you," Hayley explained as Carla excitedly ushered her inside the house.

"Don't be silly. I don't have to be at work for another hour; have some coffee with me. I'm sorry I haven't had a chance to come by your restaurant for dinner yet, but I have just been so busy."

"Well, luckily, business has been good, and it looks like we might be around for a while, so you have plenty of time," Hayley said, following Carla to the kitchen, where she poured them both some coffee.

"Milk and sugar?"

Carla scooped some sugar and poured a dollop of whole milk in Hayley's cup before she had a chance to answer and handed it to her. "There you go."

"Thank you," Hayley said, taking a sip and crinkling her nose. She preferred her coffee black. "So they've got you working overtime at Sherman's now that we're knee-deep in the summer season?"

Sherman's was the local bookstore on Cottage Street, where Carla worked behind the register a few days a week.

She gave Hayley a puzzled look. "No, I'm still only part-time; why do you ask?"

"Oh, you mentioned how busy you've been lately."

Carla gave her a conspiratorial wink. "That's not because of work. I've got a new beau."

Hayley lit up. "Oh, Carla, that's wonderful. I'm so happy for you."

To Hayley's knowledge, Carla had not dated anyone since Gray walked out on her, and that was over four years ago.

"Who is it? Do I know him?"

"We're in the very early stages. He's a local, but I don't want to jinx it by spilling all the details just yet."

"Understandable."

Carla slurped her coffee. "But Spanky's met him, and he seems to like him, which means the world to me, because Spanky is the most important person in my life."

"You must love having him still at home with you."

"He's been such a rock to me, especially after his father left us. I think he stuck around because he intuitively knew I needed his support. It was a pretty awful time, to be honest. I was in the depths of my misery, and Spanky was always there, trying to make me feel better. I am so grateful to him. But now, I think he's ready to get on with his life and not be living at home with his kooky mother anymore, and so I've been pushing him to get out there and follow his dreams. He wants to be a professional DJ; he's always loved music."

"Yes, Spanky told us when we ran into him recently."

"I can see him making a name for himself, becoming a big superstar. Of course, it's a mother's right to be a little biased. He needs a fresh start, especially after what happened."

Hayley's ears perked up. "What do you mean?"

"Miranda Fox, poor thing. She and Spanky had been dating before you found her frozen like a popsicle in Lynette Partridge's ice cream truck. Spanky was so devastated when he heard the news. He really liked her. And they made such a cute couple."

"I knew Spanky had a crush on her, but I was not aware they were actually in a relationship," Hayley said.

Carla nodded, downing the rest of her coffee and pouring herself another cup. "Oh, yes. He never brought her home to meet me or anything like that. It didn't last that long. They just went out on a few dates. Spanky was in heaven, but then, rather abruptly, she dumped him. Oh, I felt so bad for Spanky. He was inconsolable. He locked himself in his room and just blasted his music for hours. I got so worried about him. I know I shouldn't have done it, but I went down to the ice cream shop to have a little talk with Miranda." Carla picked up on Hayley's wary expression. "I know, in retrospect, it was a dumb thing to do. But I just hated seeing Spanky hurting so much. I just thought maybe I could persuade her to give him another chance, explain what a fine boy he was, plead his case. Well, I have to say, she was very polite, but didn't budge one bit. In her mind, it was over for good. She had no interest in giving him a second chance. I had a feeling there was someone else she had her eye on."

"Did Spanky ever find out about what you did?"

Carla nodded guiltily. "Apparently, he stopped by the

ice cream shop, and tried asking Miranda out again, and she told him that she had already told his mother and she was telling him now, 'No dice.' Well, you can imagine how mortified Spanky was to find out I had interfered in his personal life. He was so embarrassed and humiliated. He came bursting through that front door and yelled at me for hours. I can't blame him. I never should have stuck my nose where it didn't belong."

"He'll realize some day you were just trying to help," Hayley offered meekly.

"I've made such a mess of things. There is this rift now between us. He barely comes home, which worries me because I have no idea where he goes, or who he hangs out with, or what he's up to. Horrible thoughts go through my mind, like 'Is he doing drugs?' Or 'Will he somehow hurt himself?' I can't tell you how much it pains me that he's been distancing himself from me."

"Have you gone into his room to look for answers?"

It was a casual question.

But Hayley had an ulterior motive for putting it out there.

"Oh, I've thought about it, but after what happened, I don't want to ever invade his privacy again."

"Still, he's living in your house, and you do have a right to know if he's hiding drugs in his room."

"You know, you're right. I could be responsible if the police showed up and found illegal substances on the premises."

Hayley let that unsettling thought sink in before suggesting, "If you want to check right now, I would be happy to come with you for moral support."

Carla considered the offer.

Hayley didn't want to push too hard, but she was feeling confident that she was about to gain access to Spanky's room, where she could search for some kind of evidence that might connect Spanky to Miranda Fox's murder. It was a long shot, but she had to explore every angle.

Carla slammed her coffee cup down on the kitchen counter. "Let's go!"

Carla led the way up the stairs to Spanky's room. When Carla swung open the door and the two of them entered, Hayley was nearly overcome by a rancid stench best described as dirty socks. The room was a pigsty: clothes strewn everywhere, pizza boxes and empty beer bottles on the floor, a big blue bong sitting out in the open on top of his cluttered desk.

Carla zeroed in on the bong instantly. "Oh, dear, where there's a bong, marijuana can't be far away!"

Hayley seized the opportunity to search the drawers next to the desk, and the first thing she spotted was a sealed plastic bag with what looked like weed. She handed it over to Carla, who stared at it, vexed.

"Recreational pot isn't illegal, Carla, and Spanky is of legal age, so you're good so far," Hayley remarked, before returning her attention back to the drawer, where her eyes fell upon a glass vial. She picked it up and read the label.

Tetrodotoxin.

She had heard the name before.

It was the toxin found in puffer fish that, if not removed, would kill anyone who ingested it.

It was also the poison that, according to county coroner Sabrina Merryweather, had been used to murder Miranda Fox.

Chapter 23

As Hayley studied the label on the tiny glass vial in her hand, she noticed the word Tetrodotoxin scribbled in red pen. There was nothing official-looking about it, like it had come from a lab, so she couldn't be sure if it was the real thing, or it was just plain water being passed off as Tetrodotoxin. She certainly was not going to taste it to find out.

Carla craned her neck around to see what Hayley was so interested in looking at, but Hayley's back was to Carla, and she couldn't see what Hayley was holding in her hand. "Is that Spanky's anxiety medication? I'm constantly after him to take it, but he always forgets, and then of course we all pay for it later."

Hayley slowly turned around, fishing for some tissue in her bag to hold the vial and minimize her own fingerprints. "This is not anxiety medication, Carla. If this is what the label says, then it's the poison that was found in Miranda Fox's system."

Carla's mouth dropped open in shock, and then she sprinted forward to get a closer look at the label. "Treta-what?"

"Tetrodotoxin, it's a toxic substance found in a puffer fish."

"A puffer-*what*?"

"Like a blowfish or balloon fish. Most contain a lethal substance called Tetrodotoxin, which is about twelve hundred times more poisonous than cyanide."

Carla gasped. "Are you serious?"

"Yes. There is enough toxin in one puffer fish to kill about thirty adult humans."

"I don't understand. Why would Spanky be in posses-sion of something like that?"

There was a long, agonizing silence.

"No!" Carla cried. "Spanky would never . . . This is ridiculous! Where on earth would he even get his hands on a deadly poison?"

"If people can buy assault weapons online, I'm sure there are ways to order a lethal substance like this on the dark web. You only need a Wi-Fi connection."

"Hayley, this is crazy. That can't belong to my son. I know him; you know him. Spanky doesn't have a mean-spirited bone in his body. There is no way he would ever contemplate doing something so vile and evil!"

Hayley wanted to believe her.

She truly did.

She had spent countless nights when Dustin was younger hosting sleepover parties with him and Spanky, where they would stay up all night watching James Bond movies on DVD and gorging on pizza and popcorn and sugary sodas. He was such a sweet, polite, unassuming kid. But she had seen even the nicest boys grow up to become troubled young men. And she couldn't ignore what she had just uncovered just because she had a few happy memories of Spanky's childhood sprinkled around in her brain. She carefully wrapped the tissue around the vial and placed it inside her bag.

Carla tensed up. "Where are you taking that?"

"To the police," Hayley said solemnly.

"The *police*? I don't see why we have to bring them into this just yet. I mean, let me talk to Spanky first and try to clear all this up."

"Carla, I have no choice. This is hard evidence. Sergio needs to see this."

"Please, Hayley, no! I'm begging you!" Carla yelled frantically, blocking her exit from Spanky's room. "Spanky's very fragile. If they arrest him and lock him up, Lord knows what he might do."

"My brother-in-law is a fair, decent man. He'll take very good care of Spanky when they bring him in for questioning, I can promise you that."

But Carla wasn't buying any of this. She was growing more panicky and desperate by the second, to the point where Hayley began to fear she might try to physically detain her from leaving her house and turning over this evidence. So when they heard a car pull up outside, and Carla flew to the window to see if it was Spanky, Hayley seized the opportunity to race out of the bedroom, fly down the stairs, and out the front door to her car.

"Hayley, wait!" Carla screamed, chasing after her.

Hayley jumped behind the wheel and rolled down her window just as Carla raced out of her house, stopping at her porch steps, her shoulders sagging from the realization that she could not stop Hayley from doing what she was about to do.

"I'll call you later, Carla; just sit tight! And for Spanky's sake, if he shows up, tell him to *please* call Sergio and volunteer to go to the station, so they can question him."

Carla just stood on the porch, in a state of shock and distress, but she did manage a slight nod as Hayley pulled out from behind the UPS truck that had just been parked there while the driver delivered a package next door.

Hayley drove directly to the police station and handed the vial over to Sergio, who immediately had Officer Earl drive it over to the Jackson Lab. There, they had the right equipment to test it instead of shipping it to the police lab in Bangor, where it might take days. Then, once the substance was confirmed, Sergio put out an APB on Spanky McFarland throughout the state, so by noon, dozens of law enforcement officers, from Bar Harbor to Ogunquit, were out scouring the roads and highways looking for him. Hayley called Carla several times during the day to find out if she had heard from her son, but all of her calls went straight to voice mail.

By five o'clock, Spanky had still not turned up.

Hayley swung by her restaurant, where her manager, Betty, had everything under control in the dining room while her chef, Kelton, ran things smoothly in the kitchen. After signing off on the night's specials, Hayley left her business in the very capable hands of her staff and headed home to spend the evening with Bruce, Dustin, and MacKenzie. On her way, she stopped by Carla's house again to check on her. She rang the doorbell twice. Through the front window, she could see Carla sitting in her living room, staring straight ahead, as if in some kind of trance. She ignored the doorbell.

Hayley tried knocking.

Carla still didn't budge.

Sighing, Hayley walked back down the porch steps, across the lawn, and stood directly in front of the living room window, where Carla could not pretend that she didn't see her.

"Carla, I understand that you're upset with me, but you know I couldn't suppress evidence, it just wouldn't be right," Hayley shouted through the window.

Carla's eyes flitted briefly over at Hayley, then quickly darted away again. She was biting her lip, pensive and nervous, and was in no mood to talk.

"Are you going to make me stand out here all night?"

Carla began bobbing her knee up and down, debating with herself; then finally, in a huff, she bolted upright and marched out of the living room before whipping open her front door and confronting Hayley.

"What do you want, Hayley?" Carla spit out coldly.

"I just wanted to know if you heard from Spanky today?"

"No, I have not. Is that all?"

Hayley noticed some muddy sneakers on the floor just behind Carla that had not been there earlier in the day.

Nike LeBrons.

She had seen Spanky wearing them many times.

Carla instantly picked up on the fact that Hayley was distracted and followed her gaze, turning around to see the discarded sneakers on the floor.

Hayley took a deep breath. "Is he here?"

"No!" Carla snapped. "If you don't believe me, then why don't you call your brother-in-law and have him get a warrant and search the place?"

If Carla was truly hiding Spanky, Hayley figured she never would have made that kind of offer.

"Then he *was* here," Hayley said accusingly. "And you tipped him off that the police are after him, so now he's gone into hiding until you can figure out what to do."

"I'm tired of your guessing games, Hayley," Carla growled, stepping back inside the house and moving to close the door on her.

"Where is he, Carla? Hiding from the police will only make it worse!"

Carla slammed the door loudly in her face.

There was no doubt in Hayley's mind that Carla McFarland knew the whereabouts of her fugitive son.

But she was never going to talk.

Chapter 24

It was going on two-thirty in the morning.

Hayley punched her goose down pillow with her fist, trying to give it more fluff, then rested her head on it, hoping a new position might help her finally drift off to sleep.

No such luck.

Her eyes remained wide open, and she let out a heavy sigh.

Bruce was in a deep sleep next to her, his usual rackety snoring having mercifully subsided some time ago.

Hayley shifted to her other side, facing away from Bruce, and closed her eyes. But her mind was racing. She was consumed with thoughts about Spanky McFarland: if the police had finally tracked him down; if he was already across state lines, heading south, halfway to Mexico by now. Finally, unable to clear her mind and fall back to sleep, Hayley crawled out of bed, threw on a robe, and headed downstairs for a late-night snack.

Her shih tzu, Leroy, whose ears perked up at the sound of Hayley's feet padding across the creaky hardwood floor to the staircase, had bolted out of his cushiony doggie bed in the corner of Hayley and Bruce's room and followed her down, excited that a treat might be in his immediate future.

He wasn't disappointed.

Hayley grabbed a box from the cupboard and spoiled him with not one, but two bone-shaped meat-flavored treats. Then, she put a pot of coffee on, grabbed a carton of Lynette's Pralines and Cream ice cream from the freezer, and began digging into it with a large soup spoon. She turned on the police scanner on top of the refrigerator, and then sat down at the kitchen table to listen, but there was very little activity happening on this very quiet evening, and absolutely nothing about Spanky McFarland.

She was most of the way through the carton when she heard rustling coming from upstairs and then someone descending the staircase.

It was Bruce, yawning and scratching his bare chest.

"What are you doing up?" Hayley asked, her mouth full of melting ice cream.

"I reached over to cuddle up with you, and you weren't there, and when I noticed Leroy gone, too, I thought I might be missing out," Bruce said, grabbing another soup spoon from the kitchen drawer and making a play for some of Hayley's Pralines and Cream.

As he dug deep into the carton, scraping out what was left at the bottom, Hayley yanked it away protectively. "Hey, don't take it all."

"You barely left any for me," Bruce complained.

"There's a carton of Vegan Chocolate in there; you can go to town on that one."

"I'm not vegan."

"You don't have to be vegan to eat vegan ice cream."

"It just sounds like fake ice cream to me."

Bruce noticed the red light on the scanner and pointed at it. "Is that why you can't sleep? You're waiting on word about Spanky?"

Hayley nodded, setting the now-empty carton down on the table. "I hated turning him in like that. Carla will probably never forgive me."

"You couldn't ignore what you found in his room, babe."

"I know, but you should have seen the look on Carla's face—the horror, confusion, fear. I couldn't imagine what I would do if it had been Dustin."

"We don't know anything about Spanky, what's going through his head, what he might be capable of. You see it on the news all the time, people saying 'He seemed like such a nice kid, I never suspected a thing,'" Bruce said calmly as he grabbed the Vegan Chocolate from the freezer, popped the top open, and scooped out a big chunk with his spoon, stuffing it in his mouth. "Oh, man, that's really cold!"

"Maybe that's why they call it ice cream," Hayley deadpanned.

Bruce waved his hands around, trying to swallow. "Whoa, wow, brain freeze." He paused, waiting. "Okay, that's better. And by the way, the Vegan Chocolate, kinda tasty."

Hayley smiled, hardly surprised. "Lynette is an ice cream goddess. She can make *almost* any flavor work." Her mind wandered back to Spanky. "He used to be such a happy-go-lucky kid when he was younger. I remember he and Dustin would make their own horror movies; he had such an active imagination. But as he got older, he started to change. He didn't smile as much, he became more remote, and he and Dustin slowly drifted apart. Carla did her best with him after the divorce, but eventually, he fell in with the wrong crowd, got stuck in a rut with the drugs and alcohol. He's kind of been lost and rudderless ever since high school. But that happens to lots of kids; it doesn't mean they would resort to anything so . . ."

"Who knows? It's possible. Maybe when Spanky met Miranda, he thought she might help him turn things around, make a fresh start, give his life purpose, but when she rejected him, all that hope went out the window, and he just snapped," Bruce theorized.

"No!"

The loud voice startled both of them.

Hayley spun around to see Dustin standing in the doorway to the kitchen, in a ratty old T-shirt and sweatpants, his eyes narrowed, full of anger.

"Dustin, I didn't see you standing there. You scared me half to death," Hayley said.

"He didn't do it, Mom," Dustin insisted. "I have known Spanky my whole life, and he just doesn't have it in him to harm anyone, especially Miranda. He was totally in love with her. And even if she didn't feel the same way, he'd never do anything rash like poison her, no matter how desperate he was. That's not the Spanky I grew up with."

Dustin crossed to the refrigerator and opened the door, perused the contents, and then pulled out a jar of pickles.

Bruce raised an eyebrow. "Having a craving?"

Dustin glanced at the pickle jar he was holding. "These are for MacKenzie. She's been tossing and turning for hours. The baby's been kicking, she can't get comfortable, and now she's hungry. She's kept me up all night."

"Just wait until *after* you have the baby; it won't get any easier," Hayley said with a smile.

Dustin eyed the carton of ice cream in Bruce's hand. "You going to finish that?"

"No, I'm done. It's vegan."

Dustin shot an arm out and grabbed the ice cream away from him. "She won't care. She likes to have something to dip the pickles in. It's become a thing. Kinda gross, but it keeps her happy." Dustin started to leave, but stopped and turned back around. "Can you do me a favor, Bruce?"

"Sure, buddy. Whatever you need."

"Please don't write about Spanky in your column. Not yet, anyway."

Hayley could see the deep concern in her son's eyes.

"I'm not sure I can promise that. I'm paid to write about local crimes, and this is the biggest story we've got going in town right now."

"I know, but if you go pointing your finger at Spanky, it might make him more desperate, and he'll be less willing to come forward, and allow the police to question him. I just don't want to make his situation worse before he has a chance to clear his name. Please, Bruce, just hold off, give him a little more time. Your opinion carries a lot of weight around here, and I don't want the whole town coming out with pitchforks and torches until he has the chance to explain himself."

Bruce considered this, not sure he should agree. He glanced at Hayley, who tried to remain neutral. This was Bruce's call, not hers.

"Okay, buddy," Bruce sighed. "I will keep his name out of my column, for now. But the clock's ticking."

"Thank you," Dustin whispered, grateful but still very much worried about the fate of his childhood friend.

Chapter 25

"Hayley, I have not been dodging your calls, I have just been incredibly busy this week, trying to find a buyer for this house," Liddy said in a clipped tone, as she waved at an approaching black BMW that was barreling down the gravel road toward the Seagull House.

"I won't keep you, but we really need to talk," Hayley insisted. "I'm sorry I just showed up like this, but your office said you'd be here, and I was hoping to get you alone before your prospective buyers arrived."

"Well, as you can see, they're here, and as much as I love the Nash family, Rachel has been absolutely impossible about clearing out so I can show the house. Today, she is only allowing a half-hour window. How can anyone show a house this size in thirty minutes? It's impossible, and I tried to explain to her that in order to secure the right sale, perhaps it would be in her interest to be a tad more flexible, but she didn't want to hear it."

"I'll get out of your hair, but can you meet me later, say around five, at Drinks Like A Fish, so we can talk?"

Liddy tapped at her phone, bringing up her calendar, perusing her day. "Maybe; I'll let you know. I've been trying to schedule a dinner with George for tonight, but he's been MIA these last couple of days. I don't know what's going on with him," Liddy huffed.

A young, attractive, preppy couple emerged from the BMW. They could have been the models in a Giorgio Armani ad on the inside pages of *Vanity Fair*—rail thin, fashionably dressed, ridiculously expensive sunglasses, both of them pouting dismissively.

"Hello, so nice to meet you—I'm Liddy, the Realtor!" Liddy chirped excitedly before whispering an aside to Hayley, "The Stantons. They're from New York, looking for a summer getaway home. He runs a huge hedge fund on Wall Street; she has her own publishing arm at Simon & Schuster. Big, big money."

Hayley offered them a friendly wave, which they didn't return. "Okay, I'm outta here, but please, Liddy, meet me later, because what we need to discuss concerns George."

This stopped Liddy in her tracks as she was about to descend upon on her potential buyers. She raised a finger. "Could you two hold on a minute? I just have to consult with my associate for one sec."

Associate?

When it came to the real estate world, Liddy was always weaving a tangled web.

"What about George?"

"It can wait; tend to the Stantons."

"No, tell me now. What about George?"

Hayley eyed the Stantons nervously. People that rich were not often imbued with much patience. Mr. Stanton folded his arms with a frown and glared at them while Mrs. Stanton listlessly texted on her phone.

"Liddy, they don't look happy about having to wait."

"I'm sorry, but this is important. George has been ghosting me the past few days, and if you happen to know why, you need to tell me, because you're my best friend, and it would be wrong to withhold such crucial information from me."

Hayley took a deep breath. "Okay, Bruce and I ran into George recently."

"Where?"

"Mona's house."

"Mona's house? What was he doing there?"

"He came for dinner."

"Dinner? At Mona's house? I'm totally lost here, Hayley."

"The reason you may not have heard from George lately is because he might be afraid of how you will react to what I'm about to tell you."

"Stop drawing out the drama, Hayley—if you have something to say, then say it."

"George is dating Mona."

Liddy stared at her with a blank look for the longest time. Hayley wasn't sure if she was busy processing what she had just heard or if she was currently in a debilitating state of shock.

"Liddy, did you hear what I just said?"

"You said that George is dating Mona."

"Yes," Hayley sighed.

"But obviously, you meant to say something else, because just the idea of George dating Mona when he is also dating me is just too absurd, too ludicrous to even contemplate."

"I'm afraid it's true, Mona. But trust me, Mona had no idea he was dating you at the same time."

"Wait, didn't Mona tell you she was dating a janitor named Chuck? Now all of a sudden she's also dating a doctor named George? How is that possible? Mona's been with her deadbeat husband Dennis her entire adult life up until last year, and now she's dating not one, but *two* men?"

"No, he's one and the same," Hayley said, going on to explain Mona's nickname for George, and how she never considered he was a doctor when he told her he worked at the lab, and just assumed he was on the maintenance crew.

"Excuse me, Ms. Crawford," Mr. Stanton seethed. "But we are under some time constraints, so if we could just get on with seeing the house—?"

"Shut your face, I'll get to you in a minute!" Liddy screamed, startling them both enough for Mrs. Stanton to drop her phone to the ground. "I have a major crisis I need to deal with right now!"

"Liddy, I'm sorry, but you really should take care of—"

Liddy shot up a hand to silence Hayley. "They can wait. This is your last chance, Hayley. Tell me that this is just some sick, not well thought-out, utterly ridiculous joke."

"It's not," Hayley lamented.

"Oh my god!" Liddy wailed. "I don't know what's worse! Me dating the same man as Mona, or a man I'm dating actually being *attracted* to Mona! What does that say about his taste, *my* taste? I'm suddenly feeling dizzy, I'm seeing stars, I better go inside and sit down for a spell . . . could you tell the Stantons we're going to have to reschedule?"

"There's no need for that now," Hayley said.

"Why not?"

"You've already scared them off."

Hayley gestured toward the gravel drive, where they saw the taillights of the black BMW light up at the top of the road as the car braked, swerved to the right, and disappeared back toward town.

Chapter 26

There have been many historical peace summits in world history. The Vienna Summit, where JFK met with Soviet Premier Khrushchev, in 1961; the Yalta Conference in 1945, where FDR, Winston Churchill, and Joseph Stalin discussed post-Nazi Europe after World War II; the Geneva Summit in 1985 with Ronald Reagan and Mikhail Gorbachev, where they hashed out the Cold War and the arms race. But none of those monumental meetings rose to the challenges Hayley faced by trying to broker the Drinks Like A Fish Peace Summit with her two besties, Liddy Crawford and Mona Barnes, who were both now painfully aware that they were romantically involved with the same man.

Hayley had strong-armed both women into at least showing up at Randy's bar and making some kind of attempt to hash it out and reach some tentative reconciliation. They had both balked at first, but Hayley forcefully reminded them of their vast history as friends, the decades of warm and happy memories they had accumulated over the years, how silly it was that they would allow one man to come between them. When they both begrudgingly agreed to meet at six o'clock that evening at Drinks Like A Fish, Hayley felt confident they could arrive at some sort of détente. Honestly, how difficult could it actually be to get over this little bump in the middle of their long, winding road of friendship?

In hindsight, Hayley quickly realized, her naïveté was breathtaking.

"I should have known you would try something like this, Mona. After all, you started way back in the third grade, when I had a crush on Austin Littlefield, and you were all over him!"

"I was never all over him! We just waited at the same bus stop every day before school. It was hard to avoid him!"

"Every day when the bus pulled up, I would look out the window from my seat in the back and see you shamelessly flirting with him."

"First of all, I was in the third grade; I didn't know the meaning of the word flirting! Second, I hated Austin Littlefield! Every day for a whole winter, I'd push him in the snowbank and make him cry!"

"That was your idea of foreplay! Still is, I imagine!" Liddy cried.

"Yeah, well, I guess it worked in this case, didn't it?"

Liddy whipped around to Hayley. "See? She just admitted trying to steal George from me!"

"I didn't have to steal anything. Chuck was all over me like a cheap suit," Mona said, chuckling.

"His name is *George*!" Liddy snapped.

"Yeah, well, I call him Chuck, so deal with it!" Mona snapped back.

Randy, who was worried their shouting might frighten off his other customers, appeared from behind the bar. "Mona, can I get you a beer, you know, to calm your nerves?"

"I'm not thirsty!" Mona barked.

Uh-oh.

This was bad.

Really bad.

Mona never said no to a beer.

Ever.

Liddy held her signature cosmo, but she was shaking, and it was spilling over the side, dripping down onto her hand holding the glass.

Hayley knew it was time to intervene. "Listen to me, this should not be a war between you two. Neither of you did anything wrong. George is the culprit here. You two are just the unsuspecting victims. There is no reason to be mad at each other. Liddy, you honestly don't think Mona purposefully started dating George to stick it to you, do you?"

"His name is Chuck!" Mona yelled.

"Chuck. George. Whoever. He's the one to blame for all of this," Hayley said.

Randy, who had scooted away a few seconds earlier, returned with a Bud Light, popping the top off with a bottle opener and setting it gently down on the bar next to Mona. "Just in case you change your mind."

Liddy gulped down the rest of her cosmo and slammed the glass down so hard on the bar, it shattered to pieces, and she was left holding only the stem.

"No worries, happens all the time, I'll clean it up,"

Randy sighed, rushing off for a small hand broom and dustpan.

Hayley inspected Liddy's hand for cuts from the glass but fortunately didn't find any.

"Thank you, Hayley, I'm just very upset. Every time I think about it, I find it utterly impossible to believe . . ."

"Some men are pigs, it's as simple as that," Hayley said.

"That's not what she's saying," Mona growled, seething.

Hayley glanced at Liddy, then to Mona. "What do you mean?"

"She's not upset because Chuck was two-timing her, she's upset because Chuck was two-timing her with *me*! She can't stand the fact that he found me attractive! It just doesn't make sense to her that he could be going out with her and then also like me! She's always thought she was better than me!"

"Oh, don't be ridiculous, Mona," Liddy scoffed.

"For once in your life, be honest, Liddy. I'm right about this, aren't I? If it was anybody else, you'd be mad, but you might understand—but not me, not big, fat Mona with no makeup and a terrible haircut! That's what you think!"

Hayley turned to Mona. "That's not true . . ."

Mona kept her eyes trained on Liddy. "Go on, deny it, Liddy, say I'm wrong."

Hayley stepped forward. "Of course you're wrong—"

"I'm asking Liddy!"

A silence fell over the bar.

Except for Nick Jonas playing on the jukebox.

The other patrons were watching the whole ugly scene like a car wreck they couldn't tear their eyes away from.

Even Randy had stopped serving customers, because he was so glued to how Liddy was going to respond.

Finally, Liddy couldn't stand everyone staring at her, waiting for her to say something, and so she threw her hands up in the air and cried, "Okay, yes, maybe there's a grain of truth to that, I won't lie!"

"I knew it!" Mona said, grabbing the bottle of beer and taking an angry swig. "You've always looked down on me! I can't believe how many years I wasted being your friend!" She guzzled the rest of her beer, handed the empty bottle to Hayley, and stormed out of the bar. Liddy, in a flood of tears, retreated to the restroom in the back and locked herself inside, leaving Hayley alone. She was done trying to restore harmony. Their emotions were too raw, and neither was, at this point, willing to work on lowering the temperature on the whole wretched situation.

Randy returned and gingerly took the empty beer bottle from Hayley. "So has anyone heard from George?"

"No one has seen him for days," Hayley said, defeated.

"Maybe he's hiding out with Spanky McFarland," he quipped, before wandering back to wait on his customers, who were thirsty after watching the unscheduled floor show.

Chapter 27

Hayley knew what she was doing was wrong. But she just couldn't help herself.

When she had arrived home and headed up the stairs to change for dinner, she had heard her son's voice, soft and muffled, as he spoke to MacKenzie in his bedroom with the door closed.

And now, here she was, standing outside his room, her ear pressed to the door, eavesdropping on their private conversation.

"Are you going to tell anyone?" MacKenzie asked.

"No, if I say anything, they'll find him and arrest him and put him on trial. They desperately need someone to take the fall so they can close the case, and I'm not going to do that to him."

Spanky.

He was talking about Spanky.

And it sounded like Dustin knew where he was hiding.

"He's really scared, Mac. He swears he didn't do it."

"Do you believe him?"

"I've known him most of my life—yeah, we lost touch, and people change and all that, but I believe he's innocent. It's a gut feeling I have; he would never intentionally hurt anyone."

"Then stay quiet, don't say a word," MacKenzie advised.

Bad advice, Hayley thought to herself.

Dustin continued talking, but he lowered his voice to almost a whisper, and Hayley had to strain to hear what he was saying, pressing her ear harder against the door. She was so focused on what was going on in Dustin's room, she didn't hear Bruce coming up the stairs.

"What are you doing skulking about outside your son's room?" Bruce said in a jocular manner.

Hayley, startled, yelped loud enough for Leroy to come scampering out of Hayley and Bruce's bedroom, where he had been napping, to investigate.

"Bruce, don't sneak up on me like that, you nearly gave me a heart attack," Hayley whispered.

Bruce looked around, confused. "Why are we whispering?"

The door to Dustin's room flew open, and Dustin charged out and glared angrily at his mother.

"I wasn't eavesdropping," Hayley said weakly, fully aware no one was going to believe her.

Bruce stifled a laugh.

Hayley threw him a peeved look.

"Of course you were, Mom." Dustin sighed. "You've been spying on me ever since I learned to talk."

"That's not true!" Hayley cried, offended, still fully aware no one was going to believe that one, either.

"How much did you hear?" Dustin demanded to know.

Knowing she was backed into a corner, Hayley finally chose to come clean. "Okay, okay, enough to suspect you know where Spanky McFarland is hiding."

Dustin bristled at the suggestion but didn't deny it.

MacKenzie suddenly appeared behind him, silently watching the family drama.

"Dustin, is your mother right? Do you know where he is?" Bruce asked, suddenly concerned.

"What I may or may not know is my business and nobody else's," Dustin snarled.

"Dustin, you can't withhold information from the police. Spanky is a fugitive from justice," Hayley reminded him sternly.

"Stop saying that. He didn't *do* anything," Dustin said.

"Then he should not be afraid to turn himself in and let all the facts come out," Hayley said.

"Oh, come on, we've all seen enough Netflix documentaries to know people get railroaded and sent to prison all the time for crimes they didn't commit because the police are overly eager to close the case," Dustin said.

Hayley folded her arms. "We both know that your Uncle Sergio is a good cop who would never allow anything like that to happen."

"He already thinks Spanky did it, because you found that poison in his room! How do you know someone isn't trying to set him up by planting that evidence?"

MacKenzie was unconsciously nodding her head, in full support of her boyfriend.

"We don't, but we can't just discard it, either," Hayley said.

"Dustin," Bruce said, calm and serious. "If you know Spanky's whereabouts, and you do not inform your Uncle Sergio, that's a clear case of obstruction of justice, and you could be arrested and put on trial yourself."

That seemed to land with Dustin, who suddenly looked shaken.

MacKenzie put a comforting hand on his shoulder.

Hayley gasped. "He would never . . . I mean, I can't imagine Sergio *arresting* Dustin . . ."

"I'm just saying Dustin's putting himself in legal jeopardy if he knows something and doesn't report it," Bruce said matter-of-factly.

Unmoved by their pleas, Dustin glowered at them for a long moment, then grabbed MacKenzie by the hand and retreated back into the bedroom, slamming the door behind them.

Hayley and Bruce exchanged worried looks.

She knocked lightly on the door. "Dinner will be ready in about twenty minutes. I'm making meat loaf. Your Uncle Randy's coming over to join us."

There was no response.

After changing her clothes, Hayley went back downstairs to finish preparing dinner and found Bruce sitting at the small, round kitchen table, sipping a beer and staring out the window. At the sight of his troubled wife, Bruce offered an encouraging smile. "Don't worry, he'll come around."

Hayley checked the meat loaf sizzling in a pan in the oven, then mashed some potatoes with a mixer and stir-fried a vegetable medley with some oil in her wok. Bruce set the dining room table, and before Hayley had a chance to call up to them, Dustin and MacKenzie marched down the stairs and into the kitchen.

"Don't count on us for dinner; we've decided to go out for pizza," Dustin grumbled.

"What? But—"

Dustin kept going, but MacKenzie, feeling slightly guilty, stopped and added, "Sorry, but I'm having one of my cravings." She turned to see Dustin halfway out the door and scurried to catch up, one hand on her belly. They passed Randy on the way, who had just arrived.

"Hey, where are you going? I just got here," Randy said.

Dustin didn't respond, and MacKenzie gave him a friendly but cursory nod.

Randy turned to Hayley and Bruce. "Was it something I said?"

"It's probably for the best; dinner was going to be ex-tremely awkward now, anyway," Hayley said, resigned.

"Sergio's going to try to make it for dessert, but he's tied up at the precinct," Randy said before returning to the drama at hand. "So what's got him so upset?"

Hayley and Bruce hesitated, not sure if they should say anything just yet, but Randy was already zeroed in on finding out the cause of all the tension.

"Come on, sis, we tell each other everything. What is it?"

Giving up, Hayley sighed. "We're fairly certain Dustin knows where Spanky McFarland is hiding."

Randy's eyes widened. "Oh. That's why Sergio's going to be late. He and his officers are out there right now, scouring the whole island, trying to find him."

There was an uncomfortable silence.

Hayley had no idea in the moment that telling her brother her suspicion would set off a major explosion.

The kind that could tear an entire family apart.

Chapter 28

Hayley was already running late.

She had arranged to meet with her restaurant manager Betty to go over the week's receipts at nine a.m. It was already ten minutes to nine, and she was still waiting to get into the bathroom. That was the problem with having just one bathroom and four people staying in the house. The door to Dustin's room was wide open, and when Hayley took a quick glance inside, she found it empty. She heard the water running in the bathroom and waited impatiently, tapping her foot, worried about keeping Betty waiting.

She heard voices downstairs in the kitchen.

It sounded like Bruce and Dustin chatting, so she assumed MacKenzie was taking her sweet time in the bathroom. Finally, the door swung open, and just as she had suspected, MacKenzie waddled out, with wet hair and a teal robe tied loosely around her ample belly.

"Sorry, were you waiting long?" MacKenzie asked with droopy eyes and a half-smile.

"No, not at all," Hayley lied, slipping past her. "Just need to brush my teeth real quick."

MacKenzie shuffled into Dustin's room and closed the door to get dressed as Hayley grabbed her electric tooth-brush off the shelf, squeezed out some toothpaste, and started cleaning her teeth. She heard a door shut down-stairs and peeked out the bathroom window to see Dustin pound down the side porch steps and walk toward Bruce's car. She hurriedly rinsed out her mouth and flew down the stairs, where she found Bruce sipping coffee and read-ing the day's headlines on his iPad.

"Where's Dustin going?"

"He left for a run," Bruce said, eyes fixed on the tablet.

"Why is he taking your car? He usually just runs to the park from here."

"He wants to go around Eagle Lake, so I told him he could borrow my car, and I'd hitch a ride with you to the office."

Eagle Lake was located on the outskirts of town, and depending on which trail Dustin chose, that could be a five- or six-mile journey. Dustin had boasted he preferred a longer workout—twelve, maybe thirteen miles—so why drive to the lake? Why not just run there from the house, which was about three miles each way, to get more miles in?

Hayley grabbed her bag and rushed toward the back door. "Do you mind walking to the office this morning?"

Bruce looked up from his iPad. "Why? Where are you going?"

"I'll explain later. You can walk off those three help-ings of meat loaf you scarfed down last night!"

"Is that your way of telling me I'm getting fat?"

"Oh, and call Betty at the restaurant and tell her I'm going to be late! Love you!" Hayley chirped as she bounded out the door to her car, started up the engine, and then squealed out of the driveway, in hot pursuit of Dustin in Bruce's Volkswagen Atlas SUV. It didn't take long for her to catch up to him as he zipped along Cromwell Road, past the cemetery and Kebo golf course, turning left at the stop sign onto Eagle Lake Road.

Maybe Dustin had been telling the truth, and he was just going for a short run around the lake. Hayley felt a twinge of guilt as they drove toward the entrance. She felt like a bad mother for not trusting her own son. And even worse for tailing him and spying on him. But then, Dustin blew past Cadillac Entrance Road, driving on toward the other side of the island. Hayley continued following the Atlas, keeping a distance, staying one or two cars behind him so he wouldn't spot her through the rearview mirror. Dustin zipped past the high school and turned left at the end of Eagle Lake Road toward Southwest Harbor with Hayley still behind him, maintaining a safe distance.

Why was Dustin going to Southwest Harbor?

And why did he lie to Bruce about the reason he was borrowing his car?

Once he reached Main Street in Southwest, Dustin pulled over, parked outside Sawyer's Market, and dashed inside. Hayley parked across the street and waited for him to come out. He was in there ten or fifteen minutes before finally emerging. He carried two bags of food and was accompanied by an employee lugging two more. Dustin opened the back of Bruce's Atlas, and they deposited all the groceries. Dustin tipped the boy a fiver and slammed the door shut. He was back behind the wheel and on his way out of town again. Hayley rushed to follow him and nearly sideswiped a Southwest police cruiser passing by. Luckily, the officer just blasted his horn in annoyance but wasn't in the mood to stop and ticket her. Hayley kept her speed down to fifteen miles an hour until she was out of town, then slammed down on the accelerator to catch up to Dustin, who was now driving toward Tremont, located on the quiet side of the island. Hayley managed to keep pace until Dustin turned off the main road and down a dirt path deep into the woods.

That's when Hayley had her eureka moment.

She knew exactly where her son was headed.

Hayley's ex-husband Danny had an Uncle Otis, who'd lived for years in a ramshackle old cabin deep in the woods. When Otis died several years back, he willed Danny his property, a small lot, less than one acre, and a crumbling home in dire need of repair. Since Danny lived in Des Moines, he didn't have the desire or need to fix up the place, and pretty much left it abandoned with the intention of one day returning to Maine and restoring it as a possible future retirement home. As far as Hayley knew— she didn't talk to him often, for obvious reasons—Danny still owned the place. Although it was close to falling down, it still had running water and electricity and would be the perfect place to keep a low profile.

Especially for someone who was on the run from the law.

Hayley stopped her car and got out, deciding to walk the rest of the way to the cabin so she could maintain the element of surprise. The morning birds were chirping. She heard a persistent owl in a tree somewhere nearby and the crunching of the gravel underneath her shoes, but otherwise, it was pretty quiet. When she rounded the corner and got her first view of Otis's cabin, she saw Dustin unloading the last two bags of groceries and taking them inside. He shut the door to the cabin behind him.

Hayley crept up to the front window just left of the door to peer inside, but the glass was smudged with dried mud, and she couldn't see anything. But she could hear voices. Deep voices. Obviously two men. She cautiously moved to the door and tried the knob. It was unlocked. She took a deep breath, knowing what she had to do, and then charged inside.

She was hardly surprised to find her son and Spanky McFarland unloading the grocery bags. Both young men jumped back at the sudden intrusion, and then, panicked, Spanky instinctively grabbed a pistol off the kitchen counter, swinging it around and aiming it at Hayley. She realized too late that she had made a monumentally stupid mistake by bursting in unannounced and was about to get herself shot.

Chapter 29

"Spanky, don't shoot! It's my mom!" Dustin cried.

Spanky, his hand shaking, dropped the gun, and it clattered to the floor. "Mrs. Powell, I'm so sorry, you scared me. I thought . . ."

"It's okay, Spanky, but where did you get your hands on a gun?" Hayley asked, her voice cracking, still in shock over coming so close to getting herself killed.

Spanky stared down at the gun lying on the floor of the cabin. "My cousin Albert. He's a hunter with a big gun collection, but I don't really know how to use it, I just thought I might need it for protection."

"Mom, what the hell are you doing here?" Dustin yelled.

"I—I saw you leaving, and I suspected you might know where Spanky was hiding—"

"And so you followed me? That's wrong on so many levels, Mom! Did you call the police?"

"No, not yet. Where did you get a key to Uncle Otis's cabin?" Hayley asked her son.

"Dad gave it to me the last time he was here. He said I could use it whenever I wanted, at least until he decided what to do with it."

"Dustin, what you're doing is . . ."

"Illegal. I know, Mom, you've told me that about a dozen times already. But Spanky's innocent! He didn't do anything wrong!"

Spanky took a tentative step forward, inadvertently kicking the gun on the floor with his foot.

They all froze, worried it might accidentally discharge, but it just slid across the floor, stopping a few feet from Hayley, who walked over, picked it up, and gently put it down on a side table near the front door.

"Mrs. Powell, please, don't turn me in. I didn't poison Miranda. I have no idea how that vial got in my room!"

"Someone must have planted it!" Dustin chimed in.

Hayley studied Spanky carefully.

He looked scared and out of sorts, definitely on edge, given how close he had just come to shooting someone in the chest. But she believed him. In her gut, she knew her son's childhood best friend was not a murderer.

But the evidence to the contrary was overwhelming, and she also knew Spanky could not stay in hiding in a dilapidated cabin deep in the woods of Tremont until the police found the real killer.

"If you just come with me to the police station, Spanky, we can discuss this with Chief Alvares and try to clear this whole mess up."

Spanky shook his head. "No, I can't. The whole town

thinks I'm guilty. They want to see me arrested and sent to prison. It doesn't even matter that I didn't do it at this point. The cops need someone to take the fall, no matter what the truth may be."

"He's right, Mom. We can't let that happen," Dustin cried.

"I know it looks bad," Spanky lamented. "I did follow Miranda around after she dumped me. I was a basket case. But I loved her. I was hoping she might give me another chance and take me back. I'd never felt that way about a girl before."

"I believe you, Spanky," Hayley said quietly.

Spanky finally made eye contact with Hayley. "You do?"

She nodded. "Yes, but you can't hide from this. You have to face up to it. Come with me now. We'll drive back to Bar Harbor together and sit down with the chief and explain everything . . ."

"They'll *arrest* him!" Dustin protested.

"I'm not saying that won't happen, but if you're innocent, and I honestly believe you are, then I am sure it will all turn out okay," Hayley said.

Spanky glanced over at Dustin, who remained resolute in his resolve that Spanky not turn himself in, but Hayley could tell Spanky was slowly starting to waver.

Hayley put out her hand. "You just have to trust me."

Suddenly, without warning, the door to the cabin burst open, and Sergio, Lieutenant Donnie, and Officer Earl stormed in, guns drawn.

"Freeze, Spanky!" Sergio ordered.

Spanky instantly threw his hands up in the air as Lieutenant Donnie shoved Hayley aside, marched over, wrenched Spanky's arms behind his back, and snapped on a pair of handcuffs.

"Spanky McFarland, you're under arrest for the murder of Miranda Fox," Sergio said solemnly.

Dustin, stunned and horrified, watched slack-jawed as Donnie paraded Spanky out the door to the waiting patrol car with Officer Earl bringing up the rear. Sergio lagged behind.

Finally, Dustin found his voice, and spun around to Hayley. "Mom, how could you?"

Hayley shook her head. "I didn't, I swear . . ."

"I don't believe you!" Dustin spit out.

"Your mother's telling you the truth, Dustin," Sergio said. "She didn't knowingly lead us here."

Hayley looked at Sergio, confused. "Then how—?"

Sergio turned to Hayley. "After what you said to Randy at dinner last night, I had no choice but to put a tail on both you and Dustin to see if one of you might lead us to Spanky."

Hayley's mouth dropped open, appalled.

She couldn't believe what she was hearing.

"I'm sorry, but I was just doing my job," Sergio muttered, before heading out after his officers.

Hayley spun back around to Dustin, who was visibly despondent.

She felt awful.

This was all her fault.

Island Food & Spirits
BY
HAYLEY POWELL

One of my favorite traditions that kick off every summer season in Bar Harbor is taking a day trip with my BFFs Liddy and Mona to Down East Maine, to a little roadside diner that we discovered a few years back on the drive home from an unforgettable week staying at a camp owned by Mona's uncle in Salmon Cove. But that's a whole other story I'll save for another time. Anyway, this delightful establishment, owned and operated by the same family for several generations, boasts the freshest fried clams you will ever have the pleasure of eating.

These clams arrive at your table piled high on a plate alongside a mound of hot, crispy fries and a heaping side of coleslaw. And if that's not enough to fill up your belly, we always top it all off with a freezing cold metal bowl of their homemade vanilla ice cream, drenched with homemade strawberry sauce, for dessert.

Well, that's enough to start any tradition, so

like clockwork, every year, on the first weekend after Memorial Day, Mona, Liddy, and I excitedly hop in Mona's truck and drive out early on a Saturday morning, and head down east. We always make sure to stop at a roadside antiques store or two, but our top priority is to be first in line when the diner opens its doors to start serving lunch, sharply at 11:00 a.m. We would show up earlier, but those mouth-watering fried clams aren't on their breakfast menu, although Mona swears they'd probably be just as delicious stirred into some pancake batter.

This year, poor Liddy was feeling a bit under the weather, but she refused to postpone a week and upend our annual tradition. She insisted we go on our trip as planned, even though when she took her temperature, it registered at a worrisome 101 degrees when we first hit the road.

Luckily, by the time we hit the Trenton Bridge, Mona and Liddy were bickering as usual, so I was feeling confident that Liddy's condition was improving, and she was acting like her old healthy self. She had made herself comfortable in the truck's back seat under a pile of blankets and a pillow that she had brought from home and was already ordering Mona to turn up the heat, because she was freezing. Mona, for her part, had her window rolled all the way down to let in some cool fresh air, and was adamantly refusing to comply with Liddy's demands. This went on for at least another twenty minutes until Mona cranked the wheel onto ME-15 toward Castine and Salmon Cove, her mouth clamped shut, refusing to engage with Liddy any longer. Liddy, in a huff, covered herself up from head to toe with the blankets and promptly fell asleep.

As planned, Mona and I stopped and browsed at a couple of our favorite antique spots, allowing Liddy to sleep since she wasn't feeling one hundred percent, although, as Mona put it in her typical tactful way, "Let the big baby sleep so we don't have to listen to her yap on and on like an annoying little lapdog."

After a few of hours of poking around, we got back on the road to make it to the diner on time, before it got too crowded and we would have to wait to be seated. When we pulled into the parking lot, Liddy magically emerged from her cocoon of blankets like a freshly hatched butterfly, looking and feeling much better, and excited to scarf down a plate of those mouth-watering fried clams.

By the time we were all groaning about how full our bellies were from all the clams and fries and coleslaw, but fortunately still had a tiny bit of room left for the ice cream, Liddy and Mona were best buds again, laughing at each other's jokes, forgetting all about just how much they routinely got on each other's nerves.

After devouring dessert, the three of us waddled slowly back out to the truck for the nearly two-hour drive home. We had barely made it out of the parking lot when Liddy remarked how cold she was, and Mona defiantly rolled down her window. The two were at it again. I was way too full and tired to play referee, so I just stared out the window counting the trees as we whizzed past. Liddy eventually gave up on Mona turning on the heat and burrowed herself completely under the blankets and once again fell asleep.

After a couple of brief stops at some fresh produce farm stands, Mona pulled into a gas station so we could fill up the tank, pick up some bottled waters, and use the facilities. I suggested we wake Liddy up. Mona gave me a sharp look, and I decided to just leave her be, since we would be home within the hour anyway.

Finally back on the road, Mona and I were chatting away when I quietly mentioned that she might want to give Liddy a break and say something nice, since she wasn't feeling her best. After all, even though they were at odds a lot, she and Liddy were still close friends and loved each other and would do anything for each other. Mona begrudgingly agreed and called back to Liddy, "Hey, Princess Kate, do you want a bottled water?"

Okay, it wasn't exactly what I had in mind, but it would do in a pinch. When Liddy didn't answer, I could see Mona already getting irritated, so I reached in the back and grabbed at her blankets to pull them off. "Hey, wake up, we're almost home, and you don't want to miss Mona trying to be nice!"

It took me a moment to register what I was seeing, and I finally shouted at Mona to stop the truck! Mona was so startled she almost drove straight off the road. The truck screeched to a stop, and Mona angrily spun toward me, opening her mouth to yell, but before she could spit out one word, I screamed, "Liddy's gone!"

Mona just stared at me for a moment; then, her mouth dropped open, tears pooling in her eyes. "I didn't think she was that sick! I never should have given her such a hard time!"

"No!" I cried. "Not dead. She's gone! Like, she's not here in the truck!"

Mona whipped her head around to see the empty back seat for herself. "What in the hell happened to her?"

I shook my head as I unbuckled my seat belt and maneuvered around, frantically pulling all of the blankets off the seat.

Mona jumped out of the truck, circled around, and whipped open the back door. "Uh-oh . . ."

"What? What?"

Mona held up Liddy's purse.

"Look inside and see if her phone is in there. She'd never go anywhere without her phone!"

Mona opened the purse and pulled out Liddy's phone. We both just stared at it with a sense of dread. Then Mona tossed the purse back, raced around the driver's side of the truck, jumped in, and squealed into a U-turn. We sped off back in the direction from where we came.

Poor Mona rocked back and forth in the driver's seat, distraught and blaming herself for allowing poor Liddy to be kidnapped right out of her own truck while she was sleeping! Or did she wander out of the truck on her own in a fever-induced state at one of our farm stand stops and collapse in a ditch, and we just drove off without her? Or maybe she rolled out the back at a sharp turn? I calmly asked Mona to stop conjuring up worst-case scenarios, because it was not helping the situation at all.

Forty-five minutes later, we spotted the gas station sign up ahead where we had last stopped, and I heard Mona mumble under her breath, "Please let her be all right, please let her be all right," over and over again as she swerved the truck into the parking lot and we came to a screeching halt.

The next words out of her mouth were, "I'm going to *kill* her!"

There, right in front of us, sitting out in front of the store in an Adirondack chair as if it were her own royal throne, her shapely legs crossed, was Liddy, surrounded by a group of local men, who were all gazing at her adoringly and hanging onto her every word as she held court.

Mona and I hopped out of the truck, and

Liddy, spotting us, waved and smiled, calling out in a sing-songy voice, "I knew you'd be back eventually!"

Mona was ready to blow a gasket, and I had to grab her arm to calm her down. I asked Liddy, "What happened?"

Well, according to her, she had awakened while we were inside the store paying for our bottled water, and she thought now might be a good time to scoot into the ladies' room for just a minute. By the time she emerged feeling fresh and revitalized, we had unknowingly driven off, assuming she was still sound asleep in the back seat of the truck.

I didn't have to ask Liddy why she hadn't just borrowed one of her admirer's phones to call us and let us know what had happened. She was having too much fun flirting. I was just thankful Liddy was alive and well. Mona was already back behind the wheel of her truck, revving the engine and honking the horn, so I felt it was in all our best interest to get back on the road as quickly as possible. I had to practically drag Liddy to the truck, because she was taking her sweet time bidding adieu to the strapping men in her local fan club. The last thing I needed right now was Mona driving off without us in a fit of anger.

Two minutes into our journey home, instead of thanking Mona for coming all the way back for her, Liddy griped, "For God's sake, Mona, can you turn up the heat? It's like a tundra back here!" It was as if a bell rang at the start of a boxing match, and the two were at again, but it was in that moment I realized something. They both were enjoying every minute of it. This was how they showed how much they cared for each other. By fighting. They'll probably never see eye to eye on anything, but they do love each other, and that's what counts the most in the long run.

Ice Cream Cocktail Float

INGREDIENTS:
2 ounces of pink moscato
1 ounce strawberry liqueur
1 ounce strawberry soda
1 small scoop vanilla ice cream

Put a small scoop of vanilla ice cream in a glass.

In a shaker, add your soda and liqueur, and shake to combine. Pour over the ice cream.

Top with the pink moscato and enjoy!

VANILLA CREAM CUSTARD ICE CREAM

INGREDIENTS:
3 eggs
¾ cup sugar
3 cups heavy whipping cream
1 cup milk
1 teaspoon vanilla extract

Beat your egg and sugar until thick and light, about 5 minutes.

Mix in your cream, milk, and vanilla until blended.

Pour the mixture into a prepared ice cream maker and churn for 25–30 minutes.

Transfer the ice cream into a clean container and freeze until firm, or eat soft right away.

EASY STRAWBERRY SAUCE

INGREDIENTS:
16 ounces strawberries, hulled and coarsely
    chopped
⅓ cup white sugar
Zest of one lemon
Juice of half a lemon, or to taste

In a saucepan, combine your strawberries, sugar,
lemon zest, and juice, and cook over medium-
high heat, stirring occasionally.

Cook until the strawberries break down and re-
lease their juices, and mash some of the berries,
too.

Continue cooking, 10 minutes or to your desired
consistency. The sauce will thicken more upon
cooling. Cool completely before using. Store in
the refrigerator if not using right away.

Chapter 30

Carla McFarland was fighting back tears at the thought of her son Spanky behind bars. Chief Sergio had reluctantly allowed Carla, Hayley, and Dustin to visit Spanky in the police station's interrogation room instead of his holding cell, even permitting Carla to bring him some of his favorite snacks. Spanky sat at a rickety metal table, slumped over, dazed, chewing on a Mars candy bar as if the severity of his situation were still slowly sinking in. Carla paced back and forth, a pensive, worried look on her face, as Hayley and Dustin sat across from Spanky, both trying to remain upbeat and positive.

"Have you found a lawyer yet, Carla?" Hayley asked.

"No, they want to saddle me with a public defender, Matt Garrett, but he's barely out of high school, and I can't imagine him being an effective attorney."

"I hear good things about him. He may be young, but he knows the law," Hayley said.

"I want Spanky to have the best representation as possible. It'll be expensive, but I figure I can take out a second mortgage on my house," Carla said.

"Mom, please don't do that. I went to high school with Matt's brother Ethan. Matt's really smart. He'll be fine."

"We need more than just *fine*, Spanky. I will not have you spending the better part of your adult life in a state prison," Carla barked defiantly. "I just won't have it!"

Spanky took a bite of his candy bar, lost in thought, as if he were picturing himself twenty years from now, a hardened inmate, consumed by bitterness and hate.

"Don't worry, Spanky, I'm not gonna rest until I clear your name. The only thing they've got is that bottle of poison Mom found in your room. They're going to need a lot more than that to convict you," Dustin said, an encouraging smile on his face.

Like mother, like son, Hayley thought to herself.

"Carla, assuming someone is trying to set Spanky up for the murder of Miranda, do you have any idea how that person might have gained access to your house?" Hayley asked.

"Yes," Carla said, wringing her hands nervously. "The lock on our back door is busted. I've been meaning to get it fixed, but I never got around to it. Anyone could have just waltzed right in and planted that poison in Spanky's room."

Spanky licked the melted chocolate from the candy bar off his fingers and then reached out and took his mother's hand. "Mom, don't beat yourself up. This is not your fault."

Carla couldn't hold back her tears anymore. She burst out crying, covering her face with her hands, embarrassed. "I promised myself I wouldn't do this. I'm supposed to be the strong one here."

Spanky stood up and hugged his mother, who buried her face in his chest, sobbing.

Any residual anger he had been harboring for his mother going to speak to Miranda without his knowledge had mercifully dissipated.

Dustin stood up from his chair. "Mrs. McFarland, why don't you sit down?"

Carla hugged her son for a moment, then took a step back, reaching into her handbag and pulling out some tissue, which she used to blow her nose. "I'm fine, Dustin, really, but thank you."

At that moment, Hayley spotted Randy outside the door, breezing past, carrying a brown paper bag. She popped to her feet. "Excuse me for a minute."

Hayley bolted out the door and followed Randy down to Sergio's office, arriving at the doorway in time to see Randy standing over Sergio, who sat at his desk, opening the bag, which contained a paper basket of fried clams and a side of French fries.

Randy suddenly noticed Hayley hovering outside the office. "Oh, hi, I just stopped by to bring Sergio some lunch."

"How could you?" Hayley spit out, her voice cracking, her bottom lip quivering.

Randy glanced over at Sergio, confused, then back at Hayley. "What are you talking about?"

Sergio uncomfortably cleared his throat. "She knows you were the one who told me about her suspicion about Dustin knowing where Spanky was hiding."

The blood seemed to drain from Randy's face. "Oh."

"You're my brother. I thought you'd be the last person to betray me. We've always trusted each other, our whole lives."

"Yes, but you must realize I had no choice," Randy said. "Hayley, if I kept that information to myself, I'd be complicit, too. I had to share it with Sergio."

"Don't blame Randy," Sergio said. "I was the one who put the tail on you and Dustin. In my defense, I was just doing my job."

"But I've come to believe that Spanky is innocent. He shouldn't be behind bars . . ."

"Spanky will get his day in court. I happen to believe in the justice system we have. It's not perfect, but it works. We all have the same goal, Hayley—for the truth to come out," Sergio said.

"Well, I certainly hope that just because you have Spanky in custody, that does not mean you will stop investigating other possible suspects," Hayley snarled.

"Of course not; this is still a very active investigation," Sergio insisted.

Hayley loved her brother-in-law and was proud of his tenure as Bar Harbor's esteemed police chief, but in this instance, she was not entirely convinced he would keep hunting for answers full throttle given the evidence against Spanky already. However, she also knew in her heart that Sergio was right about one thing. He was just doing his job. It just didn't make it any easier to accept her own role in Spanky's arrest. She was consumed by guilt.

Randy, shaken by his sister's ardent anger, whispered, barely audible, "Hayley, I'm so sorry . . . If there's anything I can do . . ."

She thought about it for a second and then said, "Yes, there is. You can go back to Drinks Like A Fish and get some more fried clams and French fries for Spanky. I and his mother will feel a whole lot better knowing he's got a little comfort food in that cold, dank cell and not subsisting on a baloney sandwich with wilting lettuce."

"That I can do," Randy promised.

Hayley knew she couldn't stay mad at Randy and Sergio, but she also wasn't quite ready to let it go without a further thought, either, so she nodded curtly and then stormed out.

Chapter 31

Hayley stared at the old grainy photograph that she had found in a storage box of old yearbooks and photos shoved in a corner in her garage. The picture was of Hayley, Mona, and Liddy, probably around twelve years old, straddling their bikes with banana seats sometime during the summer in the Village Green, holding ice cream cones in their hands. Always the same flavors. Chocolate for Hayley, vanilla for Liddy, and strawberry for Mona. The ice cream shops didn't have as much imagination back then as Lynette's more progressive menu these days. Hayley got a warm, nostalgic feeling staring at the picture, from a simpler, more innocent time. She set the photo down on the kitchen table and digitally scanned it with her phone, then texted it to both Liddy and Mona with the note: **Meet me in front of Bar Harbor Ice Cream in one hour**. She knew it was a gamble. There was no guarantee either of her best friends would bother to show up, especially since there was still a towering wall of tension between them.

But Hayley had to try.

She walked through town, arriving precisely one hour after sending the text, and purchased three ice cream cones—one chocolate, one vanilla, and one strawberry—from Eric, who was working behind the counter. With all the wild and creative flavors to choose from, Eric gave her a puzzled look, not sure why she would choose such boring flavors. Hayley thanked him as he handed them to her, and then she carried them outside and sat down on the wooden bench to wait.

She immediately regretted buying the cones before they arrived, because it was a hot day, and they immediately started melting in her hand. She had to frantically lick her hands as the ice cream slid down the side of the cones and onto her fingers.

"Hayley, what the hell? Here, give those to me; you're making a mess!" Mona yelled, grabbing the strawberry and vanilla cones from her as Hayley lapped up the chocolate that was all over her hands. Mona practically swallowed the scoop of strawberry ice cream drooping on top of her cone whole, leaving her with one empty cone and a rapidly melting vanilla cone.

"Mona, I'm so happy you showed," Hayley said, smiling.

"Well, I didn't want you sitting here all alone like a fool, and besides, seeing that photo made me hungry. I miss those old days when we'd ride our bikes to Ocean Drive Dairy Bar and blow our allowance money on onion rings and ice cream."

"Those summers together were so much fun," Hayley

commented, eyeing Mona carefully. "The three of us hanging out."

"I know what you're trying to do, Hayley, and it's not going to work."

"Why not?"

"Because Liddy's not going to show up, that's why. She's too stubborn, and she's not going to fall for your lame attempt to try some stupid reconciliation with a photo from our childhood! I might as well eat this before it completely melts, and I have to throw it away!"

Mona opened her mouth wide to devour the vanilla cone, when suddenly, someone snatched it out of her hand.

"Don't you dare eat that! That's *my* ice cream cone, Mona! You don't even like vanilla!"

Mona spun around to see Liddy daintily darting her tongue out to taste the top of the drooping scoop.

"Well, color me surprised," Mona said gruffly. "I honestly didn't think you'd fall for Hayley tugging at our heartstrings, especially since you have no heart."

"I was in the neighborhood, I had an inspection nearby at one of my properties, and my sweet tooth is no big secret. I just didn't think I'd see you here, Mona," Liddy said, now violently attacking the sides of the vanilla scoop with her tongue.

"I couldn't resist sending you two that photo. You have to admit, we shared a lot of special times, the three of us, together," Hayley prodded.

Mona heaved a big sigh. "Yeah, well, times change." She turned pointedly in Liddy's direction. "*People* change. Some get meaner."

This stung Liddy. She tossed what was left of her cone in a nearby trash bin. "Mona, I was wrong to say what I did to you. I didn't mean it. I was hurt and angry, and I lashed out."

Mona stared at her warily, not sure whether to believe her or not. Once Mona's feelings got trampled, the walls tended to go up fast for her own protection.

Liddy took a deep breath. "I have been overly sensitive and skittish about relationships ever since . . . well, you all know what I'm talking about."

"You mean when Sonny ditched you at the altar?" Mona offered.

Liddy shot her an annoyed look. "Yes, Mona, I was hoping that part would be left unsaid, but yes, ever since Sonny humiliated and embarrassed me, left me a tragic, pitiable victim in front of the entire town."

"Yeah, that had to have hurt," Mona readily agreed. "I'd probably never be able to show my face in public ever again."

"Okay, Mona, you've made your point!" Liddy snapped. "So given that trauma, maybe I overreacted just a little when I realized that it was happening to me all over again, and this time, it involved one of my best friends. So I may have said some things to you out of spite and jealousy, things I don't honestly believe."

"Yes, you do. But I've heard worse. From my own kids, in fact. I mostly got mad because Chuck was the first guy since my deadbeat husband Dennis to pay any attention to me. Actually, Dennis never paid much attention to me, ever. He left me at our hotel room in Boston to go to a Red Sox game on our honeymoon. The no-good lout. Anyway, it felt good having a guy look at me for once, and not say, 'How much do you charge for your lobsters by the pound?'"

Liddy snickered.

Hayley, still sitting on the bench, leaned forward, hopeful. This sounded like real progress.

"When George or Chuck, whatever his name is and I first started going out, I kept waiting for the other shoe to drop," Mona continued. "And when it didn't, I finally let my guard down, but the moment I did, *bam*, I find out he's dating you, too, and I couldn't deal with that."

"Mona, I'm sorry," Liddy said.

"Me, too," Mona said, shrugging.

Hayley sprang to her feet. "I think this would be a perfect moment to hug it out, don't you?"

They both glared at Hayley and said simultaneously, "Don't push it."

Liddy and Mona stood awkwardly in front of each other until Liddy finally turned to Hayley. "So what do we do about George?"

"He's obviously avoiding both of you, ever since he found out you know about each other, so I think in order to get full closure, we should go over to his house right now and have it out. Make him face up to what he's done, and then you can wash your hands of that lying cheat forever."

For the first time in quite some time, Liddy Crawford and Mona Barnes were in full agreement.

"Let's do it," Liddy said firmly. "I'll drive. I'm parked just across the street."

"Good! I've been dreaming about busting his puny little head wide open, and now I'm going to get the chance to make that dream come true," Mona said, following Liddy.

"Talk, Mona! We're just going to *talk* to him!" Hayley cried, chasing after them.

Chapter 32

"**O**h, dear Lord," was all George Kittridge could manage to choke out when he opened the front door of his house and found himself face to face with Liddy and Mona, as Hayley hovered closely behind both of them, ready to intervene if either one resorted to physical violence.

"Surprised to see us?" Mona barked angrily.

George nodded, not sure whether he should slam the door, lock it, and run and hide somewhere inside his house.

"I—I can explain . . ." he stammered, fear in his eyes as he blinked uncontrollably.

"George, we are not here to cause any kind of scene," Hayley interjected. "We just came to discuss the situation calmly and rationally."

"Like hell we are!" Liddy cried. "How dare you cheat on me, toy with my emotions like that, after I confided to you all I've been through with my ex, Sonny!"

"And do you think I've been looking to hitch my wagon to a new horse after twenty-five miserable years with my deadbeat husband Dennis? No! I was happy by myself, but then you had to come along and screw all of that up! And then I find out you're two-timing me with Liddy, one of my closest friends? Are you kidding me? I ought to tie you to the back of my pickup truck and drag you through town wearing a sign that says *Lyin' Cheat*!"

"P-please don't do that, Mona—" George begged.

"You know I want to!" Mona yelled.

George nodded.

There was not a doubt in his mind.

"Mona, violence is never the answer," Hayley said.

"Since when?" Mona scoffed.

"I agree with Mona for once," Liddy said.

"Ladies, please, the last thing I ever wanted to do was hurt either of you. I was sincere when I told you both how I felt. I've spent much of my life alone. Never really found the right woman. And then, when I met Liddy, who was so fun and vibrant and had such a sparkling personality, I just couldn't imagine how I had gotten so lucky and hit the jackpot. And then, when Mona walked into my life, I had never met such a strong, opinionated, fiercely loyal woman. I couldn't resist getting to know both of you. I had to pinch myself so I knew I wasn't dreaming! How did I get so lucky? Two wonderful women! Of course, in my heart, I knew it was wrong. I should have been upfront about dating you at the same time, but the longer it went on, the harder it got, I was so drawn to both of you for different reasons, and I knew I was going to have to choose, but the idea of letting one of you go was just too much to bear. I couldn't stand the thought of losing the other."

"Well, now you've gone and lost both of us!" Liddy sniffed.

"I know, I understand, and I'm so sorry I came in between your friendship. I had no idea you two even knew each other until it was too late," George said quietly. "Can you ever forgive me?"

"No!" Mona said forthrightly.

"That goes double for me!" Liddy added. "You're a sad, pathetic, little man, George; you don't deserve a woman like me or Mona, and looking at you now, I struggle to find whatever it was I ever saw in you in the first place!"

George remained mum, knowing he deserved this brutal tongue-lashing.

Liddy spun around, taking Mona's hand. "Come on, let's celebrate our friendship with a cosmo at Drinks Like A Fish."

Mona kept her feet planted on George's doorstep. "Wait."

Liddy stopped, pivoted back around. "What?"

Mona's eyes fixed on George. "Did you ever decide?"

"Decide what?" George asked in a shaky voice.

"Which one of us you were going to dump!" Mona bellowed.

George's eyes popped open.

He hadn't been expecting that question.

Neither had Hayley, who quickly piped in, "It's irrelevant now, Mona; it doesn't matter. This whole mess is finally over."

"No," Liddy said. "I want to know." She stared daggers at George. "Whose heart were you going to break?"

George gave Hayley a pleading look, desperate for her help in avoiding this explosive question.

"Come on, George," Mona demanded. "Which one were you going to give the boot, me or Liddy? Tell us!"

George cleared his throat, stared down at his shoes, then whispered, "Both of you."

Liddy and Mona glanced at each other, confused.

"Both of us? What do you mean?" Liddy yelled.

"I—I worshipped every moment I had with the two of you, that's the honest truth, but in the end . . ." His voice trailed off.

"In the end, what?" Hayley asked, also now dying to know.

"I met someone else."

Liddy and Mona's mouths dropped open at the same time.

So did Hayley's.

"Who?" Mona growled.

George reflexively peeked behind him.

"Is she in there with you now?" Liddy gasped.

"She's making us a late lunch," George said. "I should go, but I appreciate you all stopping by."

"Oh, hell no!" Mona roared, pushing past him inside the house with Liddy on her heels. Hayley followed them, but stayed close to the door as George nervously watched his whole world crumble.

Mona marched toward the kitchen. "Come on out, we know you're here!"

Before she got halfway across the living room, Carla McFarland wandered out, wearing an apron, a surprised look on her face. "Mona, I thought I heard you at the door." Then she noticed Liddy and Hayley. "Hi, what are you all doing here?"

There was a stunned silence.

"I told them about us," George muttered.

Carla wiped her hands on the apron. "I see."

Liddy stepped forward. "You should know George has also been seeing both me and Mona at the same time. He's a serial dater, so you should beware!"

"I know, he told me everything," Carla said.

Hayley was shocked. "He did?"

"Yes, he was totally honest with me when he first asked me out," Carla said. "We didn't plan on this developing into anything romantic. Not at first. I thought we were going to just be friends when he first asked me to have dinner with him. But he's been such a rock. Especially since Spanky's been in all that trouble. George has offered me his support—emotional, financial, whatever I needed. I thought it was so sweet, and he was the only one in town who even bothered. It's so nice having someone I can lean on, especially during this very difficult time."

"It didn't take long to recognize the spark between us, and well, it just took off from there," George said warily.

"We've been inseparable," Carla cooed. "George is even working on posting Spanky's bail, hiring a good lawyer—can you believe that? He's been an absolute life-saver."

"Well, you're an incredible woman," George said with a loving smile.

"Am I the only one about to throw up here?" Liddy spat out.

"I've heard enough! Let's get out of here!" Mona shouted.

"He's all yours, Carla! Good luck!" Liddy snorted before turning to George. "You're not that handsome or charming! I can't believe you nearly destroyed our friendship. Who do you think you are, Benedict Cumberbatch?"

And then she turned on her heel and followed Mona out the door.

Hayley shrugged and said to the happy couple, "Congratulations, I think? Sorry to interrupt your lunch." And then she scooted out the door to join her two best friends.

Chapter 33

Hayley knew she had been neglecting her restaurant. She had been so laser-focused on uncovering the truth behind Miranda Fox's death and reuniting her pair of feuding best friends, her business had taken a back seat. So after leaving Liddy and Mona, she drove straight over to Hayley's Kitchen, and was excited to see about twenty cars already in the parking lot, just as her manager Betty was opening the doors to start serving dinner.

Betty happily showed her the reservation list on her iPad, another fully booked evening. Kelton, her chef, was hard at work in the kitchen, plating the night's specials for the early birds, who were already at their tables enjoying glasses of wine.

"Kelton, I'm sorry I've been MIA lately. I hope you haven't been overwhelmed with me not being here."

Kelton shrugged. "I cooked at a summer camp with over a hundred starving, screaming kids back when I was just starting out, so I think I can handle my share of persnickety tourists, no problem."

"Well, I appreciate all you do, Kelton," Hayley said with a sincere smile, then glanced at Kelton's sous-chef and kitchen help. "All of you, thank you."

The workers nodded shyly.

Hayley still had a hard time getting her mind around the fact that she was the boss. She had spent so much time in her life trying to please others; it was an adjustment transitioning to head honcho in charge of an entire restaurant staff. But she would be lying to herself if she didn't admit it felt good. She had had to fight back tears when her crew erected the restaurant's signage out in front of the building.

Hayley's Kitchen.

She had never dared dream that anything like that would ever be possible.

One of her waitresses, Christy, popped her head in the kitchen. "Hayley, one of the customers would like to have a word with you, if you're not too busy."

"Of course," Hayley said, following Christy out the swinging doors back into the dining room. Christy pointed to a small table near the fireplace.

Kimmy Nash sat alone at the table, her phone in her hand, snapping a photo of the heaping plate of rigatoni with sausage and peas that sat in front of her. She then began to furiously type with her fingers as Hayley approached.

"Hello, Kimmy, nice to see you," Hayley said.

Kimmy didn't look up until she was done typing.

Then she glanced up with a pleasant smile. "This riga-toni special is to die for. I love a tangy marinara sauce. What's in it?"

"A chef never reveals her secrets," Hayley said.

"Well, I just posted about it on Instagram. I have over a million followers, so you can expect a huge jump in your business," she boasted.

"Thank you, I'm certainly grateful for the free public-ity," Hayley said, though she suspected not a whole bunch of Kimmy's social media devotees would ever make it all the way to Bar Harbor, Maine anytime soon.

But you never know.

"Dining alone tonight?"

Kimmy nodded. "All my *real* friends are in New York. I have nobody to hang out with here in no-man's-land. My parents are always busy, and my sister is only into spending time with her boyfriend."

Christy delivered a glass of soda to the table and then scooted away. Kimmy lifted it up for Hayley to take a look at, swishing it around. "Diet Coke, see? No alcohol. I was dying for a little red wine with my dinner; my par-ents usually don't mind, but, well, you know . . ."

"I know, you're still legally underage, so I thank you for not trying to pass off that fake ID here."

"About that . . . it meant a lot to me that you helped me out that night. If your brother had called the cops, it would have been a whole crazy mess to deal with. I couldn't handle that right now, and so, I owe you big time."

"You don't owe me anything, Kimmy; just try to be-have, at least until you reach twenty-one."

Kimmy stabbed at a piece of rigatoni on her plate with

her fork. "No, I *do* owe you, that's kind of the reason I came here tonight."

"Well, I always appreciate the business and certainly you posting about it. Although I'm hopeless on social media, I know the influence it can have."

"I'm happy to do it, but that's not what I mean."

She suddenly sounded ominous, which piqued Hayley's curiosity. "Oh?"

"I heard you were, like, this amateur detective, that it's kind of your hobby."

"I wouldn't call it a hobby, exactly, but yes, I've been known to get involved in a few select cases every so often. Who told you that?"

"I overheard some kids talking. They were saying you were at a college party recently, asking questions about Miranda Fox."

Christy suddenly appeared, her eyes falling on Kimmy's half-eaten plate of rigatoni. "Would you like me to wrap that up for you to go?"

"Give us a sec, would you, Christy?" Hayley asked.

"Sure," Christy said, speeding off.

Hayley redirected her attention back to Kimmy. "Do you know something, Kimmy?"

Kimmy paused; then, biting her lip, nodded slightly.

"I'm all ears," Hayley said, leaning forward, curious.

Kimmy sighed, anxiously glanced around to make sure nobody was eavesdropping, and then said in a low tone, barely audible, "I think my sister may somehow be involved in what happened to Miranda."

Hayley snapped back, stunned, and whispered, "Zoe?"

"Yes."

Hayley took a moment to process this. She was skeptical. It was no secret that Kimmy and Zoe were embroiled in a bitter sibling competition when it came to their social media–influencing careers. Hayley had personally witnessed Zoe mercilessly teasing Kimmy about having significantly more followers online, being far more popular and famous, and perhaps this was Kimmy's underhanded way of leveling the playing field, dragging her sister down a few pegs by casting unfounded aspersions on her reputation.

Kimmy could sense Hayley's hesitation. "What, you don't believe me?"

"What evidence do you have?"

Kimmy again scanned the crowd in the dining room to make sure she could speak freely without being overheard, but no one in the immediate vicinity, let alone the whole restaurant, was paying the slightest bit of attention to them.

"I overheard her talking to a friend on the phone when we first got to Bar Harbor. She was saying something along the lines of, 'There's this ice cream chick here who is becoming a problem, and she needs to be taken care of,' something like that."

"Are you sure she was talking about Miranda? Maybe she was referring to Miranda's coworker, Bethany."

"No, she mentioned Miranda by name later in the conversation. I know it was her."

"Who was this friend on the phone?"

"I don't know, I figured it was some girl from her posse back in the city. Neither of us wanted to leave New York this summer, but our parents forced us to come. At least Zoe had her boyfriend here. I had nobody. I have been so miserable."

"Did you say anything to Zoe about what you heard?"

"Of course, I confronted her about it, especially after you found Miranda dead in the back of that ice cream truck. But she blew me off and said I was crazy. When I kept pressing her and asking questions, she said it was none of my business and warned me not to say anything. Maybe she's just worried about being linked to any kind of scandal; I mean, we all know what happened to Lori Loughlin's daughter—she lost all her endorsement deals when it came out her parents had paid bribes to get her into college."

Or perhaps it involved something far more sinister.

Hayley sat down at the table with Kimmy. "Why are you telling me this, Kimmy?"

"I know what people are going to say. I turned in my own sister to ruin her and get revenge for the way she treats me, but to be honest, that's not the truth. I met Miranda, and she seemed like a really nice girl, and she deserves to get justice for what happened to her."

Hayley studied Kimmy Nash closely.

She could see the genuine concern in Kimmy's face and believed what the girl was telling her. It could not have been easy for her to essentially rat out her sister.

But Hayley knew she now had to follow up with Zoe, knowing it was going to be a challenge, if not an impossible task, to get the more polished, image-conscious sibling to open up to her about what she knew, if anything, or even her own personal role, in the murder of Miranda Fox.

Chapter 34

As Hayley pounded down the stairs, freshly showered, tying her hair into a pert ponytail, she took in the wafting smell of bacon sizzling in the frying pan. As she reached the bottom and rounded the corner, she could see MacKenzie, in a soft and stretchy, tiered, flutter-sleeved, knee-length maternity dress, standing at the stove, flipping the bacon with a spatula as scrambled eggs bubbled up in a frying pan on another burner. Leroy sat patiently at her feet, staring up, waiting to be fed a little bit of bacon. When MacKenzie heard Hayley enter the kitchen, she turned and offered her a bright smile. "Good morning."

"Morning. Smells delicious. Where's Dustin?"

"You were out of orange juice, so I sent him to the store. I hope you don't mind me taking over your kitchen?"

"Not at all. I want you to make yourself at home while you're here," Hayley said.

"Bruce is out for a run but will be back soon. Will you join us? I made enough for a small army," MacKenzie said.

"I would love to, but I can't. I just received a text from Lynette Partridge while I was in the shower. She wants me to stop by her shop so she can show me something before she opens. It sounded important. But don't worry, Bruce always eats for two, so I'm sure it won't go to waste."

MacKenzie giggled, but then winced and set the spatula down, grabbing her tummy.

Hayley rushed over to her. "What's wrong? Are you in pain?"

MacKenzie shook her head and smiled again. "No, the baby just kicked again. I can tell already he's going to be quite a handful. Every time this happens, Dustin panics and thinks I'm going into labor. He's such a worrywart."

"He gets that from his mother," Hayley said.

MacKenzie waited a few seconds until the kicking stopped, and then picked up the spatula and went back to preparing breakfast.

Satisfied there was no medical emergency to suddenly contend with, Hayley headed for the door. "Enjoy your breakfast; I'll be back in a while."

"'Bye!" MacKenzie chirped, tearing off a small piece of bacon and blowing on it to cool it down before dropping it for Leroy to catch in his wide-open mouth.

Hayley jumped in her car and drove straight to the Bar Harbor Ice Cream Shop, swerving into an open parking space right out front. Through the large picture window, she could see Lynette inside, removing an empty carton from the display case and replacing it with a freshly made tub of Mint Chocolate Chip. No one else seemed to be around. The door was unlocked, and she swept in, startling Lynette.

"Hayley—oh, hi, I didn't see you pull up! Thanks for coming here on such short notice," Lynette said, sliding the door to the display case shut.

Hayley could see Lynette had been in the back, churning out batches of ice cream. She was in a stained sweatshirt and ripped jeans, and her long blond hair was tied up and covered with a red bandana.

"I've been here since five this morning filling restaurant orders, and I'm hurting big time. Jamie and I were up late; we had a date night and drank a little too much Merlot."

"I'm happy to hear you two are doing better."

Lynette beamed. "Now that I've retired the whole suspicious-wife act, things between us are stronger than ever. We spent the whole evening planning a trip to South America once the tourist season dies down here and before Jamie starts fall semester classes at the college. We want to hit Brazil, Chile, Argentina, maybe Uruguay if we have time . . ."

"I'm totally jealous."

"You and Bruce should come along and make it a foursome!"

"I'm tempted, believe me. Let me talk to Bruce. But fair warning. I can barely get him to agree to go to Bangor for a Luke Combs concert."

"Well, I think we'd have a blast traveling together."

"If it doesn't work out, we'd be happy to look after Sprinkles while you're gone. Leroy would love it. Whenever that upstart little dachshund of yours is around, it's like he reverts back to being a sprightly puppy again."

"Well, I'm going to hold out hope that you can talk Bruce into finally getting his passport stamped."

"Is that why you wanted me to stop by, to ask us to join you on your vacation?"

Lynette's smile slowly faded. "No."

"I didn't think so," Hayley said. "Your text sounded a little ominous."

Lynette dug deep into her jeans pocket and pulled out a wadded-up piece of paper and handed it to Hayley.

"What's this?"

"While I was waiting for my vats to freeze, I decided to go upstairs to the apartment and do a little cleaning. While I was sweeping, I found that on the floor in a corner."

Hayley unfolded the piece of paper and studied it.

It was a receipt from a key copy kiosk at the Shop 'n Save.

Hayley looked up at Lynette, puzzled. "I don't understand."

"Someone had an extra key made that I knew nothing about."

"Was it a key to open the shop?"

"No. I keep the master key on me at all times for security reasons, except when I can't be here to close, and then I give it to Bethany. But she always brings it back to me at the house before she goes home for the night. The key also says 'Do Not Duplicate,' and Alfie, who works at the kiosk, has a strict policy to never copy a key with that warning engraved on it. The only other key I can think that it could be, would be the one to the upstairs apartment. I asked all my employees—Bethany, Tim, and Eric—about it, and they all swore up and down that they didn't have an extra key made."

"Do you believe them?"

"Yes, I think so. I mean, I've gotten to know them pretty well this summer, but then again, given what happened to Miranda, who knows what they could be hiding? Still, I want to believe them; they strike me as good, honest kids."

"So if they are all telling you the truth, then the only person left who might have had access to that key would have to be . . ."

Lynette nodded solemnly. "Miranda."

Island Food & Spirits
BY
HAYLEY POWELL

I'm just going to come out and say it.

Men can be such babies!

Especially when they're sick.

That's exactly what I was thinking to myself when I pulled into a parking spot at the Shop 'n Save to buy ice cream for my ailing husband. When I got out of my car, the light rain coming down from the cloudy sky had suddenly turned into a torrential downpour, just to sour my mood even more. I fished around the back seat for the umbrella I was certain I had left there, but I couldn't find it, so I had to make a mad dash for the store using my recyclable grocery bag to cover my head.

My husband Bruce had been home a whole week now with a sore throat, and apparently the only thing that got him through his miserable day while lying in bed watching sports on TV and writing his column for the *Island Times* on his laptop was gallons and gallons of chocolate ice cream. He preferred me cranking out homemade ice cream from our maker, but one stern look from me, and he'd squeak out in a weak, disappointed voice, "But store-bought is just fine. My throat's just so sore, I need to eat something soothing."

I fought hard to hold it together, but honestly, after six days of this, my patience was wearing thin.

This had all started a few weeks ago when Bruce and I had looked after Mona's youngest daughter, Jodie, for a few days at our house while Mona headed down south to Portland to attend a lobster convention. My own kids had grown up and left the nest a while ago, so I was a bit rusty when it came to getting a young child off to school, shuttling them between sports practices and playdates, but with Bruce's help, I must say, we had a good time with Jodie. Bruce might have had a little more fun than me, since I was the one doing all the cooking, chauffeuring her around, and laundering her clothes, so Bruce could be "the fun one," up late with her playing board games, watching scary movies, and of course, scooping out extra big bowls of ice cream before bedtime.

By the time Mona returned from her trip and took Jodie home, I was ready for our household to finally return to normal.

I was up early to head to my restaurant and do a little paperwork when I pulled on my jeans and realized I was having a bit of a problem buttoning them. I stepped on the scales and nearly had a heart attack. I was up ten whole pounds since last spring! I ran back to the bedroom to tell Bruce and saw him crawling out of bed, his belly a lot rounder than I had last remembered. It was no mystery to solve. Bruce and I had spent the cold winter holed up snacking at night on bowls of ice cream and potato chips and plates of cookies while watching our favorite TV shows, usually after a hearty dinner! Something had to change! We needed to get control of our constant grazing, and there was no time like the present to begin.

Later that evening, Bruce found a car-racing movie on Netflix while I foraged for snacks in the kitchen. Imagine his surprise when he held out his hands for a bowl of ice cream, and I set down a plate of carrot and celery sticks.

"What is *this*?" Bruce demanded to know.

"Raw vegetables," I calmly replied.

In a pitiful, almost inaudible voice, almost near tears, Bruce asked, "But why?"

I explained that I had found three empty gallon containers of ice cream in the garbage just this past week alone! It was time we got back into shape! Starting now!

When Bruce tried to interject that, unlike me, he actually worked out every day at the gym and so should not be held to the same standard, all it took was another very stern look from me to convince him that he should just nibble on his carrot stick and refrain from any further comment.

We watched the movie in silence, except for some occasional sad and listless crunching.

The next morning, as I was on my way to the restaurant, Mona called and said she was so sorry, but she had just come back from the doctor's office with Jodie, and apparently, she had strep throat. Unfortunately, Bruce and I had undoubtedly both been exposed. I assured her that I felt fine, and she shouldn't worry. I had been through this with my own kids a few times, and it was never a problem with me. After hanging up, I called Bruce to let him know what Mona had just told me, and he immediately mentioned that he thought his throat might be a little scratchy. I assured him he was probably fine, since adults usually don't get this malady, but to make him feel better, I suggested he go see Dr. Frost and get a rapid strep test.

Well, so much for my confident assurances. By the time I got home from the restaurant that night, Bruce was already in bed, per Dr. Frost's instructions. The rapid strep test had come back positive.

I felt horrible for him and immediately asked if I could get him anything to help his sore throat as I fluffed his pillows and threw an extra blanket over him.

Bruce gazed at me with these sad, pathetic

eyes and muttered weakly, "I could use a little chocolate ice cream."

One week and four cartons of chocolate ice cream later, my nerves were frayed, and Bruce still wasn't showing any clear signs of improvement. The only time I ever saw him with an ounce of energy was when he was scraping the bottom of the empty bowl with his spoon.

It became a daily routine to stop at the Shop 'n Save on my way home for more ice cream. On day seven, I ran into Mona, who was there grabbing a few things in the frozen dessert aisle. I asked her how Jodie was feeling, since I hadn't had a chance to call to check in the last few days, between work and making sure Bruce was comfortably set up with his breakfasts and lunches while he worked from home.

We were still chatting in the aisle when Dr. Frost passed by and also stopped to ask Mona if Jodie was feeling better. Mona told him her daughter was right as rain, and she had bounced back in just a few days. I thought about this for a moment, and asked Dr. Frost if adults took longer to get better than kids, since Bruce was still severely under the weather after a whole week.

The doctor gave me a quizzical look and said he didn't know Bruce was sick. My whole body tensed as he went on to explain that he hadn't seen Bruce since his test a week ago and had only talked to him on the phone the following day to let him know that he didn't have strep throat, that the test was a false positive.

I thanked the good doctor for clearing things up and then bought my gallon of chocolate ice cream and drove straight home. I scooped out three giant, round mounds from the carton and went about preparing an ice cream lover's dream sundae, each mountainous scoop drizzled with a different sauce—strawberry, chocolate, and caramel—along with crushed peanuts and sprinkles and huge squirts of whipped cream from the Reddi-Wip can, all topped off with a generous amount of maraschino cherries.

I carefully carried it up to our bedroom, where Bruce sat up expectantly, his eyes lighting up at the sight of such a decadent, mouthwatering indulgence. He prattled on about what a perfect wife I was, how much he felt loved, how he didn't know what he had done to deserve such a treat—and that's the moment I dumped the whole bowl on top of his head, turned, and stormed out of the room, slamming the door behind me.

Let's just say that after a week of my husband making me breakfasts, packing his own lunches, and crunching on carrot and celery sticks at night while watching TV, all was finally forgiven in the Powell-Linney household. Much to his surprise, and honestly due to a little bit of selfishness on my part, chocolate ice cream was introduced back into our household two nights a week during movie night. So I am happy to report that things are back to normal, at least for now.

This week, chocolate ice cream has top billing, and I have an easy recipe for you to make. You can also use this ice cream in a dreamy adult chocolate shake I'm excited to share with you!

Easy Homemade Chocolate Ice Cream

Appliances:
Ice cream machine
Blender

Ingredients:
2 cups heavy cream
1 cup whole milk
½ cup cocoa powder
¾ cup sugar
1 pinch salt

In a blender, add your sugar, milk, cocoa powder, and a pinch of salt.

Blend until all of the sugar dissolves.

Add the mixture to a bowl, stir in your heavy cream, and chill in the refrigerator for two hours.

Pour the mixture into the ice cream maker and churn for 35–40 minutes.

Enjoy now for soft serve, or put in a container and freeze overnight, or until your desired consistency.

Remove, serve, and experience the true meaning of decadent!

BOOZY CHOCOLATE MILKSHAKE

INGREDIENTS:
1 cup cold milk
3 ounces your favorite bourbon or scotch
4 tablespoons powdered milk
2 cups chocolate ice cream
2 cups ice

Add your milk, whiskey, powdered milk, chocolate ice cream, and ice to a blender.

Blend until mixture is smooth and creamy, about two or three minutes. If shake is too thin, add more ice cream; if too thick, add more milk.

Feel free to garnish with some shaved chocolate and whipped cream before serving. Enjoy!

Chapter 35

Alfie Bouchard laughed right in Hayley's face. He didn't even try to hide how ridiculous he thought her question was.

"Hayley, I don't even remember how many grandchildren I have," he scoffed. "How do you expect me to recall a customer who had a key made weeks ago?"

"Because her face has been all over the local news lately. I just thought you might have recognized her," Hayley said.

"I don't watch the news—they make half that stuff up, I never know what to believe!" Alfie snorted inside his little kiosk that was set up in the back of the Shop 'n Save.

Alfie Bouchard was seventy-seven years old and getting more cantankerous with every passing year. He had worked as a fireman until he retired at sixty-five, but got bored pretty quickly after that and decided to start a whole new career as a licensed locksmith, which would help pay for his hobby of refurbishing antique cars. The previous owner of the Shop 'n Save had allowed him to set up his kiosk inside the store after the True Value Hardware business had turned him down, preferring to promote their own locksmith services. But now that the previous owner of the local grocery store, Ron Hopkins, had sold his business to a regional conglomerate, there were rumors an overhaul was in the works, and Alfie and his kiosk might be tossed out. So far, however, he was hanging on by a thread, but you would never know it from the way he carried himself, seemingly unconcerned about the precariousness of his situation. He probably figured if they did kick him out, he'd just set up shop on a nearby street corner. After all, people always needed keys made.

Hayley grabbed her phone from her pocket and brought up the front page of the *Island Times*, which had a photo of Miranda Fox splashed on it right after Hayley and Lynette had discovered the body. She hoped it might jog his memory. "I'm talking about this girl."

"Never seen her before," Alfie said, barely glancing at the photo.

"Are you sure?"

"No, I'm not sure," Alfie barked, waving her off. "I told you, I have hundreds of customers come by here every day."

That was a total exaggeration.

Alfie's best day at the kiosk probably had nine or ten people with keys to be copied. But she was in no mood to argue with him.

She held up the receipt Lynette had found.

"Well, I believe she was here on that day," Hayley said, pointing to the date and time printed on the bottom of the receipt. "And she had a key copied."

Alfie snatched the receipt and studied it. "Well, if she did, I have no recollection of it; plus, it says right here she paid cash, so there would be no credit card on file. It looks like you're plum out of luck, Hayley. Now would you mind? I have a customer waiting!"

Hayley spun around to see a doddering old woman in her eighties, in a smart gray suit as if she had just come from church services, beaming.

"Oh, hello, Mrs. Dyer," Hayley said.

"Hello, Hayley," she cooed, even though she never took her eyes off Alfie, who after all those years fighting fires, still boasted an impressive build. "How are you today, Alfie?"

"Better now that you're here, Sylvia," Alfie said with a flirtatious wink as he reached out and squeezed her hand.

"Oh, you behave." Mrs. Dyer cackled loudly, raising her free hand to her face to hide her obvious blushing.

Hayley stepped back in order to allow their shameless flirting to continue as Mrs. Dyer explained between girlish giggles that she wanted an extra copy of the key to her wine cellar made for her new housekeeper.

Hayley turned to go when she noticed a security camera in the upper right-hand corner of the ceiling just above the kiosk. Alfie Bouchard's faulty memory may not be much help, but if that camera was working, its memory would be far more reliable. She hurried to the front of the store and asked one of the cashiers if the manager was around. They had to call him over the loudspeaker, but pretty soon, Bobby Wade, a boy from

Gemma's class, who had started as a stock boy here when he was fourteen but was now running the place for the new management, arrived. Hayley had heard through the grapevine that the once shy, soft-spoken, and small-for-his-age Bobby hadn't matured much physically—he was still barely five feet—but he had tried to make up for it by becoming an aggressive, power-hungry taskmaster.

"I heard Dustin's in town," Bobby said as he pounded toward Hayley without even a hello first.

"Yes, and he is about to become a father."

"I heard that, too. I have enough of a challenge keeping my teenage bag boys in line; I can't imagine chasing after a rambunctious toddler."

Hayley couldn't imagine that, either, but she was impressed that he knew a big word like *rambunctious*.

"What can I do for you today, Mrs. Powell?"

"I was hoping you might show me the footage from your security camera in the back of the store?"

He eyed her suspiciously. "Why?"

She showed him the receipt. "I'm trying to find out who this receipt belongs to, and the camera can probably tell me if it was turned on that day. June seventeenth."

"I'm afraid we erase everything after a month."

One of his cashiers who didn't have any customers at the moment—Judy, older, weathered, and weary—piped in. "It's been less than a month, so you should probably still have it."

Bobby shot her a furious look. "This is none of your business, Judy. And by the way, the register was forty-two cents short after your shift yesterday. We'll need to sit down at some point and discuss that."

Hayley couldn't resist rolling her eyes.

"What's the big deal in just letting her take a quick peek?" Judy wanted to know.

Bobby was now shaking with anger, and Judy had bills to pay and didn't want to get fired, so she gave up and turned her attention to a kid who stood in her aisle, wanting to buy a pack of gum.

Bobby grimaced at Hayley. "I'm sorry. It's against store policy to show anyone the footage, unless, of course, you're from the police department. Have you recently become an officer of the law, Mrs. Powell?"

"No, Bobby," Hayley said through gritted teeth.

"Then I suggest you come back when you are."

"I'm sure I don't have to point out to you that if I did that, it would take a lot longer than a month, and by then, the footage will have been erased."

"Then I guess Lady Luck just isn't on your side today."

What an arrogant little brat, Hayley thought to herself.

The rumors were true.

Bobby Wade was on a full-blown power trip as manager of the Shop 'n Save, Bar Harbor's only grocery store.

"Bobby, I don't have time to argue with you about this. It's vitally important that I see what's on that security footage. Can you at least go check it for me and let me know if Miranda Fox is seen in here on the day that this receipt was stamped?"

"I'm busy running this store; I don't have time to be watching TV because you're on some wild-goose chase."

A stock boy rushed by.

Bobby stopped him. "What's the hurry?"

"Some little kid dropped a jar of pickles in aisle six. I'm getting the mop."

Bobby nodded. "Okay, get to it." He turned back to Hayley. "See, it's a madhouse around here."

Hayley took a deep breath. "Bobby, I know you're the head cheese around here, and you want to command fear and respect, and that's fine, but don't get too big for your britches, because I have known you since the day you were born. I remember the problems your parents had with your potty training and bed-wetting; your neurotic fear of swallowing hair; how you threw up every time a girl talked to you until you were fifteen years old. I have no qualms about sitting down with all of your employees and regaling them with my warm memories. And then we will see how much respect they have for you when I'm finished."

Bobby's eyes were now bulging out of his head.

Hayley didn't feel good about blackmailing him.

And she would never actually carry through with her threat.

But the fear it instilled in him finally did the trick.

He still refused to allow her to look at the footage, but he did agree to check it himself while she waited in his office, as long as she didn't speak to anybody about what they had just discussed.

After half an hour, he returned.

"I fast-forwarded through all the footage. Miranda Fox was never in the store that day."

"Are you positive?"

He sighed. "I checked it twice."

"Then who does this receipt belong to?"

"I don't know, but it wasn't her."

Hayley tried handing him the receipt. "Can you go back and check to see who was at Alfie's kiosk at this time on that day?"

He refused to take the receipt. "No, Hayley. We had a deal. I did what you asked. Goodbye."

He meant business.

She wasn't going to get anything more out of him.

But if it hadn't been Miranda, she still had to know who had that key to Lynette's upstairs apartment copied.

And she was going to need Sergio and a legal search warrant in order to get her hands on the footage before it was too late, and Napoleon-wannabe Bobby Wade erased it.

The clock was ticking.

Chapter 36

As Hayley rushed out of the Shop 'n Save, her phone buzzed with a text. It was from Kimmy Nash. Hayley had given Kimmy her number after they spoke at the restaurant.

FYI, I just left the house. Zoe is there right now with her boyfriend if you want to talk to her about Miranda.

It was obvious there was no love lost between the two sisters. Kimmy was determined to indict Zoe. Was it a ploy to misdirect attention away from herself? Hayley couldn't be sure, but she had to follow up. She jumped in her car and sped out to the Seagull House, parking alongside the gravel driveway and walking up to the front door, where she rang the bell.

There was no answer.

A slight breeze seemed to carry the sound of voices from the back, so Hayley circled around to the large outdoor swimming pool that had just been installed the previous summer. There, she found Zoe and her boyfriend Chasen, playfully splashing around in the water, laughing, their hands all over each other, lips locked.

Hayley stood near the pool's edge silently for a moment until Zoe sensed her presence. She gasped and jerked away from Chasen, who cranked his head around, curious as to what had just spooked her.

They both frowned at the sight of Hayley.

"God, you shouldn't sneak up on people like that; you nearly scared me to death," Zoe spat out, bobbing up and down in the water.

"I'm sorry, I was about to try and get your attention, but you both seemed preoccupied," Hayley said acidly.

"If you're looking for my parents, they're not here. They're at a fancy luncheon in Northeast Harbor. They said it's some kind of charity thing, but I think it's just an excuse for a bunch of rich people to drink a lot during the day," Zoe explained, hoping it would be enough to persuade Hayley to skedaddle.

"I'm not here to see your parents; I was hoping to talk to you," Hayley explained.

Chasen wrapped his muscular arms around Zoe's bare waist and drew her closer to him until she was smashed up against his bare chest. "Well, we're kinda busy right now."

"I can see that," Hayley noted with a healthy dose of sarcasm. "But it's important. It's about Miranda Fox."

Zoe was still hugging Chasen, her arms around his neck, as if she were using him for a flotation device. "What about her?"

"You initially said that you vaguely remember meeting her once and that you barely knew her."

Zoe nodded. "Yeah, that's right."

"Well, your sister Kimmy seems to think that's not entirely the truth."

"Oh, is that what this is all about, Crazy Kimmy? Is she spreading around wild stories that I was the one who killed this girl Miranda? Well, Kimmy is an unstable mess, and you're a complete fool if you listen to anything she has to say."

Chasen snickered, still holding tightly onto Zoe as they floated around in the water, both eyeing Hayley disdainfully.

"Kimmy is just jealous that I'm like a thousand times more famous than she is, so she'll do anything to knock me down a few pegs, even make up stories about me murdering some ice cream chick. I mean, seriously, I feel bad she's dead and all, but just because I didn't like her doesn't mean I killed her."

"You just said you barely knew her. How could you not like someone you didn't know?"

Zoe's whole body seemed to suddenly tense up.

So did Chasen's.

"The thing is, according to Kimmy, you not only disliked her, you had a real problem with her," Hayley said, as Zoe now wriggled out of Chasen's grasp and swam to the shallow end of the pool. She emerged from the water, grabbing a plush white towel from a chaise lounge, and nervously began to dry herself off.

Chasen followed suit.

"Kimmy needs to learn to keep her mouth shut," Zoe huffed.

Chasen flicked his eyes between Hayley and Zoe as he patted himself down with his towel before hanging it around his neck.

"Why would you downplay how well you knew Miranda if you had nothing to hide?" Hayley pressed.

"I didn't know her!" Zoe blurted out. "I mean, not well, anyway! She was around all the time. I couldn't avoid her. But after the horrific way she died, I felt like I had to distance myself. I have hundreds of thousands of dollars' worth of product endorsement deals, companies panicking at the slightest whiff of scandal—I couldn't risk losing those!"

"Do you know how many followers Zoe has on Instagram alone?" Chasen asked, coming to her defense.

"Just because I didn't want to be associated with what happened to her doesn't mean I *killed* her!" Zoe protested.

"You still haven't told me why you had such a problem with her in the first place," Hayley said, folding her arms.

Zoe dropped the towel and tried fluffing out her still wet and matted hair. "She was insanely jealous of me."

"Kimmy, Miranda—it must be difficult having so many people jealous of you," Hayley cracked. "So tell me, why was Miranda jealous?"

Zoe's mouth dropped open. She emitted a slight gasp, as if she were completely floored by the stupidity of the question. "Um, hello, I have like my own social media empire. Who *isn't* jealous? But Miranda took it to a whole new level. She was like, obsessed, always showing up wherever I was. It was so creepy."

Hayley's mind raced. Zoe's explanation definitely sounded plausible. There was no reason to doubt the fact that Miranda was totally in awe of someone like Zoe Nash, an immensely popular social media influencer with millions of fans. But there had to be more to the story that still had not come into focus yet. "Just how were you going to take care of the problem?"

"Not by *killing* her, that's for sure! I was just going to call her out, you know, shine a light on her behavior online, show everybody how super psycho she was acting."

"You mean bully her," Hayley said sharply.

"That's not how I would describe it," Zoe muttered.

"Come on, Zoe, we don't have to stand here and listen to this; let's go inside," Chasen said, taking her gently by the arm and steering her away from Hayley.

"And what about you?" Hayley asked.

Chasen stopped and turned around. "What about me?"

"You obviously knew Miranda; you both lived in the same house," Hayley said, eyes narrowing.

Chasen shrugged. "Sure. But we kept very different hours. I just rent a room there. I really don't hang out much with any of them. I have better places to be." He grinned and gestured at his opulent surroundings.

"Did you ever get the sense that Miranda had any romantic feelings for you?" Hayley asked.

"Why would you think that?" Zoe barked.

"I don't know. You said Miranda was jealous of you; there could be another reason besides your fame and influence. Maybe it was more simple, like she had a crush on your boyfriend?"

Zoe and Chasen exchanged disbelieving looks and then burst into uproarious laughter.

Hayley never cracked a smile. "What's so funny?"

"Well, it's the most ridiculous thing I've ever heard. That she would think she stood any kind of chance, that she could ever compete with me . . . I mean, it's hysterical when you think about it." Zoe snorted.

Chasen grinned as he rubbed the small of Zoe's back,

keeping his eyes fixed on Hayley. "If that was true, and maybe it was—I don't know, I never paid her much mind—it was never going to happen."

"Because she was so beneath your station?" Hayley wondered.

"Those are your words, not mine," Chasen said, still with that self-satisfied, arrogant grin that Hayley just wanted to slap right off his face. "But yeah, if we're being honest. I never would have given someone like her the time of day. I mean, come on, look at who my girlfriend is, she's so beautiful and smart and perfect. I'm the envy of millions of guys. There is no way in the world I would ever give her up for some . . ."

"Ice cream chick?" Hayley said pointedly.

Chasen knew how he was coming across, but didn't seem to care much. "Yeah, some ice cream chick."

Zoe, for her part, was eagerly lapping up all the over-the-top flattery, eyes batting, falling for her man harder than ever now. Hayley had to give him credit for knowing exactly what buttons to press.

Zoe finished fussing with her hair and walked over and slipped her arm through Chasen's. "Look, if you're trying to blame Chasen for Miranda's murder, he obviously has no motive. He's with me. It doesn't even matter whether she was pining for him or not. Miranda was never even on his radar."

Hayley thought about this for a moment. "You're right, Zoe."

Zoe sighed, relieved that she had finally gotten through to this maddeningly annoying woman.

"It makes no sense," Hayley continued. "Chasen would

have no reason to poison Miranda's Thai Chili Coconut Ice Cream."

"Exactly!" Zoe jumped in, before adding, "But you mean Indian Pudding."

Chasen visibly blanched.

Hayley had to suppress a smile.

She instinctively knew her gamble was about to pay off.

"I beg your pardon?" Hayley asked innocently.

"It was Indian Pudding, the flavor she was eating. Indian Pudding, not Thai Chili whatever," Zoe babbled on.

"How do you know that?" Hayley asked.

"Chasen told me—right, Chasen?"

"I—I read about in the paper," Chasen sputtered.

"I see," Hayley said measuredly. "My mistake. Well, I won't keep you two any longer. Thank you. For everything."

Hayley could see Chasen wobble slightly as Zoe bounded toward the house, oblivious to what had just transpired.

Hayley was now certain that Chasen knew more about Miranda's murder than he was letting on.

He knew Miranda's favorite ice cream flavor.

So did the other employees at the shop.

But Chasen didn't work there.

Of course, he could have easily explained that one of his roommates had casually mentioned it. After all, Tim, Eric, and Bethany had all worked with Miranda at Lynette's ice cream shop and knew about her favorite flavor.

But that would not explain the look of abject terror on his face when Hayley called him out on it.

Plus, he claimed that he had read about that specific detail in the *Island Times*.

Which was impossible, because Bruce had never included that piece of information in any of the columns he wrote about the crime, specifically at Chief Sergio's request.

Chasen was lying.

And Hayley wanted to know: What else was Chasen lying about?

Chapter 37

Hayley was back in her car, on her way into town, when her phone buzzed again with a text. She didn't recognize the number, so she pulled over to the side of the road to read it.

I thought you might want to see this.

After a few moments, two grainy black-and-white photos popped up on her phone. They were shots of Alfie's kiosk in the Shop 'n Save. Alfie stood behind the counter, talking to someone. It was a man, but in both photos, his back was to the camera, so Hayley couldn't see who it was. The photos were obviously taken from the security camera. At the bottom of the photos were the date and time. They matched the receipt Lynette had found in her upstairs apartment exactly.

Another photo popped up.

The man was turned slightly this time, his face partially visible. But the photo was so blurred, Hayley still couldn't identify him.

Finally, one more photo was sent.

This time, the man had completely turned around as he headed away from the kiosk.

It was definitely Chasen, with the key he had Alfie copy for him in hand.

There was no doubt in Hayley's mind that Miranda had given it to him.

But who were these mysterious texts coming from?

She still had no idea.

Hayley texted back. **Who is this?**

She stared at her phone.

There was a long wait.

Almost two minutes.

And then, just as she was about to give up, a response came back. **Just a friend who can't stand her boss. Hope these help.**

Judy.

The cashier at the Shop 'n Save.

The one the little dictator Bobby Wade was giving such a hard time about over her register coming up forty-two cents short. She must have snuck a peek at the security footage before Bobby had the chance to erase it and taken these screenshots for Hayley.

Hayley tapped a quick reply. **Thank you, Judy. I owe you. Cocktails at Drinks Like A Fish on me! Hayley.**

Hayley dropped her phone on the passenger seat and swerved the car back on the road, heading straight for the house Miranda shared with Chasen, Bethany, Tim, and Eric.

George Kittridge wasn't the only deceitful cad in town

juggling different women. Chasen was like the junior version of George, two-timing with both Miranda and Zoe. His claim that Miranda was beneath his station was obviously a pathetic cover-up to hide the fact that he was actually cheating on his famous girlfriend.

Hayley parked out front and ran up to the front door of the house, rapping on it hard.

After a few moments, Bethany opened the door, a surprised look on her face. "Oh, hi."

"Bethany, I don't have time to explain. I need you to show me Chasen's room."

"Chasen? But why—?"

"Please, it's an emergency. You just have to trust me."

Bethany hesitated a moment, but then opened the door wider to allow her to come inside. She led Hayley up the stairs to a small room a few doors down from Miranda's. Hayley was struck by how immaculately neat the room was, unlike the others. The bed was made, the floor was swept, clothes pressed and folded in an old rocking chair, a stack of books on TV broadcasting and the news business tucked on the floor in a corner.

Hayley wandered over and bent down to study the books. "Does Chasen have ambitions to be some kind of TV anchorman?"

"God, yes," Bethany said, hovering in the doorway. "It's all he ever talks about. I came home one day, and he was sitting in front of his computer, wearing a suit and tie, recording himself reading the news, like he was auditioning or something. I teased him about it, and he got really mad, so I never mentioned it again."

Hayley stood back up.

The answer was right in front of her.

She knew who killed Miranda, and why.

Suddenly, they heard the front door open and slam shut.

They heard a voice yelling, "Anybody home?"

It was him.

Chasen.

Hayley and Bethany exchanged panicked looks.

Bethany scurried to the top of the stairs and looked down as Hayley heard feet pounding up the steps.

"What are you doing home? I thought you were hanging out with Zoe today."

"I was," Chasen growled. "But then that nosy Mrs. Powell came snooping around asking questions that upset Zoe, and we got into a fight, and she sent me home!"

"What kind of questions?"

Hayley poked her head out the door and saw Bethany blocking Chasen from passing her on the stairs and going to his room.

"It doesn't matter! Zoe says she needs some space! I swear, if I ever run into that obnoxious lady, that annoying Mrs. Powell, ever again, I will wring her scrawny little neck!"

Hayley instinctively raised her hand to her throat and shuddered.

"Chasen, don't be like that. You're scaring me," Bethany said, still trying to buy Hayley some more time.

But there was nowhere for Hayley to go.

She was trapped in Chasen's room.

"Sorry, Beth, don't mind me, I'm just in a foul mood today," Chasen said, softening slightly. "Can you move so I can get by, please?"

"Chasen, wait . . ."

Hayley bolted back inside the room, frantically looking for an escape.

But there was only one way out.

Through the window.

The second-floor window.

"What, Bethany?" Hayley heard Chasen sigh loudly.

She could tell Bethany was struggling to come up with a reason to delay him from going to his room.

"Did you know there was a positive pregnancy test found in the bathroom trash bin?"

This seemed to stop him.

At least for a moment.

Bethany continued, her voice shaky. "It's not mine, so do you think it might have belonged to Miranda?"

"I don't know, Bethany! And I don't care! It has *nothing* to do with me! Excuse me!"

She could hear him push past Bethany.

Hayley was out of time.

She raced over to the window and slid it all the way open, climbing out and lowering herself down. She kicked out her right leg toward the lattice on the side of the house, getting a good footing, until she was able to let go of the windowsill one hand at a time and grab onto the crossed and fastened wooden strips. Straightaway, she realized the lattice was rickety and not secured, and her weight was too heavy. The whole thing was about to split loose from the side of the house and collapse. She could hear voices in the bedroom to her left.

It was Chasen, standing near the window. "I don't remember leaving this open."

"I opened it," Bethany quickly explained. "The house was stuffy and smelled like stale beer this afternoon from last night's party, so I opened all the windows to air it out."

As cautiously and swiftly as she possibly could, Hayley tried climbing down the lattice, but one of the strips cracked, her foot stumbled, and she lost her balance. She tried stifling a terrified scream as she fell the rest of the way down, landing butt-first in a mulberry bush. Her blouse was stained with purple mulberry juice, and her right foot was throbbing from the impact, but without wasting another second, Hayley hobbled down the front lawn toward her car, praying Chasen hadn't noticed it parked there when he had arrived home. As she started her car, she glanced back up at the window to Chasen's room but didn't see him. She was just pulling away to drive directly to the police station and update Sergio on what she had discovered when her phone on the passenger seat lit up. She noticed she had five voice mail messages from Lynette.

This time, Lynette was sending a text.

Come to the shop ASAP! It's an emergency!

Chapter 38

When Hayley pulled up in front of the Bar Harbor Ice Cream Shop and jumped out of her car, she instantly noticed a small crowd of tourists gathered outside, staring through the large picture window. She couldn't imagine what was going on inside. As Hayley pushed her way through the crowd toward the entrance, she spotted Mona, blocking the door with her bulky frame, yelling at all the people.

"Go away! We're closed! Come back later!"

"Mona!" Hayley shouted.

Mona didn't hear her at first, but Hayley managed to work her way through the throng of people until she could reach out her arm and wave frantically at Mona to get her attention.

"Where the hell have you been?" Mona growled, snatching Hayley by the arm and plucking her out of the crowd.

She glanced past Mona and saw someone inside the shop, lying on the floor on top of a white sheet.

Hayley gasped. "Mona, what's happening?"

"It's Dustin's girlfriend MacKenzie," Mona said.

"*What*?"

"She's gone into labor."

Hayley's eyes nearly popped out of her head. "*What*?"

"Get in here; we need all the help we can get!" Mona cried, dragging her inside the shop and slamming the door and locking it behind her so none of the gaggle of nosy spectators could gain entry trying to buy a double-scoop cone.

Hayley rushed over to the side of the counter, where a few tables and chairs had been cleared to make room for MacKenzie, who was lying flat on her back, breathing heavily, face flushed, in obvious pain. Lynette and Liddy both knelt by her side, each holding one of her hands, not sure what to do. Dustin was sitting on the floor a few feet away, his head leaning against the wall, his face a ghostly white, in distress, having some kind of panic attack.

"Liddy and I stopped by your house earlier to take Dustin and MacKenzie out for some ice cream," Mona tried to quickly explain. "But MacKenzie barely had a bite of her Coriander Blackberry Streusel when we all heard this splashing sound, and we realized her water broke."

"Dustin slipped on it running over to her and nearly cracked his head open!" Liddy wailed.

"Okay, let's try to stay calm . . ." Hayley said.

"Drugs! I need drugs!" MacKenzie screamed.

Hayley knelt down next to Lynette and wiped the sweat off MacKenzie's brow. "I know, dear, just relax, we'll get you some once the ambulance arrives to take you to the hospital."

"That's a negative," Mona interjected. "Not happening."

Hayley rose to her feet and pulled Mona aside and whispered urgently, "Why not?"

"We called for an ambulance ten minutes ago, but apparently there was a hiking accident out in the park and a heart attack at the town pier, so both ambulances are tied up right now. Who would've thought Bar Harbor would ever need more than two ambulances? In any event, there's going to be a delay, no telling how long, and we don't have time to drive her there ourselves, 'cause that baby's not gonna wait!"

MacKenzie screamed again, this time more desperate.

Dustin stared helplessly at Hayley. "Mom, do something!"

There was a loud rapping on the door to the shop. It was a rather put-out pushy woman with a thick New York accent. "Excuse me, but what time do you plan on opening? We'd like to order three cones but need to pick up our moped rentals at three!"

Mona charged over and yelled through the door window. "Can't you see we have a lady with a baby in here about to pop? Get lost!"

"Well, I will certainly not hold back when I write my Yelp review," the woman snorted as she whipped around and stalked off.

More earsplitting screaming from MacKenzie.

Hayley sighed, rolled up her sleeves, and then scurried over and thoroughly washed her hands in the sink, drying them off with a clean towel. Then she took a deep breath, exhaled, returned to where MacKenzie was lying on the floor, and got down on her knees. "Okay, let's do this. Lynette, do you have a pillow we can put under her hips?"

"There's one upstairs in the apartment!"

"You better go get it," Hayley said.

Lynette dashed out, returning seconds later with a big fluffy pillow that Hayley put in place.

"Are you more comfortable now, MacKenzie?" Hayley asked.

"No! I'm in agony! Get this thing out of me!"

"It's going to be fine," Hayley said calmly. "Liddy, help prop her back up and support her during the contractions."

Liddy, panicked and on edge but less of a basket case than Dustin—who, at the moment, was utterly useless—did as instructed. Hayley peered inside the birth canal.

"Are you sure we don't have time to drive her to the hospital?" Lynette asked, maybe a small part of her concerned about all the business she was losing out on at the moment.

"Um, I don't think so; I can already see the baby's head."

There was a guttural cry from MacKenzie, startling everyone. Her face was wet, her hair matted, her eyes wild, her mouth contorted. Hayley hadn't seen anything so monstrous since when she'd snuck up late one night as a child to watch *The Exorcist* on the late-late show on TV.

Hayley put her hand in front of the baby's head, guiding it out slowly, the baby sliding forward in small waves with each uterus contraction. She now had the shoulders.

"Okay, stop pushing, MacKenzie," Hayley ordered. "We're almost there!"

And then, like a miracle, the baby was out. "Someone hand me a towel!"

Mona grabbed a fresh towel they had brought from the back and threw it at Hayley, who wrapped the baby from head to toe to keep it warm, taking care to leave the face open, so the baby could breathe. She slowly rocked it in her arms and smiled at its scrunched-up little face. "You sure do know how to make an entrance, don't you?"

Liddy removed some of MacKenzie's hair from her face. "Congratulations, dear, you're the proud mother of a . . ." She paused. "Wait, what is it, a boy or a girl?"

"Gosh, I was so nervous, I didn't even bother to check," Hayley said, laughing, opening the towel enough to take a quick peek. "Boy! It's a boy!"

Through the window, the gawking crowd of onlookers outside erupted in thunderous applause.

MacKenzie happily sobbed tears of joy as Dustin finally managed to get control of himself and rushed to his baby mama's side, showering her with kisses on the cheek.

Hayley gently handed the newborn to the euphoric young parents and crawled to her feet, turning to Lynette. "I'm going to need some gauze and sterilized scissors to cut the umbilical cord."

"There's a first aid kit in back, on the shelf next to the ice cream maker. I'll go get it," Lynette said.

"No, you stay here and start scooping ice cream for everybody in here and out there," Hayley said, pointing to all the customers happily gawking at the scene from outside. "It's on me!"

Hayley hurried into the back of the shop that was used to produce all the ice cream flavors. A machine was whirring and grinding, the blades churning around and around a green goop, creating something that smelled possibly like pistachio to Hayley. She saw the first aid kit, just where Lynette said it was, and grabbed it off the shelf. Spinning around to rush back out front, Hayley stopped dead in her tracks, finding herself face to face with Chasen, a desperate look in his eye and brandishing a sharp knife.

Chapter 39

"Chasen, how did you—?"

"The back door was unlocked, so I let myself in," he said, an intense, disconcerting look on his face.

"You shouldn't be here," Hayley warned.

"But I am, so what do you plan on doing about it?"

There was a distasteful arrogance about him.

As if he were somehow untouchable, entitled. And yet, he was a local boy, from a family of modest means, with few big money connections.

Until recently.

And that was the piece Hayley had needed to finally complete the puzzle.

"I know it was you, Chasen—you were the one who poisoned Miranda!" She shouted the words, but all the whirring and grinding from the ice cream maker drowned her out. No one out in the front of the shop would be able to hear her unless she screamed at the top of her lungs for help, but if she did that, Chasen might lunge forward and drive that knife through her stomach.

"I spotted you running away from the house a few minutes ago, after you searched my room, so I just followed you here on my bike," Chasen growled. "Why couldn't you just leave me alone?"

"Whatever you plan on doing to me, Chasen, it's too late. I'm not the only one who has seen the security tape that shows it was you who had the copy made to the apartment upstairs. Pretty soon, the whole town will know. It's all the proof the cops will need to arrest you for Miranda's murder."

"No! That tape doesn't prove anything! You can't convict someone for getting a key copied!"

"No, but it fills in the blanks and helps tell the whole story," Hayley said evenly. "You were Miranda's secret boyfriend, the one she was being so coy about, but you were embarrassed by her, you were just using her until something better came along, which is why you insisted she keep your trysts on the down-low. You didn't want to be stuck in Bar Harbor for the rest of your life. You had much bigger ambitions. And then, to your utter delight, something better did come along. Zoe Nash. Rich, famous, beautiful. And the key to your future success as a network news anchorman. Zoe was your ticket out of Bar Harbor. And more importantly, if you married her, her adoring parents, who would do anything to make their youngest daughter happy—the powerful Jim and Rachel Nash—could basically hand you a successful career."

He flinched slightly, then quickly recovered, fingering the knife menacingly.

Hayley knew she was spot on.

"You just needed to make the perfect audition tape for them to watch, and you'd be on your way, probably co-hosting their morning news show by Christmas. But there was a snag. A big one. Miranda. What to do about Miranda? You tried breaking up with her quietly and discreetly, but she wasn't willing to let you go so easily. She had fallen hard for you; she was willing to fight for you. Am I right?"

Chasen bowed his head slightly.

Was there a trace of guilt inside him?

If there was, it was fleeting.

He raised his gaze at Hayley defiantly. "I got her pregnant. I thought we were being careful. But what was I supposed to do? She was threatening to tell Zoe. I figured Zoe wouldn't care I had dated other girls before her, but if one was carrying my baby, then I knew she'd dump me. Miranda had my back against the wall. I couldn't just stand by and let her ruin everything I had always dreamed about!"

"Miranda lied," Hayley said.

Chasen stared at her, confused. "What are you talking about?"

"She wasn't pregnant."

"But she showed me the test."

"She must have gotten a positive test from someone who was pregnant, a friend, a relative. The important thing was, she wanted to use that test to try and trap you into staying with her, but she didn't take into the account the desperate lengths you were willing to go to get rid of her."

"I had worked so hard, I was determined to make something of myself, and she stood in the way—she was so clingy and demanding. There were other boys who liked her, but she wouldn't give them the time of day, she wanted me, only me, and I couldn't stand another minute listening to her cloying, whiny voice!"

"As her secret boyfriend, of course you knew she was the only one who worked in the shop who ate the Indian Pudding ice cream, so you knew nobody but her would ever touch it. You somehow got your hands on that rare poison. That was a tricky one to figure out, but I assume you can get pretty much anything on the dark web."

Chasen stood stiffly, gripping the knife handle, refusing to give Hayley the satisfaction of acknowledging just how right she was about everything.

Hayley was undeterred and continued. "You injected the poison into the ice cream, knowing Miranda couldn't resist having some on nights she closed the shop. That night, after she had already left, you got her to come back to the apartment above the shop to see you. You had the key, and when she did, you made sure she had some of her favorite ice cream. After she was dead, you dragged the body to the freezer in the back of the truck and stored it there, where you figured it might not be discovered for days, just to throw everybody off. What you didn't count on was a few cartons of ice cream I had ordered for my restaurant that had already been loaded in the freezer. Lynette was planning on delivering them to me the very next morning. And when she showed up, we discovered Miranda's body."

"What about Spanky? He was obsessed with Miranda! He had the poison in his possession! Why aren't you chasing him down?" Chasen spit out.

Hayley smiled. "Come on, Chasen. We both know you planted that evidence. It was common knowledge that

Spanky was in love with Miranda, and she had coldly rejected him, so it made perfect sense for you to frame him for the murder. You waited for his mother Carla to leave for work, and then you snuck in the house and hid the vial of poison in Spanky's room for someone to easily find if they were looking for it."

"No, people will still think it was Spanky—the whole town already thinks he's guilty—I can explain away the security tape, Miranda gave Spanky that key to get copied, and he asked me to do it as a favor, that's it, nobody ever has to know I was ever involved with that awful Miranda; it was Spanky! He was obsessed, driven to do it!"

"It's too complicated, Chasen. Your story just won't hold up for long, you can't keep the lie going forever, it's over."

"No, it's not! It's not! I can do this!"

"I'm sorry, you're just not as smart as you think you are."

This was like a gut punch to Chasen.

All he seemed to have going for him was his remarkably sturdy self-esteem. And Hayley immediately regretted calling him out because, well, he was the one holding the knife.

It was a dumb, impulsive move on her part.

"This is still going to work," he snarled. "I just have to tie up one very big loose end."

He slowly advanced upon Hayley, raising the knife.

Hayley opened her mouth to let out a full-throated, bloodcurdling scream, but before she had the chance, they heard sirens above the churning of the ice cream maker.

Both Hayley and Chasen suddenly froze in place.

The sirens grew louder and louder, getting closer and closer.

"I called the police on my way over here, Chasen," Hayley said coolly. "I planned on reporting you when I got here. Now you've saved them the trouble of having to go looking for you."

Chasen's eyes darted back and forth, panic-stricken, spooked. He stepped back from Hayley, considering his options, and then, still gripping the knife, he bolted out the back door. Hayley covered her mouth with her shaking hand, about to dissolve in tears from fright. She had just come very close to falling victim to Chasen's deadly plans.

Hayley knew it wasn't a police siren approaching.

It was the paramedics.

Not a patrol car, but an ambulance, arriving to whisk MacKenzie off to the hospital with her newborn to be checked out by doctors.

Luckily, Chasen hadn't known that.

And that little fact had most likely just saved her life.

Chapter 40

Poor MacKenzie was understandably overwhelmed by the endless parade of well-wishers who began to stream through Hayley's house the day after she returned home from the hospital to get a glimpse of the newborn. There were all of Hayley's employees at the restaurant, and Bruce's coworkers at the *Island Times*, including Hayley's old boss Sal and his wife Rosana. Randy and Sergio arrived bearing a box of gifts for the baby, as well as Randy's bar manager Michelle at Drinks Like A Fish. Lynette Partridge and her husband Jamie showed up with the cutest little bib with ice cream cones on it. Hayley's mother Sheila was already busy booking a flight up from Florida to see her great-grandson.

And then there were Mona and Liddy, who had driven up to Bangor together to go shopping for baby clothes. Mona bought every size they had, explaining that he would grow into them eventually, so the new parents wouldn't have to be constantly buying a new wardrobe for the kid every few months. Hayley was pleased to see Mona and Liddy reunited and doing things together again, the painful saga of George Kittridge now long behind them, their friendship bond still solid and unbreakable.

By late Saturday morning, Hayley had ushered out the last of the visitors, with the exception of Randy and Sergio and Mona and Liddy, who were all staying for brunch. Bruce whipped up some Bloody Marys for everyone, and Hayley prepared waffles with ice cream. She was celebrating, so any thoughts of a healthy diet were promptly thrown out the window, much to Bruce's elation.

The color was thankfully back in Dustin's face after nearly fainting at the sight of the messy horror show called childbirth two days prior. Of course, in his defense, he had mentally prepared himself for the calm, sterile environment of a hospital, not the chaotic scene that had unfolded in the front of Lynette's ice cream shop, with dozens of tourists gawking at them through the window. But he was still suffering from a weak stomach and begged off one of Bruce's Bloody Marys.

As Bruce, Mona, and Liddy cooed and doted on baby Eli, who MacKenzie held in her arms, wrapped in a blanket, rocking him gently in Bruce's recliner under the watchful eye of his dad Dustin, Randy and Sergio wandered down to the kitchen, where Hayley was hard at work preparing the brunch food.

"Anything we can do to help?" Randy asked.

"No, I seem to have everything under control," Hayley said, before noticing Sergio was empty-handed. "Sergio, do you want something to drink?"

"I don't like tomato juice, so I'm not a fan of Bloody Carries."

"Bloody Marys," Randy sighed. "Bloody Carries sound like a Stephen King novel. Do you have any champagne?"

"Yes, in the fridge. And I have some orange juice, too," Hayley said.

"Great, I love Minnesotas," Sergio said, grinning.

Hayley stopped at the door to the fridge, thought about it, and then smiled. "Yes, Minneapolis is a lovely city. I'll make you a *mimosa*!" She turned to Randy. "It's funny, we're all getting better and better at understanding what he really means."

"It takes a village," Randy cracked.

Hayley pulled open the door, fetched a bottle of Prosecco and a carton of orange juice, and began pouring both into a champagne glass she retrieved from the cupboard. As she handed the drink to Sergio, she touched his arm gingerly and then reached out and squeezed Randy's hand. "I want to apologize to both of you . . . for the way I reacted about you putting Dustin and me under surveillance . . . I understand now you were just doing your job, Sergio, and you couldn't let family get in the way of that. And Randy, you were doing what you thought was right, and in the end, it *was* the right thing, and I never should have gotten angry with you, I wasn't thinking clearly . . ."

Randy patted Hayley's hand. "There's no need to apologize. You were just acting like a protective mama bear, which is what you are, and your kids are lucky to have you."

Hayley could feel a lump in her throat.

She didn't want to burst out crying, so she just pulled

them both toward her into a group hug. They stood there, holding each other for a moment, until Mona came pounding down the hall to the kitchen, gulping down the rest of her Bloody Mary.

"Oh, for the love of God, what kind of schmaltzy Hallmark movie moment is this? I'm going to need another drink if we're doing group hugs and talking about our feelings! Hey, I'm starving! Are we ever going to eat?"

"I'm working on it," Hayley said and sniffed, pulling away to check on her waffles in the griddle.

"By the way, Hayley," Sergio said, "after we found Chasen hiding on the Nash estate and placed him under arrest for Miranda Fox's murder, I drove straight over to the McFarland house and had a talk with Spanky, to let him know he was in the clear, and that I hoped there were no hard feelings. He was very mature and understanding, and he told me he has some college plans happening. I think he's going to do okay. And it looks like Carla and her new boyfriend are going to help pay his tuition. Do you know Carla's new guy? He works at the lab—"

"Sergio!" Randy hissed.

Sergio turned to him, dumbfounded. "What?"

"It's all right," Mona assured him. "Liddy and I are one hundred percent over it. And if George is going to help Spanky get a start in life, then good for him. And Carla can deal with the half a dozen secret girlfriends he's probably got stashed away all over New England! Hayley, I can't wait for Bruce to get his act together; mind if I make my own Bloody Mary?"

"Of course, Mona."

Mona snatched the bottle of vodka and started a very heavy pour, muttering to herself, "I'm completely over him . . ."

"So am I!" Liddy declared in the kitchen doorway, having overheard a part of the conversation. She shoved her own empty glass toward Mona. "Make me another one too, Mona, okay? And make it a double."

"With pleasure, dear friend," Mona said, and they smiled at each other in solidarity.

Hayley turned to Randy. "Food's about ready; just keep an eye on the griddle, so the waffles don't burn. I want to go check on MacKenzie, see if she needs anything."

Hayley bounded down the hall to the living room, where MacKenzie was still holding baby Eli. "Brunch will be ready in a few minutes—can I help you with anything? Does he need to be changed?"

"No, he's fine; do you want to hold him for a bit?" MacKenzie asked.

"Sure," Hayley said, beaming, taking the bundled-up baby in her arms and gently rocking him back and forth as he fussed slightly.

Dustin walked up to his mother and smiled. "MacKenzie thinks he takes after me."

"You were a good baby, hardly ever cried. It was when you got older when the trouble started," Hayley joked.

Then she got serious.

"I'm proud of you, Dustin."

He nodded. "Thanks, Mom."

"I know I wasn't fully on board when I first found out you were going to be a father, but you have to understand, you're my youngest, my baby; I've always had issues about letting you go. I guess I have always carried around this image of you in my head as being a boy, but now, especially now, I finally see you as a grown man, embracing fatherhood, and it's so clear to me that you are ready and up to the task, in every way. You're going to be a wonderful father."

Dustin leaned in and kissed Hayley on the cheek. "And you're going to be a wonderful grandmother."

Hayley blanched, while still rocking the baby.

"*Young* grandmother," Dustin quickly added. "You're going to be a wonderful *very young* grandmother!"

He could see she was still struggling with the word *grandmother*, so he continued, "Maybe when he's old enough to talk, he can just call you Hayley instead of Nana or Grandma."

"No, I will get there. I'm not there yet, but I *will* get there eventually," Hayley assured her son before calling into the kitchen, "Hey, Mona, make a Bloody Mary for me, too!"

Island Food & Spirits
BY
HAYLEY POWELL

All I can say is that if this month is anything
like last month, we sure are in for one long and
busy summer. Our household has been quite
the hub of activity ever since my son Dustin and
his girlfriend MacKenzie became first-time parents about a month earlier than expected, since
their son Eli decided to make an unexpected
appearance right here in Bar Harbor instead of
California, where he was supposed to make his
debut. But at least he has a great story to tell
when he grows up, since he was born right in
the middle of his grandmother's favorite ice
cream haunt.

Which brings up a sticky issue that I have
been trying to wrap my head around lately.

Grandmother.

That's such a loaded word.

It makes me feel so old.

In my mind, I am just way too young to be a
grandmother.

When Bruce and I dropped Dustin, MacKenzie, and baby Eli off at the airport a couple of weeks ago, I was so sad to see them go. I wanted to spend as much time as possible with my new grandson, but at the same time, I just couldn't imagine anyone calling me Grandma! It seems like yesterday that I had my own children! In my head, I just don't fit the mental image of a doting grandmother.

Good Lord, I'm still in my forties!

But maybe I could come up with a name that didn't make me feel so ancient that Eli could call me when he learned to talk. After Bruce dropped me off at my restaurant, I did a little research on my computer and came up with a list.

Nana—still too old.

Gram—even older.

Abuela—maybe, but I'm not Spanish.

Mémère—pretty, but I'm also not French Canadian.

MeeMaw, Oma, YaYa—all make me feel like a cartoon character.

I was determined to come up with something—anything—just not Grandma!

I was in a distracted mood and feeling sorry for myself, so after planning the night's dinner specials with the local ingredients my chef Kelton and I had bought off the dock and at a few local farm stands earlier that morning, I decided to leave my restaurant early.

Bruce and I had dinner plans later that evening with Lynette Partridge and her husband Jamie, and I thought it would be nice to have a few hours alone and try and shake off the funk that I had been in lately before going out for the evening. I headed out on foot, since my car was in the shop and I had already told Bruce I would walk home, since I needed to work off some of the many ice cream cones I had been devouring lately.

I arrived to find my dog Leroy in the kitchen, always excited to see me. I would bet I didn't look like a Grandma to him! I let him outside to do his business before feeding him a snack. After gobbling up his treat, he immediately retreated to the couch for his afternoon nap.

Good idea, I thought.

I headed up to my bedroom for my own nap, but when I reached the top of the stairs, my eyes drifted to the small narrow door at the end of the hall, which led up to the attic, my least favorite room in the house, since it was always dirty, and on my To Do List of things to clean and organize. I hadn't been up there since I had put the Christmas decorations away, and I really didn't want to be reminded that it had not been touched since.

Nevertheless, I found myself opening the door, flipping on the light switch, and trudging up the small flight of stairs. It was as if something supernatural was guiding me, and I ended up near the back wall, standing in front of a stack of labeled plastic totes.

I grabbed one of the totes, sat down on the dusty attic floor, removed the lid, and peeked inside. The first thing I saw was Dustin's baby blanket that we had brought him home in from the hospital. Further digging, I found Dustin's first picture with Santa, his first baby tooth, that important first day of kindergarten, a report card—and it went on and on.

Each tote that I opened made me laugh and cry. They all held such wonderful memories of Dustin and his sister Gemma's childhoods. Then, I happened upon a photograph of me as a six-year-old girl with my own grandmother, Grammie, and the sheer adulation in my eyes as I smiled up at this wonderful, kind, generous woman I held so close to my heart. I couldn't have loved her any more if I tried. And that's when I suddenly realized: It was a blessing to be someone's grandmother, not a curse. I needed to get over this Grandma thing.

I began to clean up my mess when my phone rang. It was Bruce. I answered the call, and he said he was just reminding me of our dinner plans with Lynette and Jamie, and asked when I'd be home and ready.

"Give me thirty minutes," I said, and hung up. I forgot to mention I was already home and up in the attic. I laughed to myself, picturing how surprised he would be when I suddenly popped downstairs.

I finished packing the totes back up and left the attic. When I reached the top of the second-floor staircase, I could hear a commotion in the kitchen, lots of whispering, and women giggling. Who was in the house? We were meeting Lynette and Jamie at the restaurant. I crept down the stairs toward the kitchen door and peeked in.

There in my kitchen were my closest friends: Liddy, Mona, Rosana, Lynette, and even my old boss at the paper, Sal, as well as a whole crowd of other friends that I could see in the attached dining room. There were gifts on the table, assorted hors d'oeuvres, even an ice cream sundae bar set up. And there was a banner draped across the dining room wall that said, CONGRATULATIONS GIGI!

GiGi?

Who's GiGi?

And why are they throwing a party for her in my house?

At that moment, Bruce started gathering everyone in the dining room and instructing them to be quiet, because the guest of honor would be arriving at any moment.

Suddenly, someone tapped me on the shoulder and said, "What are you doing here?"

It scared me so much, I let out a bloodcurdling scream, rushed forward, and tripped over Leroy on the floor. I grabbed at the nearest thing to stop my fall, but unfortunately, it was the kitchen table, which I missed, but I got a hold of the tablecloth and brought down all the platters of finger sandwiches and bowls of dips and chips with me, splattering everything onto the floor.

There was complete silence. The next thing I knew, Randy and Sergio were hauling me up to my feet. They had just come through the front door when they spotted me, spying on everyone in the hallway near the kitchen.

Bruce and about fifteen of our close friends gaped at me, shocked and confused. I was so embarrassed and didn't know what to say, so I said the first thing that popped into my head. "Surprise!" When that didn't get much of a reaction, I followed up with, "Who is GiGi?"

Liddy answered that one. "It's popular among grandmothers who think Grandma is too old and stuffy. It's a hipper, more modern alternative. Eli can call you GiGi!"

That's when it dawned on me that this party was for me, and I had just ruined the surprise. Oh, well. Once everything was cleaned up off the floor, a good time was had by all, and after they toasted my new grandson, I announced to all the guests that if Eli wanted to call me Granny or Grandma, that was fine by me, just as long as he made sure to put the word *Fun* in front of it.

I also got a couple of new favorite treats out of that surprise party—which, of course, I'm going to share with you now, and believe me, you will not be disappointed. Just remember to let me know if you enjoyed them!

GRAMMA'S FROZEN MOCHACCINO

INGREDIENTS:
½ cup sugar
¼ cup strong espresso or coffee
¼ cup water
1 cup mini chocolate chips
2 ounces Baileys
1½ cups heavy whipping cream

In a saucepan, add your sugar, espresso, and water. Bring to a boil, stirring occasionally to make sure sugar is dissolved. Boil for two minutes.

Remove from the heat and add your chocolate chips; stir until melted and smooth. Let this cool to room temperature, and then add your Baileys, pour the mixture into a blender, and blend for a couple of minutes.

Add your whipping cream to a stand mixer and whisk until stiff peaks form.

Fold your whipped cream into the chocolate mixture and pour evenly into glasses, add a straw, and enjoy.

For an added treat pour into small bowls, cover with plastic and freeze, then serve with a spoon and enjoy!

GRAMMA'S EASY OREO ICE CREAM

INGREDIENTS:
2 cups heavy whipping cream
1 14-ounce can sweetened condensed milk
1 teaspoon vanilla extract
1 package Oreo cookies

Break and crumble your Oreo cookies into smaller pieces and set aside.

In a stand mixer, add your heavy whipping cream and whisk until stiff peaks have formed.

Fold the sweetened condensed milk, vanilla extract, and ¾ of the crumbled cookies into the whipped cream and mix well.

Pour mixture into a container and add the rest of the crumbled cookies over the top cover. Place into the freezer for at least 8 hours.

When ready, remove, scoop into bowls, and enjoy!

Index of Recipes

Visit us online at
KensingtonBooks.com
to read more from your favorite authors,
see books by series, view reading
group guides, and more!

Visit us online for sneak peeks, exclusive
giveaways, special discounts, author content,
and engaging discussions with your fellow readers.

Betweenthechapters.net

Sign up for our newsletters and be the first
to get exciting news and announcements about
your favorite authors!
Kensingtonbooks.com/newsletter